ELLE HARTFORD

Tangled Up in Murder

The Alchemical Tales #8

Contents

Welcome

Long, long ago, a coven of witches created a world just
beyond ours—a realm of fairy tales.
In Beyond, humans rub shoulders with mythical creatures,
and magic mixes with science.

There are only three rules:

Happily

accept that we share the same home

Ever

remember that what you take, you must also give

After

struggle will always lead to new beginnings

So, if you are ready . . . you are welcome here.

* * *

Belville & nearby forest

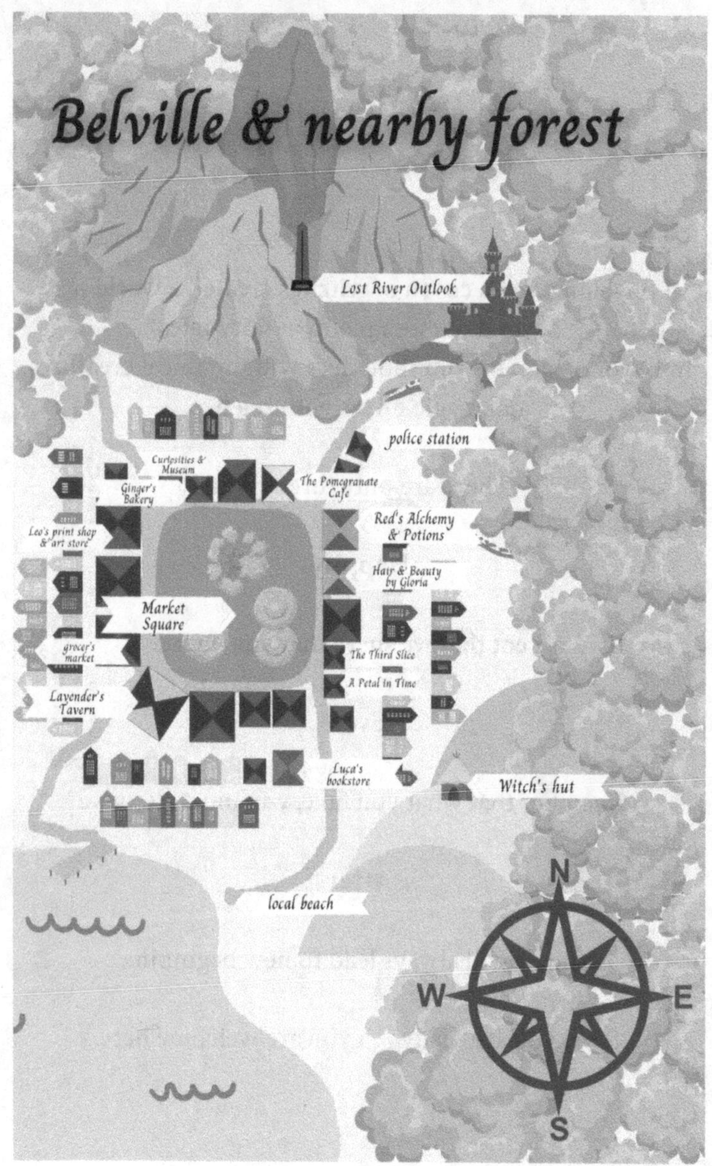

Cast of Characters

Top thirteen, in alphabetical order

Doug: faun; herb seller in Belville's market

Dusty: handy-gnome and jack of all trades, best friend to William

Jack: mysterious newcomer to Belville, much distressed

Keith: new in town; long-lost relative of Lavender, and Jack

Lavender: longtime tavern owner of Belville; relative of Jack's

Luca: bookseller and scholar, complicated past; friendly to a fault

Olivia: fresh police recruit assigned to Belville to learn from Officer Thorn

Red: alchemist and child of Seers, full name Cinnabar Sunset

Rowan, Sir: old-fashioned knight; works at Red's Alchemy & Potions; first name Rhys

Thorn, Officer: half-orc policewoman in charge of keeping law in Belville; first name Mina

Trent: official Witch, lives in a Hut outside of town; serves as healer for Belville

Vesper: reclusive sorcerer with a long history in Belville

William: canine familiar, capable of protection magic and plenty of sass

1

Waiting and Wondering

When you venture out into the world, you learn to trust your judgment. But sometimes, for one reason or another, you get cooped up and start to doubt yourself.

I'd spent yet another morning huddled in my lab. Torrential rain pounded at the back door—as it had every day for the past week. The only sound from the potions shop beyond was William snoring.

Since William and I had settled in rural Belville four and a half years ago, we'd endured our fair share of storms. But this autumn was shaping up to be in a class all its own. If it rained any more, I thought the whole town might just slide off the mountain and into the lake. That, or the lake itself would rise up and swallow us. And yet it *did* keep raining, more and more, and we'd yet to fall victim to any terrible disaster.

Of course, that's how it's supposed to go, right? All across the magical world of Beyond, people have devised spells and magitech and tricks of architecture to protect themselves from flooding. My own potions shop was no exception—

with protection magic being William's specialty, we were safe in many more ways than one. I was grateful, truly, but I was also itching for a change of scene. I'd grown up in a desert climate where storms whipped in and out of town, sometimes in minutes. Stuck under my work bench, my feet bounced nonstop. I couldn't shake the feeling that *something* would happen, and soon.

I took a sip of the steaming matcha perched on the window between my lab and the potions shop. Though I had a strict rule against food in the laboratory when I was working, I'd grown quite lax over the past seven days.

Everything is fine, I reminded myself. *It's* good *to have a chance to catch up on potion-making.*

Belville's official celebration of Samhain, otherwise known as All Hallow's Eve or Halloween, was only ten days away. As the only alchemist in town, I'd been asked to supply glow powder and weak glamour potions—not to mention a cartload of ever-sticking glue to secure the decorations that would adorn Market Square. Because of all my time spent indoors lately, I'd even managed to come up with a new kind of lightstick that shone with black light, giving an eerie effect that the local kids would love. And all this business was on top of my usual seasonal orders for things like overwintering fertilizer potions, warming powders, and holiday soaps or cleaning potions for those preparing to host out-of-town family. Autumn was a pretty profitable time to be an alchemist . . .

. . . *That's if there's actually a Samhain festival at all,* I couldn't help but think.

I took another sip of matcha and shook my head, willing myself not to be so morose. But that was the trouble: it wasn't just that I was bored. I was *worried.*

There was no reason to be, of course. Sure, our first few autumns in Belville had seen some crime—a mysterious haunted castle at first, and then a string of seriously frightening attacks the year afterward. But life in Belville was quiet and idyllic, on the whole, and it had been a long time since my friends and I had been drawn into an investigation. Months, at least. And to be fair, that one murder investigation over the summer had occurred while we were visiting my parents back in the Blue Desert Isles, many hundreds of miles away . . .

I shook my head again. No, it wasn't crime I was worried about. And it wasn't weather-related disasters either—not really. Actually, it was something much closer to home.

My partner, Luca, was what *truly* troubled me.

Out on the shop floor, William's snores ended in a snort. There was the sound of paws stretching across the wooden floor as he woke. A moment later, he had perched himself on the stool behind the sales counter—from which he could peer through the interior window at me.

"You don't look like you're working very hard," he observed.

I pushed my lab goggles up over my black hair, the better for him to see me roll my eyes. William was a magical familiar, a being that had been created by a sorcerer but had personality and power of his own. In William's case, it was protection magic and sarcasm—not necessarily in that order. He could be a pill, but he was deeply loyal. Besides, he was my oldest friend.

He also was, for all practical purposes, a big, fluffy black dog. At some times wolfish and at other times sheepish, he was, at present, just *smelly.* "Hard to work around here when it smells like wet dog," I told him, smiling wryly.

"You're just looking for excuses. I don't smell." William shook himself self-righteously, his soft ears flapping.

"Was it worth it?" I asked.

William gave me a long-suffering look, something he'd perfected over our years together. His magic, usually a deep blue sparkle, crackled faintly over his head in answer to my question. "Not even a bit. Cursed cloud cover's too thick."

"It's like having a solar-powered mining assistant," I chuckled, momentarily distracted from my own woes.

"Har har," said William, unamused. For reasons I didn't fully understand—as an alchemist, I handled scientific matters, and left magical expertise to William himself—his magic was strengthened by time spent under the stars. He was forever going out for late-night walks by himself, replenishing his power. Apparently, though, walks in the rain were not effective. "See how funny you think it is when all the shop wards fail."

I stopped laughing. "Is that possible?"

"Ha! Got your attention," said William smugly, shifting on his stool before answering. "But no, not really. I've invested so much time and power into the protections on this place that by now they're basically part of the woodwork. They'll linger a long time after we're both gone, most likely. I was just being dramatic to make sure you were listening."

He narrowed his dark eyes over that last point, and I blushed. I should have reminded him that he is *always* dramatic, but my guilty conscience spoke for me. "Why? Have I been that distracted lately?"

"You have," William confirmed. "And don't bother telling me it's because you're busy with potions. The only customers we've had for days are the ones with long-standing orders, and you could make Gloria's soaps in your sleep by now. You're just hiding back there, stewing."

Someone woke up feeling confrontational, I thought. But I had to admit he was right. My little lab room was like a safety blanket, tucked around my shoulders. I sighed, running one hand through my long ponytail. Instead of answering directly, I asked, "Has Luca seemed different to you lately?"

"Actually, I thought he seemed pretty unconcerned for a purveyor of books and guardian of old town records in the face of the rainstorm of the century," William said, glibly. I didn't bother replying; as Belville's resident scholar, Luca had certainly protected his bookstore from rain, of all things. William huffed and added, "Do you really not know?"

My head snapped up from contemplating my work bench. "Know what?"

"You *don't* know?" William stared at me.

"Know *what?*" I repeated, my worry quickly becoming annoyance.

In that moment, there was a thundering noise at the back door of my lab. It was far too familiar to be the storm.

No, I knew at once that it wasn't a force of nature—it was Belville's police.

* * *

To be fair, Officer Thorn is just as brash and inexorable as any hurricane or flash flood.

She established herself in an old armchair in my shop. Though most of my shop floor was taken up by wall-mounted shelves of potions and shoulder-high rows of dried flowers, powdered minerals, and other merchandise, I kept a cozy space in the back corner next to the register for people waiting on custom orders—or for visiting friends. Two armchairs sheltered by an old bookcase flanked a side table set with a tea tray. Most of the tea I made was sold at the local café, but I liked to offer new experimental or seasonal blends for free to brave customers.

Officer Thorn was nothing if not brave. A steaming cup of rosehip and clove herbal tea looked almost like a child's toy in her hands, and her booted feet stretched out halfway across the fluffy red area rug. Her mother was an orc, which meant Thorn had mossy green skin, long pointed ears, and a toothy grin. She was also perhaps twice my size without being much taller. She *was* tall—easily six feet—but most of her bulk was muscle. As always, she was wearing her perfectly tailored blue police uniform, and her long black hair fell straight and shiny behind her shoulders.

But today her brown eyes were worried, her brow creased. "I've had strange tips before, but never something quite like this."

"You still haven't explained anything," William reminded her. He remained on his stool behind the counter, but I'd come out of my lab to join them. Sometimes, physically pushing Thorn through the interior door to the shop was the only way to get her out of my lab, where she was akin to a bull in a china shop.

"Someone came by to see you in this weather?" I prompted, leaning against the counter with my matcha in hand.

Thorn shook her head. "Anonymous letter pushed through the mail slot. Only came a minute ago, but I didn't see a soul on the road. Brought it straight here—see if *you* can make anything of it."

She fished in her pocket and pulled out a scrap of folded paper, holding it out for me to take. I did so, settling back against the sales counter so that William could read it over my shoulder:

A child has been kidnapped and is being kept on Belville Mountain

Just one line, inked in refined capital letters. The paper itself was clean and white, but the upper part had been torn off, leaving a jagged edge.

"Not much to go on," William observed.

I have to admit—at first I was just glad it didn't have anything to do with Luca. The unfortunate timing of Officer Thorn's visit had set butterflies going in my stomach. I took a deep breath now, trying to focus. "What about the parents? Has anyone come forward to say their child is missing?" I asked.

Thorn tossed back half her tea in a gulp. "No one yet. That's the strange thing. Why write such an impersonal note about such a personal crime? Think it's just a Samhain prank?"

"If it just happened, maybe the parents haven't realized yet," William pointed out grimly. "Or maybe the kid was brought here from somewhere else. Doesn't your guild have a wire system or something?"

This comment was calculated to annoy, because William knew full well that the Police Guild *did* have a magitech system that enabled each station to communicate with the others. Because Belville Station was tiny—just Officer Thorn and the occasional new recruit getting some on-the-job training— we'd often seen Thorn reach out to other local stations for assistance. Of course, that was just for information; when it came to actual backup, she usually recruited townsfolk—like ourselves. As such, she was very familiar with William's brand of teasing.

"No active cases within fifty miles," she replied matter-of-factly. "The newbie's stationed at the desk in case anything comes in. But I don't have a good feeling about it."

"It's not a funny prank, if it is one," I agreed. "I can run some tests on the ink and paper for you, but it seems a little beside the point right now. I suppose that *is* why you brought it over, though?"

Officer Thorn downed the rest of her tea and poured herself a fresh cup from the pot. "Might as well see what you can get from it. For now, I'm treating the case as serious. It's the only way. What about you? You haven't heard anything lately?"

She squinted at William, who whined. "I'm magical and clever but I'm not *omniscient*."

"No, you're an omni-gossip," Thorn said, ignoring our groans at her attempted pun. "I thought you might have heard rumors I hadn't."

"Oh, is that why you really came over?" I asked, amused.

"Well, I haven't heard anything." William waved his nose in the air—probably indignant about having to admit that he knew nothing. He and his friend, Dusty, were definitely the prime gossips in Belville. Officer Thorn knew her sources well.

There was a pause as our guest drained her second cup of tea and we pondered what to ask next. In the muffled silence, I heard my lab door open once more.

"Good afternoon, Red, William!" a new voice called.

I was reluctant to give up thinking about the strange note, and yet I hated to be rude to my one official employee. William was a handy assistant, of course, but he got room and board and entitlement as his wages. Sir Rowan, on the other hand, could find employment elsewhere if he so chose.

Not that he would. Since his arrival in town a few years back, he'd settled in very well. Once a knight of fairy tales and legends, with all the chain mail and courtly manners to show for it, he'd relaxed bit by bit into small town life. As a result, he now managed to call me simply *Red*, rather than *Miss Red*, which had made me feel like an old-timey school teacher. He'd also invited us to use his personal name, Rhys.

I knew it was Rhys without looking, of course. He was the only person, aside from Officer Thorn, who insisted upon entering the potions shop via the back door—more pertinently, via *my lab*, which I usually kept off-limits during work. He also was the only person who had perfected the art of cloak-wearing to the point where he could open a door, even in this storm, and *not* bring in bucketfuls of rain with him. For that, at least, I was appreciative.

He'd just finished hanging said cloak on a hook in the corner beside my kiln when I poked my head over to catch a glimpse of him through my open lab window. "Hey, Rhys," I said, stowing the note for now. "How's the mountain? Still there?"

"It would take quite a storm indeed to have such a lasting effect on Belville Mountain." Rhys arched one dark brow over a friendly smile as he turned around. His skin was pale, especially compared to my brown tones, but his hair was just as dark as mine and his eyes were startlingly blue. He stood almost too tall for my little lab, and yet he had a way of moving that made him seem instantly suited to whatever space he entered. Even now he bowed slightly, as though it was entirely natural. But even in a crisp white shirt and green shop apron, his posture said *try anything and you'll be beat before you begin.*

He was very handy around the shop. Not for beating

miscreants—we rarely had any of those—but because he adored organizing things.

And William, in turn, adored him. "Rhys! Officer Thorn needs your help."

"Does she?" Rhys emerged from the lab and turned to find Officer Thorn, as though he had known all along she was waiting in that armchair. "I would be happy to be of assistance after my shift."

"*She* can make her own calls, thanks very much," Thorn retorted, eyeing William. But then she turned to Rhys with a more professional air. "You and Daisy haven't seen anything amiss? Strangers on the trails, new campsites popping up, that kind of thing?"

"None. One would have to be very foolhardy to camp in this weather." Rhys lingered by the door.

"Are the pixies worried about all this rain?" William asked.

This was enough to distract him momentarily. "Not as of yet. But you know how my lady Daisy is," Rhys answered fondly.

Rhys and his "lady," Daisy, lived high on the mountain along with a magical tree and a bunch of tiny pixies. Daisy had inherited the task of looking after all that magic, and tended to be reclusive—and worried. Personally, I didn't blame her in the least. Looking after a shop was the extent of my power; I couldn't imagine looking after a herd of magical creatures who considered the entire mountain to be their home.

"You might as well tell him everything," I said to Officer Thorn. "He and Daisy could keep an eye out, at the very least. And he'll see me running tests anyway."

"I wouldn't pry," Rhys said, mildly.

Nevertheless, Thorn filled him in on the possible kidnapping case.

"How terrible. We will naturally do everything we can to help," Rhys said, once she was finished. "But as of this moment, no useful information comes to mind. You might consider going to Daisy herself, however. At this moment, she and Luca should still be in the Pomegranate Café."

"What?" My mug slipped in my hands, even as I tried to sound casual.

"Didn't you know?" Innocently, Rhys turned to face William and me. His eyes were clear, his tone bland. "Luca went out to see the old keep with Daisy today."

2

The Usual Lineup

The Pomegranate Café was a one-minute walk from Red's Alchemy and Potions, sitting on the same corner of Market Square. As I made the trek in my rubber boots and large umbrella, it seemed to take ages. And that was even with Officer Thorn next to me, hurrying us along.

The potential case should have been my first priority, I knew that. But I found it difficult to feel as urgent as Thorn did. I was, frankly, distracted. I wouldn't say I'm a jealous person. I'm not even the sort of person who gets regular *feelings* about things—premonitions, gut instincts, and the like. My parents are Seers, but I don't have a divining bone in my body. I've gotten better about recognizing my feelings, and yet . . .

Luca had been my best friend since I settled in Belville, and we'd been dating for two years. He basically lived in the apartment above my shop with me. Until a few days ago. Suddenly, he started having evening meetings and staying over at his bookshop apartment instead.

Who has meetings in rain storms like this? I wondered for

the umpteenth time as we splashed through puddles on the cobblestone street.

Fortunately, the rain was loud enough that Officer Thorn didn't bother trying to talk over any more of her case.

In fact, the white siding and plum pink trim of the Pomegranate was hardly visible through sheets of water. Its little porch and patio furniture, usually an adorable outdoor space full of customers reading books from the nearby lending library, looked about as gray and forlorn as I felt. But the light pouring from the café's windows was a soft yellow, friendly and inviting.

As soon as Officer Thorn opened the door, in fact, some of my melancholy was *whoosh*ed away with the warm air. Sofas and tables under the front windows to either side of me were full of people chatting. Even the second floor balcony brimmed with tea drinkers and readers. Scents of cinnamon and pumpkin wafted out from the kitchen at the back, and behind the counter to the left side, I could see Sakura's white head bobbing back and forth as she worked her tea pots and espresso machines.

I also spotted Luca and Daisy standing at the register. Without thinking about it, I wove through the café tables to meet them, the officer trailing behind. Rhys had *told* us we should come find them here, and yet still, somehow I felt like an interloper.

"Red!" Luca's dark face shone with a wide smile as he turned and saw me. No one could possibly feel unwelcome around Luca. He wore the long black robes of his scholarly profession, as usual, the hood shading his bright green eyes. "What are you doing here? I thought you'd be busy at your shop. Hi, Officer Thorn."

"Rhys just got in, and suggested we find you here," I mumbled. "Hey, Daisy."

Daisy, a tall woman with red hair and freckles, smiled shyly at me. As usual, she was under-dressed for the weather in cutoff shorts and an oversize sweater. She and Rhys came from practically immortal heritage, and along with long lives, they both seemed to have developed a disdain for passing fads like seasonal attire.

"I need a minute to talk with Daisy," Officer Thorn said, doing her best to be discreet. Her best was still loud and official enough that several people at nearby tables craned their necks to look at us.

"We're almost done here," Daisy said quietly, biting her lip. Most people in town were so used to Officer Thorn that I rarely saw anyone get nervous around her. But it was truly uncommon for Daisy to come down from the mountain, so perhaps she'd not had the chance to become accustomed to our bold officer.

"You have good timing," said Luca, agreeably. "Do either of you want something? I haven't paid yet. We just ordered cocoas. Would you like one too, Red?"

"I have matcha back at the shop to finish," I said, unreasonably reluctant to join in anything as nice as hot chocolate.

"One wonders why you came here then," Sakura called in a singsong voice from behind the counter.

I glowered at her. Sakura, owner of the Pomegranate Café and also a dear friend, was entirely unflappable. She beamed angelically back at me. Ironic, considering that she was actually a shadow witch and had once been under suspicion for murder. With her big blue eyes, rosy cheeks, bobbed white hair, and penchant for frilly dresses, looking innocent came naturally to her. Unfortunately, so did insight and confrontation.

"Red?" Luca asked, when I didn't reply verbally. "Is everything okay?"

"Try not to hold up the line, won't you?" Sakura added with a cheeky grin.

This time I stuck my tongue out at her. The Pomegranate was probably the only business in town—aside from Lavender's Tavern, perhaps—that was *busier* because of the massive storm. There wasn't actually a line at this moment, though, and I knew she was just doing her best to stir the pot.

"I'm fine," I said finally. "I don't want anything. Thanks though. I just, um, wanted to . . . help out Officer Thorn. And hear how your meeting went?"

Alright, not my best effort. I never said alchemists made great liars.

"Meeting?" Luca looked uncertain, and busied himself with paying Saki for the drinks. While she turned around to gather some mugs, black sparkles crackling around her as she used magic to lengthen her prosthetic legs and help her reach a high shelf, the rest of us drifted along the counter to the pickup section at the end. Officer Thorn crossed her arms, practically tapping her toes. Daisy remained silent. Luca cleared his throat. "Ah, that is, it wasn't anything important, you know. Just checking on the old fort up on the mountain. There's some interesting local history there, right, Daisy?"

"I first met Rhys there," Daisy agreed in a low voice, so soft it was hard to hear her. I doubted that moment was exactly what Luca had in mind when he talked about town history, but then again, Daisy was the single most powerful protector of Belville Mountain, so maybe it *did* matter who she associated with. Under her thoughtful green-eyed gaze, I squirmed.

"Well," I managed, trying to wedge myself into the corner where the wall met the counter top, "were you worried it was flooding or something?"

"Oh, no," said Luca, "it definitely won't flood." At this, a thought seemed to strike him, and he looked up at Daisy nervously. "Er, that is, it *has* taken on a lot of damage in recent years. The outer wall is still a bit broken in places. So we decided it's really not suitable for, uh, keeping any records there."

Keeping records there? Please. Even if the bookstore was running out of room—which was perpetually the case—I knew Luca would never consider storing important documents so far away from town. The "old keep" was an ancient stone fort hours away, straight up the mountain. Scholars, apparently, could be even worse liars than alchemists.

"Did you see anything while you were out there?" Officer Thorn finally burst. She stood at the corner of the counter, crowding the rest of us in. "Anything unusual?"

"No," said Luca, looking at Daisy again, "at least, I don't think so?"

"It depends what you mean by 'unusual,'" Daisy whispered unhelpfully.

"Any other *people*?" Officer Thorn asked pointedly.

"Oh. No," said Daisy, as Luca shook his head. "I would know if there were strangers around."

"Aren't we *all* strangers, in one way or another?" Saki observed, her eyes dancing with mischief as she slid two piping hot cocoas, one covered in thick whipped cream and sprinkles, one drizzled with caramel, over the counter.

"We were just, um, doing a bit of a survey," Luca explained, reaching for the mugs.

"There's still the Lost River Outlook," Daisy said. She accepted her caramel cocoa demurely as Luca passed it to her, his hand shaking a little. After a preliminary sip, she focused on him rather than on the officer nearby, adding, "Perhaps Red would like to go with you to see that one."

Luca sputtered and his cup clattered back to its saucer, leaving whipped cream on his nose.

"Careful," said Saki. "They're hot." With a little wave, she left us to loiter and returned to her register to help the next customers.

"Yagggh," said Luca, expressively. "That *is* hot. Um, that's not such a bad idea though, Daisy. What do you think, Red? I was planning to go see it tomorrow. Daisy says it's about an hour out of town. Would you like to come too?"

"She'd better," said Officer Thorn, eyeing me over their shoulders. I got the feeling this might be payback for William telling her what to do earlier. But underneath that, it was clear that she really was concerned. She went on, "Because I'm about to ask Daisy to help me with a search effort. I can't promise it won't last through tomorrow."

I watched both Luca and Daisy, still uncertain exactly what I was stepping into. "Sure, that works," I said at last. "Rhys comes in at lunchtime tomorrow, so I could go then. We can keep an eye out on our way, too."

Strange notes about kidnapping aside, how much trouble could one old "outlook" really be?

3

Off on Adventure

Apparently, Officer Thorn wasn't ready to commit to a full-scale search just yet. After talking a little more with Daisy, she left to check in at the local school and at the police station, in case her "newbie"—Olivia, an older recruit who was hoping to make the police guild her second career—had heard any news. She left us all under strict instruction not to go spreading rumors before she was able to cover all her bases and figure out if the note was true. Given how packed the café had been, I privately thought that much of the town had probably put two and two together. But, I was grateful for a quiet evening inside, and curious about how the next day would develop.

Despite my cautious hopes, the morning's mail brought even more confusion.

Though this particular confusion had nothing to do with Luca, I found myself sharing it with him as we set out from town on foot that afternoon. He was always a good listener, and it was a nice, neutral topic.

"Zady has been gossiping about me," I announced. My

breath huffed white in the air, and a light rain *still* fell on my umbrella. But somehow, the dirt road out of town was reassuring under my boots. My next words didn't come out quite so petulantly. "I got a box from Paracelsus this morning and he mentioned her specifically."

"She did warn you that she writes to him, too," Luca said at my side. On our trip to the Blue Desert Isles, he'd become fond of both my parents.

I sighed. We passed the police station, squatting quietly at the edge of town, and headed for the thick forest. Much of the woods around Belville were evergreen, the trees old and tall, their tops disappearing into the mist today. It was such a different sight from the lab bench I'd been staring at for a week straight. I could practically feel the knots along my spine untangling. "I know, she did. And I know you think it's cute. You're not wrong. But it is a *little* unnerving to realize that your mother and your old mentor still talk about you. Still! I've been out on my own for years!"

Luca chuckled, shaking droplets from his dark umbrella. "That's fair, I guess, but you *do* lead a pretty interesting life. You can see why they'd talk about it."

"It was never my intention to start crime solving." I caught Luca's eye from the corner of mine, and finally smiled. Even the rain didn't seem so bad. "You know what he sent me? Notebooks. And a task. He said, since he'd heard so much about my investigations from Zady and I was clearly becoming 'even more talented than anyone had predicted,' maybe I could find the source of a strange glowing wildflower for him. It's rumored to come from Belville Mountain, but it's not from the pixies' hideout—I already asked Rhys when he came in today, and he didn't recognize its description."

This time, Luca tipped his head back and laughed outright. "You've been given homework!"

"I have," I agreed, though I didn't feel miserable about it any more. "Because I've done too well in all my other 'extracurricular' activities, according to him and Zady."

"I suppose that's the risk you run," Luca mused. As we followed the road into the forest, the world became more muffled, the rain on the leaves above our heads falling without reaching us—as though we were walking along the bottom of a lake. His voice steady, if a little quieter, Luca added, "I wonder if Officer Thorn was feeling the same way. Aside from this new search effort, it's been peaceful around town lately."

When Thorn had questioned Daisy on the Pomegranate's damp porch, Luca had naturally been involved and heard the whole tale. It seemed more like a puzzle to me than ever. "She stopped by early this morning to see if I'd learned anything helpful from the note, which I hadn't. But she did say no one's been able to figure out what child might be missing. So it does seem like a wild goose chase at this point."

"Maybe she *could* use some homework, then," Luca said.

"Her homework is running the volunteer effort for the Halloween fair, and she assigns it to herself every year," I pointed out dryly. "I'm surprised she hasn't insisted everyone hang up fabric streamers and paper skeletons around the Square already, even with the search and the rain."

"Give it a few days. I just finished the bookstore displays this morning," Luca said, modest satisfaction creeping into his voice.

Modest satisfaction was about as close as Luca ever came to being proud of himself. He had a tumultuous past and had inherited his bookstore from someone who'd treated him terribly. Even so, he'd come a long way toward regaining confidence since I'd known him, and he'd always remained optimistic.

Reminded of how we'd both grown together, I smiled over at him. "What theme did you go with this year?"

"I set up the children's section with spooky stories again," Luca said, eyes alight. "But I thought it might be fun to try something even scarier for adults. I pulled together all our archived news articles and books about true crime topics from all over Beyond. Did you know there's a few old cold cases right here in Belville?"

"And William assured me it was such a sleepy town when we moved in," I observed, amused mostly by Luca's enthusiasm. The forest around us was so still, like we were the only people on the mountain. It was hard to think seriously about crime. "Does Officer Thorn know?"

"I'm sure the Police Guild has a system for keeping track. Here, we're supposed to take this path—Daisy gave me instructions," Luca said, interrupting himself to point out an overgrown trail that led up the mountainside, above the main road. I followed him onto it, my breath quickening as the path began to climb. In front, his face hidden, Luca added, "Anyway to be fair, one of the cold cases was actually mine, so she definitely knew about that one. And solved it, with your and William's help."

I frowned at the roots and dirt beneath my feet. It made sense—Luca had been entangled with a dramatic case involving curses, a lost castle, and an ancient secret society when we'd met him. But I was surprised any record remained of that at all. "Are all the unsolved cases really that old?"

"There's one even older." Luca's voice turned speculative.

"Belville's been here a really long time, and even though it's difficult to be certain of anything the farther we go back into history, we do have *some* records from centuries ago. Given how long-lived some people are, there might even be people in town who remember those times."

I thought this over. I was breathing heavily now, stiff and sore from too much sitting in recent days. Talking was no longer easy, but I could ponder. Daisy and Rhys were suitably long-lived, but Rhys was a relative newcomer in Belville, and Daisy's family had actively hidden from the town for centuries before she finally made the choice to reveal herself to us. The only people I could think of in town who were also rumored to be ancient were a handful of vampire families and Lavender, the tavern owner. Rumors abounded about Lavender, actually, and I had no idea which ones to believe. She'd always been welcoming and wise with me, but of course, she was probably privy to all kinds of secrets as an innkeeper and restaurateur.

There *were* ghosts to consider, too. Samhain had originally become a holiday because it was a time of year when, as witches would say, "the veil is thin"—meaning that ghosts might have an easier time contacting the living. There was much debate in Beyond about how, why, and even *when* some people became ghosts. By and large, though we did get ghostly appearances in town around Halloween, they kept out of town affairs. Still . . .

"Are you going," I huffed at last, "to try to solve one? For Samhain?" Maybe this was why he'd seemed so distracted lately.

"Seems like I should ask *you* that question," Luca panted back. He'd given up carrying his umbrella, and thrown his hood back, too. Realizing that I was feeling quite warm myself,

I followed suit.

"Don't say that too loud," I admonished. "Or Officer Thorn will hear. I don't need her getting more ideas. One mysterious note and a glowing flower is enough."

The trail abruptly flattened along a ridge, and Luca stopped to rest. Turning, he grinned at me. "Don't forget the nosy friends, family, and old mentors, too."

"As if I could get the chance." I rolled my eyes and returned the grin.

At that moment, through a gap in the trees, a large shape flew just under the cloud cover. A white scaly body as big as a house, and green-blue dragonfly-like wings. Daisy, in her true form as a dragon.

With her on the case, it was difficult not to feel reassured.

* * *

By the time we emerged in a damp clearing, we were joking and teasing as if we had no cares in the world. I'd almost forgotten why we were on the mountain at all, except to get some exercise and a change of scene. Our dirt path had wound up and up through the forest, tracing switchbacks and trailing along ridges, and in the dense forest it was often impossible to see more than twenty paces ahead. When we arrived at the end of the old road, it took me by surprise.

The path ran out as soon as it emerged from the tree cover, dissipating into the long grass of a clearing. The clearing itself was long and narrow, stretching up to the left until it came to a point. We stood at its widest section, gazing across at a great stone tower.

"Lost River Outlook," said Luca, stowing his handwritten

list of directions. "That's definitely it."

I had to tilt my head back to see its top. The tower was an obelisk, four sides that started to lean into each other as they went up, so that the top was much smaller than the base. It must have been ten stories tall at least, and yet it seemed sturdy enough. The rain made its old rocks look dark and slick. At regular intervals, windows marked where floors or staircases must be inside.

That was all it was—just a tower, rising out of the clearing like it had been there forever. Other local relics tended to have walls or gardens, like the old haunted castle or the fort Luca had been to see with Daisy. But this one stood totally alone.

As we walked closer, I realized that it wasn't just alone—it was on the edge of a cliff. The far side of the clearing dropped abruptly into a canyon. I paused to look at that first, distracted by the thirty foot drop . . . and the fact that there was no water in the rocky gorge at all. Not even in this stormy weather.

"That's why they call it Lost River, I think," Luca said as he came to stand beside me. "Stories say there's never any water there, not even rain or snow melt. No one knows why. Of course, the popular theory is that it's cursed."

I glanced at my partner. With his hood thrown back, its magical glamour spell was removed. Instead of looking like an average dark-skinned scholar, Luca now sported a twisted, shadowy horn rising above his forehead and deep green tattoos. *He* had been cursed. But this canyon?

I tugged my goggles down over my eyes and took another look, pursing my lips. "I don't see any reason to jump to that conclusion. It's not like the gorge is actually dry. You can see wetness on the rocks and dirt—it's just that there's no actual running water, which *is* pretty weird. But maybe the soil here is super absorbent, or something."

"Another bit of homework you can add to your list," Luca said, his eyes crinkling as he smiled. "Want to check out the inside? Daisy gave me a key."

"Sure." I followed him over to the tower door, which was surprisingly simple. Solid oak with one little pane of aged glass for a window and a heavy iron lock, it didn't look like the sort of door that would give easily.

And yet, when Luca touched it to steady himself as he pulled out the key, it swung open of its own accord.

"Whoa." Luca leaned back, startled. Then he shrugged and looked back at me. "Maybe I'm just jumpy?"

"Maybe Daisy came by and opened it up for us?" I suggested, hesitant to agree. "It does seem odd. But I can't imagine why anyone else would be up here."

"Well, you can rent it," Luca said, reasonably.

"What?" I shook my head, realizing I'd never asked exactly what we were doing. "Is that why you're going around—to check up on rentals run out of Belville or something? Isn't there a town official for that?"

"Um, not exactly. It's really more of a favor," Luca said, rubbing his hands over his robes. "Well, what do you say? Want to go in, and up? I bet the view is amazing."

I couldn't imagine coming all this way and *not* seeing the inside, but I was still wary. "Maybe knock first."

Luca grinned. "You're just hoping someone's there to pull you up so you don't have to climb all those stairs."

4

Out of the Blue

Hopes or no, there was no answer to Luca's knock. After another moment for our nerves to settle, we decided to head in.

Inside the tower was like an entirely different world. It was warm, first of all—warm, dry, and cozy. The walls were plastered, and the plaster itself was colored, creating a forest mural that stretched from wooden floor to ceiling beams. A thick woven rug of deep green covered most of the first floor. Two doors lined the back wall, presumably bathrooms or closets. There was also a side table nearby supporting a mirror, almost as if this was an ordinary entrance hall for a pleasant manor house.

"This is *not* what I expected," I admitted aloud.

Luca grinned as he settled our umbrellas in a large glazed pot by the door. "Just wait til you see the rest. I've heard it's really impressive."

The staircase ran around the outer edge of the room. We began climbing and soon emerged on another floor, this one with a deep blue rug and walls painted with mountain scenes.

26

An old sofa and some armchairs were clustered near a fireplace on one side, and on the other, built-in bookshelves with glass doors displayed colorful titles.

I half expected Luca to stay there, but he kept climbing up. In another few turns, we were on the third floor—this one sporting a yellow rug and cloud murals, along with a quaint old kitchen and sturdy dining table.

"This is amazing," I said, lingering by a window. The glass was set in small panes laced together in diamond shapes, making it difficult to see the outside world but still clearly showing the tops of trees and the bellies of low-hanging clouds. We were already pretty high up.

"Come on, let's keep going," Luca insisted, taking my hand as he headed back to the stairs.

The fourth floor opened up onto a small landing, from which two doors branched in opposite directions. One led to a charming bathroom tiled in pink, and the other opened into a large bedroom with a massive canopy bed and a recurring rose motif.

"The grand bedroom," Luca explained, unnecessarily, before dragging me to the fifth floor to find a larger landing with a few more armchairs and two smaller bedrooms with baths.

The furniture and details were amazing, but by this point, we'd climbed a *lot* of stairs—and that was on top of hiking up the mountain. I paused, leaning against the wall. "Okay, I might just have to stay here while you do whatever you came to do."

"Nonsense," Luca declared. "We have to at least peek at the top."

"How does that even work?" I protested, feeling certain that this was only a prelude to convincing me to climb five more stories.

Still, his enthusiasm was infectious. He convinced me up onto the sixth floor, at least, where we found a white rug and constellation patterns on the walls. A telescope stood by one window, and a desk nearby clearly had drawing materials.

"You could do your homework here," Luca teased.

"I certainly could. As much as I love my lab, I was just thinking it's getting a little bit *too* familiar these days," I confessed. The entire tower so far had been marvelous, and I was tempted to ask Luca just how much the place rented for. There was a scuff above, though, and on impulse I added, "What was that?"

"Let's go see," said Luca, with the fearlessness of someone whose curse allowed them to fade into the shadows in a pinch.

I followed him more carefully up the stairs, recalling that note about a kidnapped child. It turned out that my caution was needless, however. Before I'd made it to the landing, Luca was already relaxed and chatting.

"We were just coming by on Daisy's advice," he was saying, "and we did wonder why the door was unlocked!"

I took a surreptitious look around. The sixth floor was bare except for maps laid into the walls—clearly, it was an observation novelty only. There was no rug, only a few chairs which had pushed to the side as a housekeeper cleaned the floor and windows.

He was shorter than Luca and me, but only barely, his dark skin peeking out at the edges of his gray, ill-fitting coverall uniform. In one hand he held a bucket and rag, and with the other he leaned on a windowsill as he chatted with Luca. His knitted cap was tucked tightly around his head, holding back any hair from his work. A fabric face mask obscured his nose and mouth. But his dark eyes were open and friendly—perhaps even a little relieved to have found someone to talk to.

"Oh, she does send people from time to time," he was saying, his voice slightly muffled. "Some folks like to look at a place before they rent it. It's always best to be prepared, that's what I say, myself."

"Yes, I think my partner, Red, can agree with you on that." Luca smiled at me as I joined them. "We were thinking of going to the top to see the view. How much farther is it, do you think?"

"Quite a ways, but that's not the problem." The man gestured up, and we followed the suggestion, looking toward the ceiling—only to see that there was no ceiling. And what in the lower floors was a stone staircase instead became iron steps set into the walls, with only the barest suggestion of a railing. As the outer walls of the tower came together toward the point at the top, the space inside the tower became smaller and smaller. The effect was several floors of rickety-looking spiral staircase before a shadowy platform far above our heads.

"Most people prefer to look from here," the housekeeper concluded.

Just *looking* at those iron steps made my legs shake. I was used to running, but that was on mostly flat surfaces. I felt certain that climbing this tower was going to give me a case of sudden-onset vertigo. "You don't *need* to go up there, do you?" I asked Luca.

"No, I've seen everything I need to." Luca glanced back down at me, smiling. "Save it for another day?"

"I'm happy waiting til somebody else goes up and sends me a postcard," I admitted, with more feeling than I'd realized.

The housekeeper chuckled.

"At least some of us are smart," he said.

"You come up here often, I guess?" As he nodded, I thought again of Officer Thorn's latest case. "Have you noticed anyone lurking around, or any signs someone was here when they shouldn't be?"

"Gods, no," the man said easily. "It's a tight ship, here. No one could get in without a key. There's spells and everything."

"And you didn't see anyone?" Luca repeated, curious.

"Not a soul, save Daisy, and the last renters a while back," said the housekeeper. "There's not many as like to come out in this weather, eh?"

"True," I agreed, with feeling. "I just wondered. Thank you for your time."

He nodded, smiling. "You want me to show you anything else?"

"Oh, no, we didn't mean to interrupt you," Luca assured him. "We'll be on our way. Should we lock up behind ourselves, or—?"

"Leave all that to me," the man assured us. "You have a nice vacation, now, alright?"

We exchanged polite goodbyes and headed back down the staircase. But something he'd said stuck in my mind. When we'd made it outside again and it was safe to turn around and confront Luca, I asked him, "What *is* all this about? You hardly ever take vacations, and anyway, we were just gone over the summer. Are you putting together another tourism brochure for the town?"

Standing by the tower's solid front door, Luca looked sheepish. "Well, I did think—you know, they don't even have one at all for the mountain properties, yet, and it's not such a bad idea—"

"*Luca.*" I crossed my arms. "You can't make fun of me for taking on all kinds of work and then go and sign yourself up for more projects than you need, too."

"They would pay me if I did," he offered.

"In peace of mind and time to de-stress?" I shook my head ruefully, smiling. "Come on. It's Samhain. Shouldn't we just relax and focus on having a good time, instead of all this other stuff?"

Luca hesitated before returning my smile. "Don't worry," he said. "That's sort of what I was thinking, too. I won't take on any new projects just yet."

* * *

That's one *mystery solved,* I thought, as we headed back down toward town.

While I did my fair share of helping people and taking on unusual tasks, Luca practically made it his mission. He did good work, but that was part of the problem. He'd made a great brochure last year about carnivals, which then made the mayor ask him to make one about Belville's fairs; he'd adopted an ancient mink as a store assistant, which then led to him being on the town committee for talking animals; he'd once done story time for the Halloween fair, which then led to him reading books for kids at pretty much any town event. He loved all of it, but sometimes, he didn't realize he was signing himself up for too much.

I was hardly one to talk, of course, with my impressive record of getting dragged into police affairs. But at least I made sure Officer Thorn had to drag me. I didn't *volunteer* for these things. Usually.

The rain returned with a vengeance just as we made it onto the main road into Belville. I fumbled for a moment with my umbrella, getting soaked, until Luca tugged me under his.

"You're safe with me," he said against my ear. I could feel his lips curving in a smile.

"Safe but damp," I retorted, smiling despite myself.

"Damp is fine, as long as you don't get sick. That's not allowed," he informed me as we began moving again. "At least here we can walk side by side. Want to stop at the Pomegranate? Or make tea at home?"

"I do have a new immune-support blend I've been working on," I said, thinking of the jars of dried herbs and flowers in my lab. "You can test it out for me."

"I'll be your tester any time," Luca agreed lightly.

"You might regret that." As I was reminding him of all my mishaps in making stock for my shop, we slowly came upon the police station. It marked the edge of town, and normally was a landmark I was glad to see. Today, though, the door was wide open.

Another strangely open door?

I stopped mid-recollection and looked up at Luca. "That's odd, don't you think?"

"I do," he confirmed. Worry creased his brow. "Especially after the news yesterday. What if the note was some kind of trap? Maybe we'd better go to the Pomegranate after all and see if Saki knows what's up."

"Hold on." I dashed out from under the umbrella to close the station door, peeking around it quickly. Officer Thorn and her trainee Olivia were nowhere to be seen.

"I just got an even better idea," Luca said grimly as I returned.

He gestured down the street. Through a break in the rain, we could see that a crowd had gathered in Market Square.

And as we jogged over to join them, we heard the rumors: Thorn's searches had turned up yet another mystery.

5

Talk of the Tavern

We got to Market Square just in time to see the local Witch, Trent, escorting a stranger away from the park.

The stranger was slight, with tousled brown hair and a limp that was painful to watch. Trent, on the other hand, was tall and spindly, his pale skin contrasting starkly with his dark rain jacket. Purple magic sparkled around him as he helped the injured man walk. Officer Thorn cleared a path for them through the crowd, Olivia at her heels.

"What happened?" Luca asked the nearest person, who turned out to be Dusty, the local handy-gnome. What he lacked in height, he more than made up for with experience—and tall tales.

"He stumbled out here not five minutes ago," Dusty told us, gesturing at the departing stranger. "No umbrella, no cloak, no nothing. Came right down from the mountain on the old mining trail. Managed to get himself all the way here to the park before someone noticed him. Soon's he saw us running over to him, he collapsed."

"So you were one of the first people on the scene?" I expected no less. Dusty had a habit of appearing wherever he was most needed. He did all the maintenance for my shop that I couldn't do myself, and he was William's best friend in town aside from Rhys.

"Finishing up a job over at Lavender's when I spotted something," Dusty confirmed. This explained his lack of weather-appropriate clothing: Dusty wore the overalls and floppy cap that made up his usual uniform, no umbrella or coat to be seen. His blue eyes stood out under the cap's brim, though, and his skin was so weathered already that he didn't look cold.

And because Lavender's Tavern took up the southwest corner of the Square, I understood exactly why he'd seen the disturbance in the park. Setting that aside, I asked, "What kind of help did he need?"

"Trent's gonna patch him up," Dusty said. This, too, made sense. Our young Witch had been working on his healing spells for several years, and was becoming quite proficient. In a town without an actual doctor, this was immensely helpful. Dusty added, "He didn't even know where he was, or what year it was."

"Did he have a head injury?" Luca asked, worried.

"Dunno. We were all asking him questions, and he couldn't answer a single one."

"Well, at least with Trent, he won't be overwhelmed by multiple onlookers," I said, wryly. Though it was nice of Dusty and the others to want to help, I doubted the experience of being yelled at by strangers had been reassuring for the newcomer.

"Thorn'll be interested, though," said Dusty. "One of the

only words I *did* catch from him was 'murder.'"

"Murder?" Luca glanced around as though looking for clues. "I thought I heard somebody saying he was involved in the search."

"He was," Dusty agreed. Naturally, as a consummate gossip with connections all over town, he spoke about Officer Thorn's "discreet" case with total confidence. "Because he's the one they were searching for."

"What?" Luca and I asked in unison.

"He must be the kidnapper," Dusty explained. "We all figure he was injured when the kid got away."

* * *

As preposterous as it seemed, Dusty's explanation of recent events *was* what everyone in town believed. Or so it seemed, at least.

Luca, William, and I had headed straight for the tavern as soon as we closed up shop for the day. By that time, stories of the newcomer had spread like wildfire despite the storm. Somehow, the town grapevine had learned some new things: the man was staying with Trent while he recovered, and he'd gone suspiciously quiet the moment he'd seen Officer Thorn. Those two tidbits seemed like fact, but everything else was wild speculation.

The three of us sat at one end of the bar and listened as we nursed hot ciders. Lavender's Tavern was a Belville institution, its one long room a beloved, cozy space. Huge fireplaces blazed on either end. Wooden tables and chairs filled up the floor, with gossip and shouts ringing up to the rafters. The polished bar ran all along the back wall, until it hit a staircase in the corner that led up to rented rooms on the second floor. Tonight, the place was so packed with news-hungry patrons that even around the tables and hearths, people stood and talked. The tavern was the sort of place that had no real menu, only a set of seasonal specials and old familiar favorites. Mine was gnocchi, and when it came out from the kitchen I found I was starving. Luca had opted for the spicy fall chili and William, perched to my right, was digging into a plate of samosas.

"Dusty said there's still no sign of any kid," William said between bites, his tone low under the rumble of the crowd. "Sounds like some people think that could be why the stranger came into town saying 'murder.'"

"They think it was an accident? Or he has a guilty conscience?" Luca frowned as he blew on a spoonful of soup.

"Or that he was delirious and accidentally admitted his crime," William, ever the pessimist, suggested.

"Everyone is making a *lot* of assumptions," I said, and paused as Lavender herself came over to us.

The tavern's owner could almost always be found behind the bar. I'd never known her to take a vacation, let alone a day off. She was matronly but ageless, with smooth pale skin that never wrinkled and silver hair that never thinned. Though she was an ample, rounded woman, I'd also never seen her eat. People said that her beautiful amethyst eyes and the occasional white feather in her hair were proof that she was an angel— essentially, an immortal spirit dedicated to helping others. I had no idea if it was true, but she was certainly in a good place to do so.

Tonight, though, her normally open and friendly expression was wan and drawn. "Red, love. I hear you and Luca were involved in finding that poor man today?"

"Not exactly," I said, glancing at Luca. "We were up on the mountain and only just got to town as Trent was escorting him away."

"I see." She settled her arms against the bar between us, her white apron stretching over her chest. "Which of the rumors do you believe?"

She glanced at all three of us as she spoke, but it was Luca who piped up first. "We're still trying to make sense of them. Have you heard a lot of different stories?"

"Ahh." Lavender waved one calloused hand. "That he was part of a criminal gang; that his comrades turned on him; that he stole a wealthy person's child in an act of revenge; that he's a notorious outlaw, or maybe an innocent on the run from his problems; or even that he's some kind of farmer or gardener who got caught up in something too big for him. Then others say he was a police informant or even a criminal mastermind who's just pretending to be injured to get access to the town . . ."

"Wow," I said, as her voice trailed off. "All of that sounds really ominous."

"Maybe it's Samhain making people nervous," Luca said, though his worried eyes belied any lightness in his tone.

"Either way, I'm sure Officer Thorn will get to the bottom of it," I added.

"She's got to show Olivia the proper way to do things, after all," William agreed.

Lavender smiled at us. "My three most practical customers!"

"Sorry we couldn't actually tell you anything," I said, even though I wasn't sure how much Officer Thorn would want known anyway. Lavender just seemed so affected by it all.

"We came here ourselves hoping to learn something, but it seems like everyone's just making up scary stories."

"That is it exactly," Lavender concluded, rising. "Let me make your night a little more satisfactory, at least. I'll get you another round of ciders, on the house."

"Oh, you really don't have to—" Luca and I spoke at once, gratitude and embarrassment mingling in our voices.

Lavender was already turning to her task. She smiled over her shoulder at us, and her eyes looked a little less sad. "None of your protests. Consider it my way of returning a favor."

I exchanged a glance with William, wondering how much of a favor we'd really done. Maybe it *was* a strain on Lavender, stuck behind her bar, hearing all these stories—each more sensational than the last. Maybe the worst part was wondering which was actually true.

6

Casting Shadows

The next morning, I woke with a start. What I'd thought were dragons' roars and kidnappers' footsteps chasing me down the mountain were William's snores.

Even though William slept in the bench seat in the window, like usual, his snores were so loud that they echoed through the studio apartment. In the bed next to me, Luca was sleeping like nothing was wrong. It probably helped that he was piled under a pillow and several blankets.

No wonder it was snowing in my dream, I thought, looking down at the lone flannel sheet that covered my pajamas.

Sometimes my loved ones were my comfort and my safety net . . . and sometimes they were the problem!

I stood, stretching. The bed stood along one side wall, separated from the bathroom in the corner by a wall and a bank of dressers. To my left was a fireplace and cozy seating area—not to mention William, the magical nightmare-enhancer. Along the front wall, there was a bank of windows looking out over Market Square. The sky beyond them was dark still, but it didn't appear to be actively raining anymore. In the far corner was my dining nook, and my kitchen was across from me, separated by the entry hall, which opened out onto a landing with two sets of stairs, one to descend into the shop and one to go outside. With all the bad weather lately, I hadn't made much use of that staircase in a while.

When I emerged from the bathroom more alert, dressed in warm wool tights and a burgundy tunic, neither William nor Luca had moved . . . but I noticed a sparkle in the kitchen.

"Morning, Sugar," I murmured as I padded around the kitchen island to open the bread box. This was our morning routine: I would feed Sugar a little bread for her breakfast, and she cast enough light that I could make tea and *actual* breakfast without waking anyone else.

She took a crumb of bread from my fingers with her customary delight. Sugar was a pixie, just like the ones Daisy looked after. She stood about as tall as my palm—if she ever stood; most of the time she was either hovering on her glimmering, insect-like wings, peering down from some hidey hole atop the cabinets, or perched in my hair. Her skin was nut-brown and she tended to wear little white toga-like dresses, so she could blend in with the woodwork whenever she wanted to. She'd found William and me two years ago over a harsh winter, and had taken up residence in my kitchen. Fortunately, her appetite was tiny, though her pranks were sometimes exasperating.

Sugar followed me as I drew water from the sink, her natural glow illuminating my work. I set the kettle to boil and rummaged in the icebox for cream cheese. The last of the season's chives stood in a glass of water in the little kitchen window, and there was just enough pumpernickel bread left for everyone. Actually, there were several kinds of bread, all stuffed in the bread box on the counter. I tended to bake when agitated. Cooking has always been a stress reliever for me—it's like alchemy, but the stakes are lower. Unless we're talking about poisoning . . .

Naturally, it was at that very moment as I was musing on natural poisons that the door below resounded with a loud knock.

Across the room, William startled awake. "I'm gonna set a ward that keeps her out of the yard as well as the shop," he growled.

"Who is it?" the pile of blankets on the bed asked in a muffled voice.

"It's got to be Thorn," I said. The knock was characteristic enough. I was just glad she wasn't already yelling. "Don't worry, sleepyheads, I'll go down and talk to her."

I turned off the stove and left Sugar sitting on my cutting board, playing with a sprig of chive. The knock sounded again as I closed the hall door and hurried down the stairs.

"*What?*" I asked as I yanked open the back door.

"Hello," said a voice that was definitely not Officer Thorn.

I leaned on the door frame, squinting a little. Somewhere behind the clouds the sun was rising, but the shop's back yard was in deep shadow. It took me a second to process the fact that the uniformed officer on the patio *wasn't* my friend—instead, it was Olivia, the trainee.

"She said I had to make sure to knock loud," she was saying. "I thought maybe you were hard of hearing—"

I sighed. "No, she's just teaching you to be exactly like she is," I said in a friendly, if resigned, manner. I didn't add *annoying,* or *effective,* both of which were true. "Is something wrong?

Where is she?"

"At the Witch's Hut," Olivia said promptly. "She asked me to come here and tell you to go over there and bring several bottles of antiseptic potion and a packet of warming powders. And to go to the bakery, too."

I frowned. "She wants me to go to the bakery?"

"No, me," Olivia said, holding up a scrawled list.

"Ah. That makes more sense." I considered Olivia. She was older than Officer Thorn, and myself, by a decade or two; Police Guild training was a change-of-life decision for her. With her black furry ears and slightly too large, yellow-green eyes, it was clear she was catkin. Many kinds of "kin" wandered Beyond, their blood mixed with magic that gave them animal-like qualities—they could come in many varieties, including phoenixkin, like my neighbor Gloria, or snakekin, like Ryuko, another friend in town. Catkin were fairly common. I wondered if William had known it was Olivia, not Thorn, he'd been threatening to ban from the property.

I also wondered what exactly was going on at the Witch's Hut. What had happened to the stranger, that he needed *bottles* of antiseptic? "Is this an emergency?" I asked.

"I'm not sure?" Olivia bit her lip.

I hesitated, then nodded. Olivia had made it clear upon her arrival in town a few weeks back that she often missed subtext or inflections in others' voices. I personally thought that might have been why the Guild sent her to Thorn—with Officer Thorn, there was usually *no* subtext. Everything was said, in a very direct manner. I doubted Thorn had forgotten to tell her trainee something important like 'this is an emergency,' but then again, in the heat of the moment she might have neglected to spell everything out. "Okay, I'll get moving," I decided. "Meet you there?"

"Bye!" Olivia agreed.

* * *

I showed up at the Hut fifteen minutes later. Sometimes, that tiny bit of magic in my blood that allowed me to run fast came in very handy.

As the official town Witch, Trent had moved to town and been given the official residence—the Hut. It sat on a hillside just outside of town. Since Trent had moved in, he'd actually managed to improve it quite a bit. The chimney no longer leaned at a dangerous angle—just a mild one. And the herb garden now sprawled across the yard between the little round house and its fence, leaving only a narrow stone walkway for visitors looking for the front door.

I closed the gate behind me and listened with interest to the raised voices as I made my way to the house.

"If you won't keep him I'll take him to the station!"

"That's not the issue here, I said I *would* take him!"

"You don't sound very certain to me!"

"Well that's probably because you already made up your mind to haul him away!"

It was concerning, but also a *little* amusing. Technically, the "town Witch" position was administered by a worldwide school of Witchery, and Witches were only responsible for being on hand to help townsfolk across Beyond. But in our little corner of Pastoria, where the Police Guild presence was small, Officer Thorn leaned on Trent as often as she leaned on me. The young Witch bickered with the officer like they were siblings.

When I opened the front door, I found Officer Thorn and Trent glaring at each other across the kitchen table. Drying herbs hanging from the rafters fell across Thorn's face, and she batted them away. Trent, who was tall but stood with a perpetual stoop, blew strands of shoulder-length black hair out of his eyes.

"I don't have breakfast," I announced as they turned to me. "Just the potions. You sound like you could both use something to eat, though."

"We didn't ask for opinions," Officer Thorn huffed.

"Yeah, Thorn's not hangry, she's just bull-headed," Trent agreed, setting his hands on his narrow hips.

"Well then. How's your patient supposed to be recovering with all this racket?" I asked, trying another tack.

"You mean criminal—"

"The *patient*," Trent interrupted the officer with a pointed glare, "is in the spare room. Probably *not* recovering. We *were* being quiet until *someone*—"

"Ooookay," I interrupted. I wasn't trying to start the war all over again. "Never mind. Trent, I assume you asked for these things because you need them. Is there something I can help you with?"

"Yeah," he said again, relenting a little. "Come on. *You* stay out here," he said to Officer Thorn. "Keep watch for your croissants or whatever."

I waited until we'd crossed the wooden floor past the hearth and Trent was knocking at the spare room door before murmuring quietly, "Wow, Trent."

"Just wait," he said, his jaw tight. "You'll see."

There was no sound from within, but after a moment, Trent

opened the door and went inside.

I followed to find a bare room—just a small bed, a table, a chair, and a window. Not even a rug or curtains. Trent wasn't much of an interior decorator. However, it was clear he was worried about his patient. He sat on the chair and leaned toward the stranger, who sat upright on the bed.

I'd been half worried that his injuries were grievous, given Officer Thorn's requests. But actually, the man on the bed looked like any average convalescent patient. Trent had wrapped gauze around his head and one of his feet was splinted, but other than that, he looked fine to my untrained eye. His thick brown hair was wild around his face, standing on end and brushing his neck, but the look suited him. His ears were pointy, both present and accounted for, and freckles danced across his tan face. He seemed to be wearing one of Trent's cast-off t-shirts and a pair of pajama pants in a purple plaid, which indicated that there had been some effort to make him comfortable. As we walked in, though, he did not respond.

"Listen," said Trent, his voice heavy. "I'm really sorry about her. She's just doing her best."

I realized he was talking about Officer Thorn, and watched the stranger curiously. He didn't even blink.

Trent tried again. "We got you some warming powders. I think they might help with the shock."

"I made them," I offered, when the man made no move. "My name's Red—I run the alchemy shop in town. They're totally safe."

He looked up at me then, his eyes a startling deep green. But I couldn't read his expression.

"We'll show you how to use them," Trent said, with a sigh, "and then we'll let you rest. Breakfast should be here in a little bit."

I lingered for a few more minutes with Trent, showing the stranger how to use the warming powders if he wanted. Since they were very simple, this only needed to take a few seconds, but Trent worried over the man like a mother hen. Given the situation, I understood.

We emerged back into the main room of the Hut to find that Officer Thorn had moved to sit on the front stoop. Taking advantage of the quiet moment, I asked Trent in a low voice, "What is going on here?"

"He won't talk," Trent said, needlessly. "I mean, he *did* talk, a little bit, in the beginning. But as soon as Thorn started spouting off about kidnappers and jail, he shut up. I can't get anything out of him now."

"What do you think happened to him?" I asked.

Trent ran his hands through his hair, which was unkempt from a night spent caretaking and arguing. "His ankle just has a bad sprain—like maybe he took a fall. But his head, that was more serious. He definitely got hit with something hard. He had a concussion when he came in. I was able to do a lot for it with magic, but he might still be feeling it."

"Like maybe he doesn't remember anything?" I suggested.

"It's possible," Trent agreed. "I keep trying to explain that to Thorn, but she won't listen to me."

"You should hear what they're saying about him at the tavern," I told him. "People are pretty scared."

"I get that, but there's no *proof,*" said Trent, losing his cool. "He's a patient—nothing more, nothing less. Maybe if she backed off, he'd be able to trust me enough to at least say if he's feeling better!"

"Hmmm." I thought for a quick moment, then laid a hand

on Trent's shoulder. "Let me try. Take a break, maybe clean up a little—just try to think of something else for a moment, okay? And, Trent?"

"Yeah?" he asked, looking suddenly defeated.

I smiled at him. "For a Witch new to this whole doctoring thing, you're doing a really great job."

7

Hidden Sorrows

"Don't you think you're going too hard on this one?" I asked as I sat beside Officer Thorn on the Hut's front stoop.

She sighed, her massive shoulders rising and falling and still inches above mine. "I'm worried about him."

Ahhh. Now that *makes sense.* I smiled faintly to myself as we looked out across the town together. The sun had risen, but under the heavy cloud cover the peaked rooftops still looked dull and damp. As did Trent's garden, which smelled like sage and moss under the morning dew.

"He says *I'm* stubborn, but he's the one who's trouble," Thorn added petulantly.

"You're peas in a pod, honestly," I said with some humor. "And I'm feeling left out. Want to explain everything to me? Luca and William and I went to the tavern last night for news, but you can imagine what that was like."

"Even worse than reading Leo's paper." Officer Thorn seemed cheered by the opportunity to make a scornful remark about Leo, our local reporter—another very colorful and determined character. "You know about the note? I did have you look at it," she reminded herself.

"Not to mention the whole town knows about that already, or thinks that they do," I supplied. "So what's happened since?"

"Olivia reached out to the local stations, and Daisy helped me search the mountain. But none of us came up with a thing. I was about to let the whole thing go as a Samhain prank yesterday when this new trouble rolls in." She jerked one manicured thumb over her shoulder, indicating Trent's patient.

I wrinkled my nose. "Has he really been trouble? Aside from town gossip."

"He's not right, Red," Officer Thorn said heavily. "There's something off about him."

"Well," I said, trying to think reasonably and impartially about my own experience with the stranger so far, "it seems like he might think the same of us."

Officer Thorn let out one startled bark of a laugh, surprising several nearby crows into flight. "Have you been talking to Maggie? She's always telling me I should be more kind."

The mention of Maggie made me smile. Officer Thorn had been head over heels for the ex-acrobat for over a year, and just this past spring, they'd started dating. Maggie was short, slight, often a little nervous, and absolutely perfect for Thorn, in my opinion. They brought out the best in each other. "I've barely seen anyone lately," I admitted lightly, "so no. But you should bring her over more often. Not to mention *listen* to her."

"Oh, I know it." Thorn tugged at one long ear, a fond expression on her face. "It's just—it's an odd case, you have to admit."

"Do you actually know that this new man is related to your kidnapping note?" I asked.

She answered thoughtfully, her eyes on a pair of distant figures that could be seen on the road leading out of town. "The timing is too coincidental. I can't rule it out. And before you say anything, yes, I know that Trent is right and we should give this newcomer the benefit of the doubt. But if he *is* tied up in a kidnapping case, and for some reason he decided to come into town to gather information or even another victim, I don't want Trent to be the one at hand. I don't want *anyone* to be at hand. Maybe I wouldn't be so worried if he hadn't rambled on about the mountain and murder before taking one look at my uniform and gluing his lips shut."

I could see how it was a complicated and frustrating situation, but the image still made me chuckle a little. "Gluing, huh? Well, he didn't use any potion of mine. Why'd you want all those antiseptic potions, by the way?"

"For Trent's stores," Thorn answered, still watching the two figures. They were clearly coming up the dirt path that led to Trent's place. "I promised him I'd get him something for his trouble."

"You're paying the local Witch for his cooperation using *my* merchandise?" I shook my head. "I don't think that's how any of this is supposed to work. And if you think I'm going to be party to bribery, then you—"

"Red," Thorn interrupted, "who do you think that is, coming here?"

I glanced at the figures, distracted. The hill was misty, but they were quite close now. One looked like Olivia—her dark ears were clearly visible, as were her shiny uniform buttons and polished knee-high boots. But I couldn't make sense of the other. It was a large figure, dressed in light colors and carrying a white umbrella, moving slowly but gracefully up the path . . .

"No way," I said, as the image finally clicked into place in my head. "Did Lavender really leave her tavern to come see *us*?"

* * *

It was perhaps the first time that I had seen Officer Thorn *not* be wholly distracted by the arrival of pastries. She took a handful of croissants and mini quiches from Olivia, passed some to me, and then waved her assistant through the door to deal with Trent. Meanwhile, Lavender lingered in the garden, clearly anxious about something.

"I looked for you at the station, but you weren't there," she said.

To me, this made the encounter even stranger. I'd never seen Lavender outside of her tavern. Now suddenly she had been to the police station *and* the Hut? She might as well have flown to the moon and back.

"Is there an emergency?" Thorn asked, clearly thinking along the same lines as me.

"No, nothing so urgent." Lavender looked through the dark doorway, then at Thorn, then at me. "I believe there is something I need to tell you, dears. I thought it best to do so sooner than later."

I exchanged a glance with Officer Thorn, still confused. "Want me to leave? I can catch up with Trent and Olivia. Or, honestly, get back to my shop."

"You should stay," Lavender said firmly, before Thorn could respond. "If the officer has no objections, of course."

"None yet," said Thorn, cautiously. Swallowing half a croissant, she added, "Do you want to talk here or back at the station?"

"The kitchen garden will suffice." Lavender moved away, through unruly rows of yarrow and thyme. She still seemed unusual to me, almost unearthly, like she was gliding. *Probably because I always see her behind the bar and never actually notice her legs,* I thought, reminding myself to calm down. Lavender's long skirts were definitely touching the ground. Probably. It was a little hard to tell with the mist and the plants . . .

"Eat while you can." Thorn nudged me as she moved to follow the innkeeper.

I looked down at the pesto quiche in my hands and found that I *was* hungry. I ate it in rapid bites as I followed along, too.

Lavender settled herself on a large rock that had been rolled up to the fence—no doubt Trent had needed it out of the way, and had never gotten around to actually moving it fully *out* of the yard. Thorn and I stood in front of her, pastries in hand like children on a snack break. We were ten paces from the back of the Hut, and in the cool misty air, no sound seemed to travel.

For once, though, Lavender looked a little uncertain.

"You know something about the newcomer?" Officer Thorn prompted.

"I . . . do." Lavender took a deep breath and smiled up at us, though her smile looked distinctly sad. "It's no use me seeing him; he won't remember me. Olivia was telling me he has been . . . unhappy. I wouldn't want to trouble him."

"But you're sure you *know* him?" Thorn asked, all at attention now.

"Yes, I . . . I saw him through the tavern doors as he came into the Square last night. I knew I would one day," she added wistfully. "But of course, he did not make it all the way back."

Officer Thorn glanced at me before brushing away the last of her crumbs and pulling her notebook from her breast pocket. "You'd better start at the beginning."

"The beginning was a very long time ago," Lavender said, her eyes distant and unfocused as she remembered. "We came here many, many years ago . . . my daughter and I."

Daughter? I'd never known Lavender had family. My eyes were probably wide as saucers, but no one was paying attention so I didn't bother to hide it.

"Three hundred years ago," Lavender continued. "It was only pixies and elves living in the woods then, but we knew Belville could become something special. *She* knew it—Violetta. She convinced me it was the perfect place to make a home. And so we did—a home for all who came through here; an inn where all would be welcome and the hearth was always burning . . ."

A tear traced Lavender's cheek as she talked, though she made no notice of it. "Many years later, once her dream had been built, a sorcerer came to stay at our inn. She was in failing health, this sorcerer, and her own magic had deserted her. She was looking for something that would save her life . . . In those days, there were all kinds of rumors about the Tree of Life and Belville Mountain. She said she had come to find a way to heal herself. Instead, she fell in love with my daughter.

"Violetta did not return her affections. She had grown very fond of a local boy, one of the elves. They were so very close . . . It was just over two hundred years ago now that they were married, in the spring. And soon after, their baby boy was born."

This time she did notice her tears, and broke off her story for a moment. I stepped in, handing her my handkerchief without a word. She nodded and, for a brief second, gripped my hand.

"She was so happy," Lavender sighed. "So happy here. But before he was a year old, her boy was taken from her. He vanished—and so did the sorcerer, who had stayed on at the inn . . .

"I should never have let her stay." Her face hardened for a moment, but soon fell. "But Violetta would never stand for me turning someone out. She thought the sorcerer would come around and accept the fact that she was happy with someone else. Instead, she was gone, and the precious little baby with her, and—and Violetta—

"Neither she nor Kieran could bear it very long," Lavender said quietly. "They spent all their time searching. Like many of the elves who lived here at that time, Kieran had a magical connection to plants, especially the local forest—they hoped that would help them . . . They must have gone over the mountain a million times. But they could never find anything, and in time, it ate them away. Kieran died first, of grief, in the fall. Violetta followed him that winter.

"That was more than a hundred and fifty years ago," Lavender said, wiping at her face with my handkerchief. "And I . . ."

"You've been here ever since," I concluded, deeply moved, when she could not. "Always in the tavern your daughter built."

"I promised her I would wait for him," she agreed, brokenly. "I knew one day I would look up and he would walk through that door . . ."

Officer Thorn sniffed conspicuously before pulling herself together. "You're saying that, roughly two hundred years ago, your grandchild was kidnapped, presumed hidden somewhere on Belville Mountain?"

"They couldn't have gone far," Lavender said, though it was unclear why she thought so. "They wouldn't have left the mountain."

I shivered as I looked up at Thorn. "Then the note that you received . . . Do you really think?"

"The man you saw yesterday," Thorn said, focused on Lavender though her eyes looked much more shiny than usual. "You're sure it was him?"

Lavender sighed deeply, reaching for my hand again. I held on, surprised by her warmth. "It was like seeing both of them at once," she said. "Kieran's height and build, Violetta's coloring. There is a trace of magic about him, too—forest magic, plant magic. Just like both his parents. I—I just *know*."

Officer Thorn's pencil paused over her notes. "His name?"

"Purslane," Lavender said, her voice cracking over the unused syllables. "She called him Purslane."

8

Stories and Silence

Though we offered her breakfast and a chance to officially meet our patient, Lavender left soon afterward. She maintained that she did not want to cause him more trouble, and while I understood that, I also wondered if his abrupt reappearance and all the rumors had been too much for her, too. Given the depth of her emotion as she told the story, she clearly had her own reactions to sort out.

To wait for more than a hundred years—and then to feel so helpless in the face of a convoluted police investigation . . . Part of my heart went with Lavender as she returned to her tavern to wait for news of Purslane's recovery.

Officer Thorn filled in Olivia and Trent as I packed up what was left of breakfast. Before I returned to my shop, though, I made a point of pulling Thorn aside.

"Purslane is another plant name," I told her quietly, as Trent and Olivia checked on the patient once more. "Its leaves are edible."

"I do occasionally eat a vegetable, you know," she retorted,

57

flipping her hair over her shoulder. "What are you getting at?"

I raised one eyebrow, making a *come on, be serious* face at her. "Rather famously, *rapunzel* is a kind of lettuce."

"I did wonder." Officer Thorn tapped her notebook on her chin as she thought.

Beyond being a world where magic and myth are woven into the dirt beneath our feet, the water and even the air we breathe, it's fairly common for fairy tales to repeat themselves. I myself was given the nickname Red as a nod to the story of Little Red Riding Hood. Nobody set *out* to be in a fairy tale, exactly, but they had a way of sneaking up on people despite everyone's best intentions. And while they were in no way predictive of villainy or heroics—a tale could always twist in unexpected ways—it was the sort of thing the Police Guild took seriously.

"Also, I bet you only eat vegetables when Maggie makes you," I added.

"Pretty much." Thorn cast a glance over her shoulder, at the spare room door. "Based on Lavender's information, we could be looking at a victim rather than a perpetrator here. But why wouldn't he want to talk to us?"

"Most likely, he's been in seclusion with only one person to trust for a very long time," I pointed out. "Maybe he wasn't in a tower letting down his hair, but still, he could have been told anything. Maybe he was taught to think police are the enemy, or even that we *all* are some kind of monsters."

"Then why come here?" Thorn shook her head. "And who exactly was keeping him *there*? I have a bad feeling about whatever happened on the mountain."

"I agree it must have been something dire," I said. "But, just to look at it from another angle, the fact that he's probably a victim doesn't mean he didn't also commit some kind of crime."

Officer Thorn ran a hand over her face. "That's what I am still worried about. I told Trent and Olivia to see if he reacts at all to his name, just his name for now. Maybe we can get some corroboration, at least. But—"

The door across the room opened, and Olivia came over to us, followed by Trent. Olivia looked a little excited, but Trent looked perturbed, his dark brows drawn.

"He doesn't know the name Purslane," Olivia said, with the air of an apprentice describing a successful experiment to her schoolmaster. "He said so outright."

Officer Thorn and I both gaped, and I beat her to talking. "He spoke again?"

"Actually," Trent put in, "he didn't, until Olivia called him Purslane. He seemed kind of taken aback by it. Like he expected Olivia to know his name, and that wasn't it."

"He said 'Don't lie, you already know my name is Jack,'" Olivia reported. In her neutral tones, the words sounded almost eerily commonplace.

Trent coughed. "Like I said, he got kind of upset."

"I thought that might be the case since that's all he said," Olivia added.

"Jack?" Thorn turned thoughtfully to me. "Well, now. How does that fit into your story?"

I grimaced. "First of all, he could have been lied to. But still . . . that does open things up quite a bit."

* * *

I was still pondering the whole affair several hours later, as

I arranged a Halloween display in the shop's front windows. Spiders, ghosts, shimmering orange potions, and yet *more* stories coming to mind featuring a hero named "Jack" . . .

I'd managed to get back to my shop just at opening time. Luca, who had been waiting for me, lingered long enough to get the bare facts and promise to look up information on Lavender's story—a case he immediately recognized from his cold case exhibit. Though Lavender's name had not been mentioned in the record, he put two and two together immediately, and set out to research.

That at least was perfectly normal. I smiled to myself, thinking of it, while listening to William sell glow powder to a dwarf family. Soon, Rhys would be in for his usual afternoon shift, and he'd promised to reorganize the goo collection today. Business had picked up as the rain held off, and everyone was chatting about the festival and costumes. Some strands of life went on as usual.

It was apparent that Officer Thorn had not found any such comfort, however, when I caught sight of her marching up to the front door.

"You," she said, poking her head around the frame. "Outside. You'll want to see this."

That sounded ominous. I sat up from the stepladder I was using as I created the display, glancing back at William to make sure he was okay before following her outside.

"I thought you'd grown past ordering people around," I protested vaguely as we stood on the corner. Though it wasn't actively raining, Market Square was still muddy and damp and mostly deserted. Officer Thorn looked like she was standing under her own personal storm cloud.

"After listening to Trent complain about me all morning,

you still think that?" She didn't smile; in fact, her hair was mussed and there were still crumbs on her jacket collar. She had definitely not had the break I had. "I left Olivia to watch the patient, and finally got back to the station after taking statements about his arrival in town last night. None of which, by the way, shed any light on the matter. No one claims to have ever laid eyes on him, aside from Lavender. So I went back thinking I'd have time to check the Guild records. Only to find *this*."

For the second time in two days, she thrust a note at me.

And actually, this note seemed strangely similar to the first. The paper felt much the same, anyway. But the upper edge was cut cleanly, the ink was drier, and the handwriting was different, an archaic cursive. *Check the Lost River Outlook*, it read, *for important information on the case.*

"Shoved through the mail slot like the first one," Thorn added as I looked it over. "I'm gonna have Trent put up some kind of observation spell."

I glanced up. "That's not a bad—"

"And why won't anyone just *talk* to me?" she burst.

"Have you had lunch?" I asked. Seeing her glower, I added quickly, "It's alright, we'll sort things out. Anyway, Lavender did talk to you, and I feel like I've been talking to you all morning."

"It's Lavender I'm headed to see next," Thorn said. "I stopped by the post office, but Mel knew nothing about the note. Just like the last one. Someone's been hand-delivering them, and it isn't a postal employee."

"Why go back to Lavender?" I asked, curious.

"Didn't you know?" Officer Thorn stopped tugging at her ear to look surprised. "The Outlook belongs to Lavender. She owns all kinds of rental properties around here, not just the tavern."

"Really?" Somehow, I'd assumed it belonged to Daisy. But now that Thorn said something, I did recall Rhys alluding to Daisy working a side gig for Lavender, looking after the properties on the mountain. I'd known the old keep was one, but I'd never thought to wonder about the tower. *Still, if Lavender really has been here for three hundred years, she's certainly had the time to acquire all kinds of places,* I thought. *So maybe Luca was actually doing his brochure for Lavender herself? But she didn't mention anything about it last night. Of course, she was pretty distracted . . .*

"I want to see if she knows anything," Officer Thorn continued, back to business. "And from there, it looks like I'll have to go up there myself. Seems like Olivia is the only one who can get Jack or whatever his name is to say anything, and I don't want to jinx that. Or leave Trent alone out there in that Hut with him. You were there the other day, weren't you? Mind coming along?"

"To make sure you don't get lost?" I thought about it for a moment. I had no idea what might be waiting on the mountain, but Officer Thorn was clearly worked up, and I hated to leave her alone. Besides, at such a remote location, she'd definitely need backup—even if it was just an alchemist with solidifying goo in her toolbelt. Daisy might make more convincing muscle, but she was nearly impossible to get a hold of, whereas I was standing right here. "Sure, I remember the path. Just let me tell William and then we can be on our way. But you're buying me lunch to go from Lavender's."

"What is it with everyone today and *food?*" Thorn grumped.

I smirked. "If Trent gets to be bribed, then so do I!"

9

A Sudden Drop

Lavender passed two steaming hand pies wrapped in cloth napkins across the counter. I took charge of both of them, inhaling scents of cheese and broccoli and potato, while Officer Thorn did the talking.

It was the middle of the lunch rush, and the tavern was full to bursting. Lavender looked more tired than ever. When Thorn mentioned the Lost River Outlook, she didn't seem too surprised.

"I'll have someone get the key for you," she said, glancing pointedly at a fellow bartender who nodded and ducked into the back room. "I'm afraid there's no telling what you'll find up there."

"You haven't had any renters lately?" Officer Thorn asked.

Lavender shook her head. "I mostly rent the mountain locations during the summer. Though we've had so many people coming into town for the Samhain festival, I have been tempted to book those further rooms out . . ."

Her voice trailed off, leaving an unspoken conclusion amongst the three of us: *good thing she didn't.*

Meanwhile, the other bartender returned with the key, and Lavender duly passed it over the counter. Officer Thorn pocketed it as I asked, "Can *you* think of any reason someone would send in a tip about the tower, Lavender?"

She hesitated, and then shook her head. "I was last up there ages ago, when Violetta had just finished fixing it up. These days I leave the maintenance of the mountain properties to Daisy."

"If you see her before I do, tell her I'm looking for her," Officer Thorn said grimly. "We'll be on our way. Thanks for your cooperation."

"And lunch," I added.

Lavender smiled faintly. "Wait just one minute." She fished amongst her glassware and brought out two ceramic traveling mugs, which she filled with hot cider. "For the road. Be safe out there," she said.

"We plan to be," I promised. Officer Thorn was already turning for the door.

I caught up with her on the tavern's porch, looking out over the Square. As I handed her one of the savory pies, I thought aloud. "When Luca and I went up there, we left by the main road going east, and then cut up along an old trail. But according to Dusty, our stranger—Purslane, or Jack—came down from the north, like he had been at the mine."

"Believe me, I tried questioning Lark that very night." Officer Thorn's voice sounded as weary as Lavender had looked, and I could understand why. As owner of a large and profitable mine, Lark was cool, professional, and not afraid to butt heads with local law. She and Thorn had had run-ins on multiple occasions. But Lark genuinely cared about her operation and fairness, so I trusted that if she hadn't had much to say about Jack, then he wasn't involved with the mine.

Officer Thorn clearly shared my opinion. As we set out across the park, she went on, "No one there said they'd ever heard of anyone fitting his description, and they hadn't seen or heard a peep out of the ordinary, either. And usually Lark knows *everything* that happens on that side of the mountain."

"I'm with you there. So the tower really does look like a good prospect," I mused. "Although, I have to tell you, it seemed perfectly nice when Luca and I went up. Granted, we didn't actually go all the way to the top . . ."

"Why were you there in the first place?" Thorn asked. As she spoke she finished off her pie and then looked vaguely surprised that it was gone.

"Luca's gotten himself involved in another tourism project," I answered, eating more carefully as we walked.

Officer Thorn frowned up at the cloudy sky above us, then sighed. "First a tip with no crime, now a crime with no scene."

"Not yet," I reminded her. "Just think of the impressive presentations you'll be making to the Guild when you figure it all out!"

* * *

Our walk up the mountain was relatively quiet, but it quickly became torturous when we made it to the tower.

Officer Thorn approached the Lost River Outlook like the walls were hiding skeletons and the furniture might jump out to bite her at any moment. It looked just as lonely and inviting as it had the day before to me. Nevertheless, I duly assisted in peering around corners and drawing a little sketch of the layout of each floor. Trailing along after the officer with notebook in hand wasn't too unlike exploring with Luca, to be honest.

Except that Officer Thorn insisted we climb *all* the stairs.

We stood on the observation floor six stories up, staring at the gloomy spiral staircase overhead. I sighed.

"You should have known," Officer Thorn reminded me.

"I should have," I agreed.

"And you should have warned me," she said, with a sigh of her own.

At that, I chuckled. "Well, it's not like I would have changed your mind. Too bad neither of us can fly."

We began dutifully climbing, up and up. The steps shook under Officer Thorn's weight and the thin railing creaked in protest as I tugged on it for support. My leg muscles were already sore. After we'd left the observation floor behind, the stairs seemed to go on forever. Regular windows let in air and light, but nothing more—we were high enough that to look straight out was to see only clouds. And I didn't dare look down.

At first we paused at each new story, marked by a square iron landing. Then we paused at every corner. Finally, just when I was contemplating crawling up the last few steps on my hands and knees, we emerged onto a bare wood floor.

There was nothing but windows—no benches, no murals or maps, no immediate clues. I leaned heavily against one of the window sills. It was easily six inches thick, cut straight through the rock of the tower wall. An iron lattice served in place of actual window panes. I could hear the wind whistling over the treetops below.

"This should be one of your frights for the Halloween fair," I panted.

"Too easy," Officer Thorn panted back. "Hardly the *height* of horror."

I groaned, and straightened up to look around a little more. The only light was from the windows, a muted, overcast glow. Pulling my goggles down over my eyes helped: the magicked lenses could enhance my vision in the shadowy areas. But even so, all I saw was cobwebs, wood, and stone.

"Nothing to write home about," Officer Thorn said, looking around.

I glanced over at her, wondering if she was making another pun. She did live behind the police station. "Too bad your tipster wasn't more specific."

"We'd have needed to check up here anyway," she insisted, still gazing at the walls.

"Fair enough. But do you even want me to bother drawing it?" I asked, looking down at the police notebook I still carried. "What would it be, just a square with a little cutout where the staircase comes up? I could mark where the windows are, I guess, but there's just the one on each wall and they're far too narrow to let anything in, even without the bars. It's all pretty predictable. I don't see anything of note either."

"Your fancy glasses don't show you everything," Officer Thorn said. She, too, was leaning against a wall, but when she caught my eye she pointed up.

"What?" I asked incredulously. "It's just the ceiling. The stairs ended!"

"It's a ceiling," Thorn agreed. Her tone had changed, becoming brisk—a sure sign she was on to something. "Not a roof. From the outside, the top of the tower looked pointy."

I shook my head, shivering a little as the autumn wind came through the windows. "So?"

"What we're seeing is flat," she insisted. "So it can't really be the top of the tower."

At this, I looked up again. I couldn't imagine there were yet *more* stories left, but I did survey the ceiling, even as I complained. "You've got to be kidding. You don't really think—"

"Ha!" Officer Thorn said when I paused. "You see something up there, don't you?"

"I thought my 'fancy glasses' weren't good enough for you," I retorted, light-hearted, before shaking my head and trying to make sense of what I'd noticed. "It's a normal wooden ceiling, I think, but there *is* the faint outline of a square above us. Right there, next to this wall. It seems to be magic."

"Called it," Thorn said smugly. She looked up where I had indicated and bellowed, "Hello! Police!!"

No answer came except a faint echo from the rocks far below the windows.

I shivered again. "You don't really think there's anyone up there? Surely Lavender would have said something. Unless somehow she doesn't know . . ."

Officer Thorn shrugged. "I think it's a good thing I had Trent make me some magic-banishers. You're not the only one who makes useful things," she added in response to my questioning look. She pushed off the wall and came over to look up toward the trace of magic I'd seen.

This time, I resisted the urge to comment. I was, quite frankly, curious about what a "magic-banisher" might be and how it would work.

It turned out to be a small black fabric pouch, stuffed full and tied shut. Officer Thorn drew it from her pocket and weighed it in her hand for a moment before lobbing it straight up at the ceiling. She had a good eye. The pouch hit squarely within the little square of magic I had seen with my goggles and exploded in a puff of dark smoke, a shower of ash, faint glimmers, and an acrid, unpleasant smell.

Once we'd finished coughing and waving the ash away from our faces, we looked up to see a hatch in the ceiling . . . with a rope ladder hanging from it.

"Trent promised it'd dispel any common spell," Thorn said, pleased, "and it looks like it did. Eh?"

"Agreed." I looked up at the opening through my goggles again and could see only the faint patterns of sunlight that might come from any window. Whatever illusion spell had been hiding the ladder and door was totally gone. Nothing magical, nothing stirring. "It still might be nothing more than an attic."

"Okay, *Rapunzel*," Thorn said. She rubbed her hands together, clearly riding high on the success of having found a trap door. I had to admit she had a point, but I was concerned when she added, "I'm going up."

"I'm right behind you," I said quickly. She might be properly trained and annoying, but still, she wasn't going into the unknown alone.

Officer Thorn nodded and flipped her hair back from her face. She clambered up the rope staircase. I might have wished for a more covert approach, but sneakiness had never been her style. Resigned, I followed, listening intently—but I still could not hear anything other than her breathing and the wooden steps of the ladder bouncing off the stone wall. If anyone was above us, they were being very still. Or we were all alone and very, very high above the mountainside.

Briefly, I wished for Luca.

But in the next moment, Officer Thorn had hauled herself through the opening, and my head came level with the new floor. As I emerged, I could see that it wasn't an attic at all: it was a fully furnished room, smaller and much more utilitarian than the floors far below, but still reasonably cozy and obviously inhabited. A muddy rug lay on the floor nearby. There were cloaks hanging on a nearby wall, and some kind of counter and cabinets to my right that suggested a kitchen. There were more stairs in the far corner, and larger windows, though their panes were opaque. There were the lingering scents of lemon and thyme . . .

And there was, in the middle of the floor, resting beside a crouching Officer Thorn, a body.

10

A Sheltered Life

If I hadn't been clinging to a ladder, I might have fallen over.

"Definitely dead," Officer Thorn said, answering the one question I *didn't* have.

"I figured that." I looked up at the ceiling above us: plain wooden planks. "Who is it?"

"No idea." Thorn glanced back at me, rising to her feet and rubbing her hands together. "First things first: I need to search the place and make sure our culprit isn't hiding somewhere. Maybe some clues about who this is will turn up, too."

I swallowed hard. "Culprit? You're sure?"

"Not one hundred percent," Thorn admitted. Glancing down at the body on the floor, she added, "Looks likely to me, and it seems fairly fresh. But the culprit's long gone if they know what's good for them."

"*Long* gone?" I repeated.

Thorn tugged at her ear. "Maybe not that long. I'd guess a few hours at most." She returned her gaze to me and asked, "You going to be okay? You could head back to town, you know."

"It's a shock, but I'm not leaving you here alone when there may be a 'culprit' around," I told her. After taking a deep breath to recenter myself, I climbed up the last ladder rungs to sit on the floor facing the wall. I'd helped Officer Thorn examine a body a few times before—usually back in Belville's police station though. Encountering one "in the wild," so to speak, was abrupt and unpleasant. I couldn't help but wonder aloud, "Was *this* what your tip-writer wanted you to find?"

"Questions for later," Thorn said, in an *I wonder too but we have to focus* voice. "You brought the notebook up, right?"

I got to my feet and held up both notebook and pencil. "Ready."

We began by skirting the body, walking around the edges of the square room. While I sketched the floor plan, Officer Thorn opened cabinets and peered at the windows. It didn't take long before she decided we should head up the stairs.

Thorn went first, not necessarily stealthy, but careful. This new floor, though, was more empty than the first. A dining table with an open paint set sat in one corner, a half-finished canvas propped up on an old vase. The picture was a vividly imagined forest. Paint had dried on the palette nearby, and the brushes were unwashed, gummed up with green and blue pigments.

There was an armchair in the opposite corner, accompanied by a stool and a thick rug. The entire floor was strangely quiet.

But of course, there were still stairs leading up. We ascended on high alert, only to find an empty landing with two doors. One led into a bedroom where the walls were covered in paintings, mostly of colorful landscapes and plants. The other led into the messiest room yet: an office of sorts, with a massive desk and piles of old tomes covering a threadbare carpet.

We lingered in that room—it took Officer Thorn longer to check all the nooks and crannies, seeing as there were more nooks and crannies to check. While she poked her head under the desk, I worked on my floor sketch. By this point, I was fairly confident we weren't going to find anyone else. And I was heartened by the fact that we hadn't found any more stairs.

"Make sure you take a peek around with those goggles on," Thorn said, coughing on dust.

"Yes, Mother." I dutifully pulled my lab goggles on again and scanned the room. "I do see traces of magic, but it's faint."

"Makes sense. All the spell books are ancient," said the officer. "It's not much of a library."

I began filling in the last corner of my sketch and paused. "Maybe it's not meant to be one. I think what I thought was a workbench over there might actually be a bed?"

"Let's see." Officer Thorn turned her attention to that cluttered corner next, peering under a pile of rags, a velvet carrying case of crystal balls, and a jumble of scrolls. She got down on her knees and came back up coughing again. "Definitely a bed. There's a bedspread under all the junk, and a monster underneath."

"That's not funny," I said, making notes on my sketch.

"Just the dust bunny variety," Thorn admitted. "Wonder why the other rooms were clean and this one isn't."

"*I* wonder why there are two bedrooms up here and only one person so far," I replied.

Officer Thorn tugged at her ear as she stood. "Seems doubtful it was a guest room, when someone went to such an effort to hide this apartment. If it weren't for the timing of it all, I'd be thinking our culprit has run away from home."

My pencil paused. Many people had arrived in Belville lately for the upcoming Samhain celebration, but only one had been conspicuously *running away* from something—or at least, from the mountain.

Thorn met my eye with a knowing look. "You're the one who always says we shouldn't jump to conclusions."

"I know," I said, clearing my throat. "And since you said that, there's something else I should tell you. When Luca and I came up here the day before last, we *did* run into someone—a housekeeper. I don't remember if we got their name or not."

"Add it to the list to ask Lavender about. It's probably nothing, but it could help narrow down the time of death if need be. Although," Thorn said, tugging at her ear, "it's a stretch to think Lavender or her staff knew about this apartment at all, given how high up we are."

"And how hidden the entrance was," I agreed. "Even so, it seems this tower was a lot less secluded than everyone thought."

* * *

After Officer Thorn insisted I double- and triple-check the ceiling for more trapdoors—even though there *was* a sloped ceiling this time, just like the roof outside—we trooped back to the lower level to see if we could find any more clues about the deceased.

While Officer Thorn took her notebook back from me and began a thorough examination of the body (following a Guild procedure that listed things like "visible injuries," "suspected age," and "evidence of magic?") I was directed to look at the cloak hanging on the wall. I kept my goggles on, just in case. Now that we knew that someone in the apartment had studied magic, I couldn't help but think of Lavender's story . . .

But I did my best to remain empirical and unbiased. Officer Thorn, meanwhile, was developing her own opinions.

"Wound to the back of the head," she muttered aloud as she made her notes. "Someone didn't like this person, that's for sure."

"Do you know they didn't just fall backward?" I asked, rifling through the cloak looking for pockets.

Thorn, too, was hunched over her work. "It'd have to have been with a lot of force."

I shuddered. There *was* blood on the floor behind me, but I'd been doing my best not to think about it too much. After discovering a crime scene on my idyllic home island over the summer, that sort of violence particularly affected me. Before, it had been easier to keep an objective mindset. Now, it felt closer to home—literally. And in a home that was a tower, to be a victim of falling of any kind seemed like a cruel irony.

In the lining along the front of the cloak, I noticed a pocket. While I put on my gloves and prepared to investigate, Officer Thorn activated her torch for better light. What had been a dreamlike, pale colored light from the windows was now bright white.

It didn't make much difference to me just yet, but I heard Officer Thorn suck in her breath.

"What is it?" I asked, fishing in the pocket.

"Odd," she said decisively. "At first I would have figured this person to be maybe thirties, tan-skinned, long dark hair, human. Recently deceased. But she looks different in the light."

"How different?" Curious, I finally turned around to look.

"Like a hundred years different," Thorn said, her voice dry.

She was hardly exaggerating. The person illuminated by her torchlight looked wrinkled and sunken, with thin white wisps of hair and too few teeth. For the briefest of moments, I thought Officer Thorn had pulled some kind of Halloween prank on me.

Before I accused her of anything, though, I glanced at the windows, my goggles still enhancing my vision. "I do see traces of magic, but again, it's quite faint. I don't think the lighting exactly was to blame."

"Can you tell what the magic on the windows is for?" Thorn asked.

"For that you'd need William," I told her. "And honestly, it might not be a bad idea to have him look at the books upstairs."

"Could be that she had some kind of fancy glamour on herself," Officer Thorn said thoughtfully. "The Guild puts out updates on glamours every year. I just got the new one in—Olivia and I were going to go over it before the kidnapping business came up. As I understand it, most of them disappear when someone dies. No need for looks in the afterlife."

I rolled my eyes at her humor. "It'd be interesting to see what the victim looks like in natural light, maybe."

"Once I document the scene I'll take her down to the station," Officer Thorn agreed. "We'll see what comes up then. For now, looks like I'll just have to have two sets of notes."

"Too bad Olivia didn't come along, huh?" I commented, turning back to my own search. There was something small and square in the pocket, but I hadn't gotten a proper hold of it yet.

"I feel better knowing she's in town. Folks are unsettled, and she's my best recruit so far. Even better if she can get that Jack fellow to talk."

As Officer Thorn continued talking, I finally clasped my hand around my prize. I pulled it out to find it was a small leather-bound wallet. The style was very old, patched and resewn many times. It opened up to reveal two pockets—one was empty, but there was a thin bronze medallion in the other. I delicately fished it out and recognized the logo etched onto its face.

"Hey," I said, interrupting the flow of talk about Olivia and her various strengths. "There wasn't anything in the cloak except a wallet, and nothing in the wallet except this. Take a look."

"I'll get to everything in—" Despite herself, she did look up as I held it out. And I saw the moment realization clicked behind her eyes. "That's the coin that approved merchants at the grocer's market carry. The grocer gives it to new merchants as a 'first coin' or good luck charm as much as for identification."

"I thought those vegetables looked familiar," I said, speaking of the design on the coin—which echoed the design on the grocer's sign in town. It featured a basket overflowing with vegetables of all kinds.

"This is perfect. It gives us a place to start," Officer Thorn said. "Judging by the age of that coin, she must have been selling at the market for a while."

"Or she only did a long time ago," I put in. "Because, no matter what the lighting is, I still don't recognize her. And I go there every week."

Officer Thorn made a hand waving gesture. "She wouldn't be the first person to avoid the local alchemist."

"Hey! What—"

"What I want to know," she went on over my protest, "is if she was holed up here on the mountain, and if she wasn't paying rent because Lavender didn't even know she was here, and if she was the one to set those spells and go to such trouble to hide this place—then what was she doing selling things at the market in Belville an hour away?"

"I don't know," I said simply. "But that's a lot of *if*s."

11

Cozy Spaces

We got back to town around tea time, Officer Thorn with her gruesome discovery in her arms. It wasn't perhaps the *most* official way a victim has been transported to a police station, but it was practical. Officer Thorn was very strong, and more than that, she knew her limits—under her uniform she wore a back brace which helped support her on the trip down the trail.

I, too, knew my limits. I declined to help with any more investigations that night. Thorn would need to identify the body before Guild procedure allowed her to do much more, in any case, and I didn't feel like tagging along to check on Olivia, Trent, and Jack. Instead, I stopped by my shop to check on William, and then I just kept walking.

Luca's bookstore was a block south of Market Square. It was a straight shot; I knew the path by heart at this point. It was raining again, and I hid under my umbrella rather than greet the other folks on the street walking home or out to dinner. I wasn't in the most friendly of moods.

The chime on the bookshop door put me more at ease.

Aside from Luca's festive seasonal displays, the bookstore had remained much the same since the first moment I arrived in Belville. The rows of shelves were stacked high and chaotically, and the lighting was shadowy at best. To one side of the door a large desk served as a sales counter. Usually the place smelled like old parchment and dust, but today I detected an undertone of chocolate.

Frank, a wizened old mink, was curled atop the desk. His plush white fur and beady black eyes gleamed in the glow of a nearby lamp. Though he looked exactly the same as any other mink—aside from the fact that he was missing one back leg—Frank had lived for thousands of years, and sometime during that lifespan, had acquired the ability to talk. It was uncommon but not unheard of in Beyond for animals to acquire magic, and it went a long way to explaining why most people ate largely vegetarian diets.

Frank's general reluctance to deal with strangers didn't feel uncommon these days, though. I'd always wondered why he decided to take up residence in a shop if he didn't like people.

"Oh, it's you," he told me, with a yawn.

"Yep," I agreed. I hung up my cloak and set my umbrella in a stand by the door. When Frank offered no further insight, I added, "Do you know where I can find Luca?"

There was a pause, and in that pause, my heart skipped a beat. But then he said, "He's in the back room researching cold cases."

"Oh." *Of course.* "I'll just head back there, then."

"Go on. Tell him I'm locking up in a minute," Frank said, calling over his shoulder as I moved past him. His croaky voice sounded a little warmer then. I smiled faintly. Talking about Luca did have that effect on people.

Perhaps that's why Frank settled here, I decided, as I moved past towers of books.

The back room was technically where children's books were kept. But there was a nice roaring fire in the hearth there, and Luca often used it as a sort of work room when business was slow. I found him sitting cross-legged on the floor, leaning over old journals and books, while the rain tapped at the windows above. An empty mug of hot chocolate sat beside him.

"Sakura should offer you discounts on cocoa, at the rate you're going," I said by way of hello.

"Or dental care, more likely," he replied, turning to look up at me with an easy grin. "I'd offer you some, but I ran out. Want to sit with me a while? Or did you want to go somewhere?"

"I want to sit." I collapsed next to him with a heavy sigh. After a moment, I leaned my head on his shoulder while he continued reading.

At this, he glanced over again. "Not a good day?"

"Very long and emotional day," I said. "Officer Thorn and Trent needed an intervention about Jack, which you knew, and then there was Lavender's story, which I guess I told you about earlier. Then at lunchtime Thorn came by again asking about the Lost River Outlook, so we went there too. We found an apartment hidden at the very top."

"Whoa. You went all the way up?"

"Yeah. And we found someone murdered in the hidden space."

"Seriously?" Luca sat up straight, though I refused to be dislodged.

"Seriously," I confirmed. "No idea who it was, but she had a marketer's coin in her wallet, from the grocer here in town. So Thorn's working on identifying her now."

"That would mean she was living somewhat as a local. Jack appeared as a total stranger, but somebody must know this other person," Luca reasoned.

I nodded against his shoulder, watching the flames in the fireplace. "That seems to be Officer Thorn's thought. I thought maybe though that she was only a merchant at the market a long time ago. She looked like she could be pretty old."

"I guess that's possible . . . people do carry keepsakes." Luca's voice was thoughtful. He shifted to put his arm around me. "Was it very bad?"

"Not as bad as it could have been. I think it's the randomness of it that really gets to me. Plus I am tired," I admitted.

"Hopefully with more investigation the randomness will seem a lot less random," Luca said. "But as for tiredness, that makes sense, what with all the work—and homework—you've been doing lately."

"Ha ha," I said weakly, though I did smile. "I haven't even started the project Paracelsus sent. Aside from asking Rhys. It's more just—worry, I think. And being cooped up doesn't help."

"The weather, you mean?" Luca glanced up at the windows. "I can see that. It sure is cozy, though, don't you think?"

I sighed again, more softly this time. "It is."

Luca tightened his arm around my side. "How about dinner in tonight? I had promised Frank I'd get him a pizza sometime. He might be willing to go pick it up."

"Can minks eat pizza?" I asked skeptically.

"I figure he's lived long enough he can eat whatever he

wants," Luca joked. "After all, I'm not his keeper. Just his employer-slash-landlord."

"I think you mean *friend*," I told him.

"Well, obviously that. Come on, it's probably been forever since you ate. What toppings do you want?"

I didn't miss the fact that I'd been bothering Thorn with the same observations that morning. Knowing that he was probably right, I helped decide on a white pizza with broccoli before lapsing back into comfortable silence while Frank and Luca made the arrangements.

After Frank had darted off into the night, Luca started organizing all his research into stacks—the better to make room for dinner. I watched this with interest. "Find anything useful?"

"I did actually find some things related to Lavender's story," he answered. "Once I knew to look for 'Violetta' and 'Kieran,' it was a lot easier. The *Still Missing* book from a few years ago includes their case—it has a few quotes and reprints from local papers at the time. But the closest paper in those days was in Pine."

Pine, the county seat for Pastoria, was across the lake—near enough when we needed something, but far enough that their reporters probably had not been 'on scene' at the time of the disappearance. I pursed my lips. "What did they say?"

"Nothing to contradict what Lavender said," Luca replied, "but nothing much more, either. Except, um—"

He hesitated, and I sat up, concerned. "What is it?"

"I think Kieran may have been Drus," he said at last, his eyes on the carpet.

I blinked as I thought this over. Lavender had said that Kieran had plant magic, and that he was a local elf . . . so that did make sense. And at the same time, it was strange. Luca himself came from the group of local forest-dwelling elves who called themselves the Drus—in fact, he was the only one we knew of who still lived in Belville. I was so accustomed to thinking of it being his heritage alone that this possibility had never occurred to me.

I shifted forward so that I could look at his face. "How do you feel about that?"

"Well, I appreciate you asking." Luca's smile flashed momentarily before he became thoughtful again. "But I'm not really sure. It's not like I remember him or anything—what with everything that's happened since, my memory of that time is still a little hazy anyway. It's just strange to think about it at all. I don't think it has any connection to what happened . . . Every reporter or researcher is fairly certain, like Lavender, that the sorcerer is the one responsible. Vesper is the name she told the town, but I saw one scholar say that might have been a pseudonym from the beginning. Anyway, she and the child, Purslane, disappeared at the same time. There's never any mention of Drus politics or anything. Maybe Kieran had chosen to distance himself from that."

"I certainly wouldn't blame him if he did," I commented. "But if everyone is so certain they know what happened, why were Purslane and Vesper never found?"

"They talk about that in this one," Luca said, fishing a book titled *Mysteries in the Mountains* out of his pile. He flipped through the encyclopedic pages until he came to one with the heading "Beloved Child Disappears." "This writer spent a lot of time looking at Police Guild reports from back then," he explained. "At the time, there was only the station in Pine. Some people have theorized that the police officer assigned to the case just didn't like coming up to Belville . . . but it's probably more than that. For one thing, Vesper *was* a sorcerer. Even if her magic was faint, like she told Lavender."

"Wait, is there an explanation for that?" I asked. The only sorcerers I knew were powerful to the point of egotism—and one outlier whose magic had suffered because of a punishment imposed by the sorcerer community.

"Not exactly," Luca said, meeting my gaze and no doubt referring to the case on my mind. "Of course we can't say for sure, but most people think she was just quite old and sick. The person who wrote the book about her potential pseudonyms pointed out that her magic was probably fading just as her physical strength was fading—that's not necessarily *always* how magic works, but it does happen, especially with some illnesses."

"Okay, but I can't imagine Vesper was going around telling *everyone* that," I said, again thinking of what little I knew about sorcerers. It took a certain temperament to dedicate one's life to learning arcane spells from ancient texts. "I can see how Lavender and Violetta would have found out, but everyone else?"

"No, it sounds like she just told a few people, people she thought might be able to help her. Like Lavender," Luca agreed, his eyes troubled. "Lavender's not mentioned by name, but reports do indicate she was running the inn and Vesper told her why she'd come to stay. Basically, she was traveling around looking for ways to bring back her magic and extend her life."

I pondered this. "Vesper definitely wouldn't be the first to want something like that. That in itself doesn't seem nefarious. But I don't see how kidnapping a little kid would help that."

"No, I don't think she came to Belville expecting to become

a criminal." Briefly, Luca's eyes crinkled as he smiled. "But it does seem like she was, in general, very focused and determined . . . and most sources do agree she fell in love with Violetta."

"Still not a reason to kidnap someone's kid," I said.

"Well, I don't think *reason* comes into it, exactly," Luca returned.

"Fair enough." I smiled wearily at him. "This sounds like a lot of interesting stuff, though, Luca. What a long day it's been, all round."

"True," he sighed. He leaned back on his hands and stretched his legs out to the fire, books forgotten once more.

"At least your brochure project will probably be put on hold," I said, as the thought suddenly occurred to me. "I doubt they'll want any tourists up there while it's a crime scene."

"What? Oh, right," Luca murmured.

He opened his mouth to say something more, but whatever it was, the shop chime drowned it out. In a waft of garlicky air, Frank had returned, bearing an oversize pizza box.

The less-than-social mink quickly stole a few slices for himself and disappeared to his quarters upstairs, leaving Luca and me to ourselves. As we sat there with our warm dinner and our fire, and the rain still falling outside, all thoughts of crime were set aside.

12

Botany and Business

The next morning found me doing my own version of research. In the quiet hour before the shop opened, I sat at my workbench with my journals scattered and open.

I'd tacked Paracelsus's letter to the low cork board that ran under the window to the shop—a very handy place for recipes, reminders, and in this case, reference material. Paracelsus had included a drawing of the plant he wanted me to look for. At first glance it looked like a little wildflower, perhaps six inches tall on a slender stem. But the fern-like leaves and unusual heart-shaped petals made it distinctive. Neither Rhys nor I could remember seeing something like that on the mountain— and I made a point of foraging all the ingredients I could. During my years in Belville, I'd been pretty good about keeping journals of the plants I found on the mountain, so theoretically if I *had* come across the plant and forgotten it, I should still be able to find it in my records . .. .

Theoretically. But now as I was going through my journals, it was clear how my organizational skills had failed me. My journals were a bit haphazard, filled out randomly when I had the time, or only containing the briefest notes from moments when I *hadn't* had time. Notes on minerals were mixed in with notes on plants. Even the details I recorded varied from entry to entry. Clearly, no matter how well-maintained my lab might be, I did not quite have my act together.

I was starting to understand why Paracelsus had chosen to send me *new* journals along with this project. My former mentor had probably foreseen this frustration with myself!

Before I tackled reorganizing my writings, though, I wanted to make sure I addressed Paracelsus's question. And so far, I had found no drawings or pressed flowers in my journals that matched this mysterious plant.

As I continued flipping through the pages, William sauntered down from upstairs. He clambered up onto his stool and flopped his chin onto the windowsill overlooking my lab table before he spoke. "Looking for more murder victims?"

"Looking for a *flower*," I retorted. "You're just jealous Officer Thorn doesn't drag you along more often."

"I see plenty of Officer Thorn." William yawned. "I'd rather be here in the shop than out getting muddy, anyway."

"I guess mud is a little easier to shed when you have boots instead of furry feet." I decided to take a break, stretching out my shoulders and smiling at him. "You said there was some good business yesterday?"

"Lots of orders picked up," he confirmed. "Apparently a big storm is supposed to roll in today or tomorrow."

I sighed. "Just what we need. I wonder if it'll clear up for Samhain."

Much as I might complain about town events, I did love them. It made me sad to think that the holiday this year might be rained out—especially when several people in town, Lavender and Luca included, could use a bit of fun.

But apparently William wasn't worried about the fair. "So," he said. "What does Officer Thorn know about the victim so far? And whatever happened with the stranger who collapsed in the Square?"

"You probably know more than I do." I eyed him warily. "Are you just asking so you have something to gossip with Dusty about later?"

"What, I can't be concerned about town affairs?" he asked innocently.

At that moment, as though he had conjured her, Officer Thorn's knock sounded at the back door.

I got up to let her in and was met with an enormous basket covered in a tea towel.

"Maggie's taken up baking," said Officer Thorn's voice. She couldn't be seen behind the pile underneath the towel, which smelled like sugar and yeast.

"For an entire carnival?" William asked.

With some difficulty, Thorn maneuvered herself through the doorway and turned so that she could see us, smiling fondly as she said, "She misread the recipe and thought 'spoons' were 'cups,' or something. I told her, the more the muffinier."

I grinned despite the awful joke. "Well, next time you could tell her to ask me if she wants any tips. I'm no Glacial, but I do pretty well in the kitchen."

"She actually gets along with Glacial too, believe it or not." Officer Thorn sounded just slightly worried: Glacial, the baker for the Pomegranate Café, had long been rumored to be an ex-mercenary. She certainly wasn't outgoing, but she did make a very good cupcake. "Are you going to let me into the shop so

I can put these down?"

Pleased that she had remembered not to encourage eating in my lab—or perhaps she had seen my pile of journals and decided there was no room left—I hastened to open the next door for her. She and William immediately congregated around the sales counter. I followed her into the shop and made for the tea kettle in the corner, turning on the magic burner underneath.

When I turned around, a small mountain of muffins had taken over the counter. Above it, Officer Thorn grinned widely. "This is to say sorry for getting you mixed up with a surprise body yesterday."

"Did Maggie put you up to that, too?" I smiled as I joined them. "It's alright. You had no more idea than I did what we might find."

"So both your tips have turned out to be truer than you thought?" William prompted, his tail wagging—whether about the chance to ask Thorn for info directly, or the muffins, it was hard to tell.

Officer Thorn flipped hair damp from the misty morning over her shoulder. "The notes were too vague to tell. One was two hundred years too late, if it's about Purslane or Jack, and the other wasn't very urgent for something referring to murder."

"Now you sound like me," I teased as I sorted through the muffins. There were pumpkin nut muffins, cinnamon ones, and something that looked like it might be dried raspberry and chocolate. I set one of those aside, knowing Luca would be intrigued.

"You do come in handy," Thorn said. "In fact . . ."

She pulled a glass vial out of one of her uniform's many

pockets. I set down my pumpkin muffin and examined the soft yellowish glow coming from it. "Some kind of residue you want tested?"

"I don't know what you would call it, but I do want it tested," Thorn agreed. "Found it on our victim's boots."

While that was hardly appealing, I was curious about what the substance might be. It didn't look like any potion I recognized, and it was too delicate—not to mention too glowy—for mud. I held it up for William to see. "Magic?"

Blue sparkles flared in his eyes as he looked at it, but then he shrugged. "Probably, yes, but not the spellwork kind. Something more natural."

"Natural, hm?" I examined it again, considering my options for testing.

"And speaking of natural," Officer Thorn cut in, half a muffin in her hand, "I'm headed to the grocer's market next. Who of you wants to come?"

"What about Olivia?" William protested.

"Watching Jack," she explained. And before we could ask, she added, "He's recovering just fine, but he still won't talk. Trent said soon it'll be time to let him go."

"*Are* you planning to let him go?" William asked. I tensed, remembering Thorn's fight with Trent the day before.

"He's a flight risk," the officer replied firmly. "And a person of interest. As soon as he's healed, I want to take him up to the Lost River Outlook and find out if that's where he came from. If it is, then he's a suspect—although I'm still thinking the death occurred *after* he showed up in town."

I agreed with Thorn that at least it seemed likely Jack *had* come from the hidden apartment. Where else could he have been so secluded? But the idea of waiting for confirmation in a case which so far was mostly hearsay made me itchy. "You could try giving him paints," I said slowly. "See if he makes pictures like the ones in the tower."

Officer Thorn tilted her head. "Tricky. I like it."

"It's not that I'm trying to be underhanded," I blushed. "It's just, that would also help prove which room was his, which—"

"Which implies that the other room was the victim's, and based on the contents of the room, that our victim was a sorcerer," Thorn finished.

William's ears perked up. "*The* sorcerer? Lavender's story is true?"

"I don't doubt Lavender, I would just hesitate to jump to conclusions when neither of the people involved is actually talking," I said.

"Sounds to me like you're the one who should come along for questioning merchants," Officer Thorn said, smirking at me. "Plus you can come along to the tavern and see if you spot the housekeeper from the other day."

I put my hands on my hips. "I do run a shop, you know." It was a longstanding joke between us. Turning to William, I asked, "Is that okay?"

"I *would* rather be here," he said reluctantly. "But I expect a full report when you get back."

* * *

While Officer Thorn and William chowed down on muffins and tea, I slipped back into my lab to set up some tests on the mysterious glowing material. I put some of it in my distillation setup, a system of glass tubes and bulbs over a small burner, which would break the sample down into its component parts.

On a whim, I also put some of the unknown substance into a clean terrarium and set it under a grow light just to see what might happen. William had said he thought it was natural, after all.

With that done, I traded my lab coat for a thick woolen cloak and pulled on my boots. After promising to check back in at lunch time, I let Thorn lead the way out the front door.

She showed me the coin in her hand as she walked. "I didn't make it to the grocer's last night. But that's for the best," she said. "It's a morning market anyway, and better practice to interview bystanders with a clear head."

"I'm not a trainee," I reminded her wryly. She'd lapsed into the teaching voice she sometimes used with Olivia. "But for the record, I do agree. You probably wouldn't have found anyone around last night."

"We might find too many people today," Thorn observed. As we crossed Market Square, we had ample opportunity to notice people in the park and on the streets. The café and the bakery were busy, as was to be expected, but so were many of the little stores that lined the Square.

"William said another big storm is coming, so everyone's probably trying to prepare," I said.

"Not a bad idea. But still, I don't want this getting around too much. We've already got more rumors than we know what to do with." Officer Thorn pocketed the coin with a quick glance around.

I glanced, too, though only the old oak trees and fallen leaves were nearby. The morning fog was lifting, but the sky was still heavy and gray. I turned back to Thorn. "So, you're saying be discreet?"

"*You* I don't have to worry about as much as that dog," she replied cheerfully.

"I wonder why." I chuckled to myself. As a magical creature with no small ego of his own, William hated it when anyone called him just a *dog*. "If he'd come along, he would probably be giving you a hard time about not having the Square decorated yet."

"I'll get to it," said Officer Thorn with confidence. "We could even get in some work this afternoon. Once we get identification on the victim, I have to wait for the Guild to contact any remaining family for instructions anyway."

I was familiar with the Police Guild policy on contacting first of kin before conducting autopsies or invasive magics, but I still thought Officer Thorn was being far too optimistic about her timing. I shook my head. "Between experiments and interviews, my day is all booked up."

"Just you wait," Thorn said. "If my hunch is right, you may find that's actually true."

13

At Market

The grocer was *not* my favorite person in Belville.

Ages ago, when I'd first arrived, I'd been mixed up in a little drama involving him and his family. Since then, he and his sons had generally avoided me—and that was perfectly fine. But Belville was a small town, and there was only one place to go for fresh local produce.

And I had to admit that the grocer's market was actually quite pleasant—the exact opposite of the grocer himself. The market took up a full block along the western edge of town, away from the bustle of Market Square. While this might have seemed a strange business decision, it was effective for keeping customers focused. People wove through the stalls with purpose. On one end was the grocer's stand, a year-round building with a wooden roof and two walls forming a corner at the edge of the lot. The front-facing sides of the stand were open to the rest of the market, though in storms they could be closed off with weather-treated canvas and spells.

Across the rest of the lot, individual stalls were arranged in orderly rows. Local farmers or merchants, like our unfortunate victim, could reserve a space for themselves, but they had to furnish it. The result was a hodgepodge of old tables and colorful tents. This time of year, most were brimming with baskets of squashes, apples, hardy greens, and mushrooms. A few stands sold wood harvested from the forest or ready-made wreaths, as well. In the far corner was my favorite stand of all: an enterprising young merchant had rigged up a little hotplate and sold fresh candied nuts.

I could smell the sugar in the air as we neared the market—as well as more vegetable scents, garlic and fresh leaves. Just as William and Thorn had suspected, the market aisles were full of shoppers. The sound was a little intimidating. Usually, I preferred to do a week's shopping on a quiet morning, before so many people descended upon the produce.

Officer Thorn headed straight for the grocer's stand first. She found him behind his cash register, barking orders at his adult sons, who were attempting to stack pumpkins into a pyramid. I hung back behind the officer—not only to avoid any additional confrontation, but also to hide my amusement.

"What's your business?" the grocer asked Thorn bluntly, only half distracted from his managerial efforts. Many people in town knew him only by his nickname, Bull, which matched both his broad chest and flat nose as well as his demeanor. Even so, just referring to "the grocer" was usually enough to paint a picture in everyone's mind.

"I'd like your opinion on something," she replied smoothly. No amount of shouts or barks would intimidate her. Drawing the coin from her pocket, she held it up for the grocer to see.

"On what? On that?" Bull squinted at it, then shrugged. "It's a market coin. So what?"

"Definitely one of yours?" Officer Thorn asked, professional but amiable.

"Course it's one of mine." The grocer turned and yelled at his sons as a pumpkin went tumbling.

"Do you have any way to identify who you gave it to?" asked Thorn.

Bull's look was sour. "No."

"Has anyone reported one missing?" Thorn pressed.

"No," the grocer repeated, with emphasis. "What're you getting at?"

His complete lack of curiosity about the coin, essentially a physical representation of one of his own business deals, made me want to shake him. It seemed irresponsible at best. *And yet,* I couldn't help but think, *maybe he already knows why and where Thorn found it . . .*

Officer Thorn tried once more. "You don't put any kind of tracking or binding spell on them?"

"No need," said the quarrelsome grocer. "Had this stand for generations. My ancestors didn't need magic, and neither do I."

How quaint, I thought dryly. *And yet, a potential sorcerer was selling things here?*

"How many have you given out?" Thorn asked.

"As many as there are merchants here." Bull amended this incredibly unhelpful statement by adding, "They turn 'em in when they want to break the contract to sell here."

Aha, thought I, *perhaps the only useful thing from him: we know this is probably not a spare or a keepsake.*

"Have any merchants failed to turn up lately?" Officer Thorn asked casually.

"I send my sons after 'em if they do," the grocer said. Perhaps he saw something in Thorn's look that cowed him, because he added a bit hastily, "If they don't send notice aforehand. Just to check up on 'em. Some only show up once a fortnight."

"I see." Officer Thorn tucked away the coin and said, "Do you have a list of everyone who does business here?"

"That's what the coins're for," said the grocer querulously. Across the stand, several pumpkins broke loose and rolled into one of the unfortunate sons.

"Thank you," Officer Thorn said firmly, drawing the man's attention back to her. "That'll be all for now. My assistant and I will just do a little survey of the merchants."

"Assistant?" Bull's small eyes widened as he peered around Thorn's shoulder and finally spotted me. "Say, no rabble-rousing—"

He caught one look from Officer Thorn and fell silent.

The moment we turned our backs, though, he was shouting at his sons with vigor. Thorn was clearly keeping one ear trained on them as we drifted toward the stalls. After a moment of purely pumpkin-themed talk, she huffed—not unlike William—and said to me in a low voice, "Here's hoping some of the regulars will be more helpful."

"He does seem to have a strange aversion to writing anything down," I said. "And to following through with people. Unless it's intimidating them with his sons."

"Whom we have had not a few complaints about over the years," Thorn murmured wryly.

"Is it suspicious?" I asked. "Not being able to identify the coin. Not even asking how you found it, either."

Thorn shrugged one broad shoulder. "We'll see if a motive develops."

Any further musing was cut short. We'd emerged out from the cover of the grocer's stand and now made our way down the first of three aisles full of merchants and shoppers. The hard-packed dirt had been churned into mud, and a cold breeze was whipping between the tents. There was a buzz of desperation in the air as people made their purchases with urgency. Rumors of the coming storm must have been pretty bad.

Thorn took one side of the row, and I took the other, eager to hasten our search. Periodically we'd glance back at each other, but each time, we both shook our heads. The first few merchants I spoke to were relatively recent additions to the market and had not noticed anyone missing lately. One only came once a month. Another was too busy selling goose down to spare me so much as a glance.

When we made it to the end of the row, I consoled myself by purchasing a paper cone filled to the brim with candied cashews. After a grateful smile at my friend behind the stall, I turned to find that Officer Thorn was speaking to a neighboring herb merchant while she waited.

". . . looking for a fight," the white-haired faun was saying as I joined the little group. He glanced up at me and smiled. "Hello, there, Red."

"Doug," I said with another smile. His wasn't my favorite stall to buy from—I usually grew or foraged for my own herbs—but I did enjoy talking to him when our paths crossed.

As a faun, Doug stood only as high as my elbow, and in fact often hopped up onto an old box in order to be seen over his table, which was overflowing with bunches of lavender, sage, wizard's hemlock, and moss. Despite his childlike stature, he had a grandfatherly bearing which agreed with the wrinkles around his eyes and the wispy white beard on his small chin. His eyes were pale and watery, contained by wire-rimmed glasses, but his smile was wide. His small ears were hidden amongst white curls. He wore a long tunic and short pants, and behind the table, his legs ended in goatlike hooves.

He lived outside of town, keeping to himself, and seemed to prefer life that way. However, today, he looked quite willing to assist Thorn and me.

"Doug here was just telling me there *is* someone he's hoping not to see around," Thorn told me, confirming my thoughts.

"*Hoping* is a strong word," said Doug, shimmying not unlike a nervous sheep. "But if there's been trouble, I wouldn't be surprised if she was at the bottom of it."

"No one else has mentioned any drama," I said, intrigued.

A pained expression crossed Doug's face and he readjusted his glasses. "They don't see her the way I do. Most barely seem to remember her. But if you had to share your table with her for two full days twice a moon, you'd remember."

"Can you describe her?" Officer Thorn leaned in, rustling up the scent of lavender as the wind whistled by again.

"Red's height," Doug said, promptly, though his gaze flickered between us. "Red's age. Dark hair and skin like her, too."

"Hey, there," I said, just to break the tension that was growing as each detail corroborated with our victim. "You're making her sound like my twin."

"But not at *all* like you, Red," Doug said in a rush. "She's always unfriendly and making a fuss."

Officer Thorn was intent, smiling grimly. "Is this the person you've come to the station about?"

"She took several baskets from me," Doug explained, sidestepping back and forth as his voice rose in pitch. "I know she did. But she will never admit it. And she's always shedding leaves and moss all over my wares. But if I say anything about it she'll pick a fight. She accused me of trying to trick her into sharing trade secrets. I thought I'd have to go to the station first in case she—in case I—"

"We never got any complaints about you," Thorn assured him. To me, she added, "I was never able to find the merchant and follow up—each time I showed up at the market, she was suddenly missing. At the time I let it slide, but I had a feeling it might be relevant now."

"How long ago was that?" I asked, glancing at Doug to include him.

"Back in spring," the officer answered.

"But she *has* shown up since, and she is always like that!" Doug bleated indignantly. With another quick shuffle, he adjusted his glasses again and took a deep breath. "I'm sorry to get twitchy with you nice folks. But she—she just—"

I glared at Officer Thorn, *hard.* If even I had to stop myself from suggesting the phrase "gets my goat," then I knew it must have been even harder for her.

"Her behavior does sound unpleasant," Officer Thorn agreed, carefully avoiding my eye. "Remind me of her name?"

"The Hermit," Doug said, as though it pained him. "That's all she ever says. It's written on her tablecloth and on her cart. I'm not one to pry, and *I*'m not rude, no matter what she said!"

This time Officer Thorn did meet my gaze, her brown eyes interested. I had to agree it sounded promising. Encouraged, I leaned over the herbs and added my own question. "Doug, did you say what she sells?"

"Pan protect me," Doug mumbled piously, one hand on his round chest. "*I* surely wouldn't know, and it's more than my life is worth to ever ask her. But it wasn't normal forest plants, I can tell you that. It was expensive. And that moss she was always spreading around? It *glowed.*"

14

From the Chorus

Naturally, I was eager to see a sample of that moss. But it had been days since The Hermit's last appearance, apparently, and there were no scraps left to be found and tested. Doug said most of his neighbor's buyers were merchants traveling through, folks who bought wares and were long gone—another dead end. I smothered my disappointment with more candied cashews.

We chatted a little longer with Doug, and he confirmed something else Officer Thorn had teased me about—that "The Hermit" avoided not only the local police, but the local alchemist, as well. If either Thorn or I made an appearance in the market, Doug said, his reclusive table mate would immediately whisk up her wares and be gone.

It was a startling image, and one I was still thinking over as Thorn and I moved aside to chat. "I can see why someone might have that reaction to me *these* days," I admitted, casting a glance askance at her. "What with the local police besmirching my reputation as an impartial shopkeeper. But why would she have avoided me in the early days?"

"And for that matter, why avoid the local police," Thorn added. She was firm in her belief that every police officer across Beyond must be a credit to their Guild. "It wasn't until this year that a complaint was made against her."

"That you know of," I pointed out.

"Exactly." She inclined her head. "Then there's the way Doug described it. Almost like a magic vanishing act."

"It certainly speaks of desperation," I agreed. "And if The Hermit is Vesper, then I can see why she'd be eager not to talk to the police. But I still don't see what *I* have to do with it."

"The description matches our victim, but we need more. Preferably someone who can link the two names together," Officer Thorn said.

I frowned, pulling my cloak tighter against another gust of wind. "The whole point of using a dramatic pseudonym was probably to *obscure* her original name. Which some people think wasn't even her real one to begin with."

"Some people?" Officer Thorn lifted her head, distracted.

"Luca's been reading cold case reports," I explained. "There's not a lot about the kidnapping, but there is a little."

"I'll add him to the list to visit," Officer Thorn said, pulling out her notebook. "And we may end up bringing Doug into the station to identify the body. But I'd still like to get some corroboration. Wait here a moment, and then we'll move on."

She turned back to Doug's stall briefly, and in snatches, I could hear her asking Doug when he was done for the day and if anyone else had run-ins with The Hermit. If anything, the market was busier and louder than before. No one was paying us any mind; so far, Thorn's wish to be discreet had been successful.

And then I saw Dusty cutting through the crowd toward

me.

"Morning, Red!" he called cheerfully, waving with a hand clenched around a bag of his own homemade trail mix.

"Morning," I chuckled, waving with my own paper cone of nuts. "Did you come looking for a snack, only to decide you've already got a better one?"

"Not here for myself," Dusty corrected, though his eyes crinkled in a smile as he looked up at me. "'M showing Keith around. It's his first day."

"Keith?" I looked up curiously to see a stranger emerge from the crowd. Keith wore a long, embroidered traveling cloak and an optimistic smile. He was a little taller than me, his frame so thin and wiry that it seemed like the wind just whipped right around him, passing him by. His deep brown hair had been pulled into a low ponytail, and his eyes were a matching dark, dark brown. He had dark brown skin, too, and pointed ears, and immediately I couldn't help but think of Luca's findings about another forest elf—Kieran, a possible member of the Drus.

While Dusty introduced me, I struggled to get a hold of myself.

"Good to meet you," Keith said, in a rough-edged but friendly voice.

I nodded, smiled, and downed the rest of my cashews in an effort not to say something about his heritage. It was hardly appropriate marketplace talk.

"Keith's related to the boy who came down from the mountain," said Dusty.

Thank goodness for Dusty. With my immediate question answered—if a bit abruptly—I could relax. "Really? Did Lavender reach out to you?"

"That's it," Keith agreed companionably. "Got her message yesterday afternoon. Lucky I happened to be in the area. I'm a bit of a drifter these days. Never had the heart to come back before, though," he added, glancing at the market, the peaked roofs beyond, and then the mountain itself. His expression was very readable. It said, *this place has changed more than I thought.*

I knew the feeling of returning home with unresolved issues. "It has to be tough. But no one knows the town better than Dusty these days. You're certainly in good hands."

"That's what Lavender said," Keith said, smiling down at the gnome.

Dusty tucked away his trail mix, and as he looked up at me, his gaze slid over to Officer Thorn's back. "You folks on the case?"

"Something like that," I agreed, cautiously. Unable to help myself, I asked more quietly, "Have you been to see Jack? Purslane?"

"Not yet," Keith answered, stepping closer, so we formed a little circle. "Poor boy wouldn't know me anyway. I was there for his parents' wedding, and then I was on a job at a gardening outfit in Pine until—"

"I didn't mean to pry," I said hastily, when his low voice became choked with emotion.

"Don't worry yourself," he said, shaking his head. "There's no helping it. I'd meant to come back sooner. I didn't know I wouldn't have time. How could I?"

"Kieran was his brother," Dusty told me confidentially. I accepted this without wondering how suddenly Dusty knew the names of every player in the old story.

Player—and yet, Keith was playing no role, that was certain.

Tears came away on his sleeve as he wiped his face. "I'm sorry," I said. "I didn't mean to bring painful things up."

"It happens just by walking around this town," Keith told me ruefully. "But like you said, I'm lucky to have Dusty."

"And on that note, we better keep moving," Dusty said. He let Keith say a hasty goodbye as he ushered him away, and in a second I realized why. Officer Thorn was done talking to Doug.

"What's he up to now?" she asked over my shoulder, eyeing Dusty's retreating back.

"I see you two still have some patching up to do," I teased. "Did Doug have anything more to say?"

"I gave him a look at the coin," Thorn said, "just a thought of mine. Turns out he noticed something Bull didn't. Just like you thought, it's an old version—archaic, he called it."

"Odd that the grocer himself didn't notice that," I said, thoughtfully.

"Odd, or just unhelpful as usual," Thorn said. "So what *is* Dusty doing? Didn't look like handy work."

I shook my head. "He's showing around Keith, who is apparently Jack's uncle. Sounds like he was in and out of Belville a lot, back in the day, and just came back now because Lavender reached out to him. But it made me think—why don't you just ask Lavender to identify the body?"

"Not good practice," Thorn said, steering me toward the next row of stalls. "I want a third party."

I paused, refusing to be steered further. "Meaning—?"

"Exactly what you think," she confirmed. "Aside from Jack himself, who has a pretty good alibi so far, Lavender's the most obvious suspect."

* * *

While Officer Thorn singled out a few merchants based on Doug's recommendation, I played "clean up" and checked with the rest of the market regulars, just in case anyone had anything to say. It was a little easier now that I knew what stall to ask about—though I was careful to ask if they'd noticed anyone else missing, too. It never hurt to cover every angle. Most of my alchemical training had been one repeated lesson of *don't count on outcomes before you've done the experiment.*

Most people had no new information to offer, and by the end of the next row, I was dying for something warm to drink. Even though it wasn't raining, the threat of an incoming storm was now present in the air, like the town had been possessed by a huge, damp ghost. When someone yelled my name I jumped, squelching in the mud around the stalls.

"Red," Marguerite repeated, coming over from the grocer's stand. "How nice to see you!"

Though the sentiment was much like what Keith had said earlier, it was much louder—and a little less friendly. Marguerite was serving her second term as Belville's mayor, though she was a glassblower by occupation. Using her breath to mold glass had gifted her a strong set of lungs, and several years serving the town council had left her with an entirely business-like attitude. Though our paths usually only crossed at the town business association meetings, she always greeted me by name.

"Good morning," I said, swallowing to stop my teeth from chattering—from surprise as much as from the cold, which was working its way into my bones. "Or is it afternoon?"

"Still morning," she informed me briskly. Her graying hair

was pulled back, as always, in a tight braid, and she wore a buttoned-up pea coat. "How's the shop?"

"During the breaks in the rain, doing well," I said honestly. "William and Rhys are looking after it now."

Marguerite nodded. "It's the same for most businesses in town."

"Yes, I imagine so." I peered at her, wondering why she wanted to chat. "Did you come out to check on the market before the storm?"

"I try to come by once a day," she told me. "I make a lap of town."

"Oh." I blinked; I had no complaints about Marguerite as a mayor, but I hadn't realized how deep her devotion to duty extended. "In that case, have you noticed anything unusual lately? Anyone missing, or causing trouble?"

She eyed me keenly. "Helping the police? I saw Officer Thorn talking to the Jonskid's Potato farmers just now."

"Well—Olivia's busy looking after Jack; I suppose you heard about all that?" I offered, hesitantly.

"Yes, I got the latest update this morning," Marguerite said, her voice shrewd. "Tell Officer Thorn to let me know if she needs help from the council. But at the moment, I can't think of anything to tell you. It's been business as usual here. Although—"

She stopped, looking at me with her head to one side. I shifted awkwardly. "What is it?"

"The storms bring out all kinds of people," she said eventually, carefully. "I noticed Luca came by a few days ago, with Sakura in tow. I thought you did most of his shopping these days?"

"I do, for vegetables at least," I admitted, my face flushing.

Luca could add sums and categorize books in no time flat but he wouldn't know a ripe tomato from a seedling, so we'd long ago divided up our household chores. But did the mayor care? Was she trying to get gossip out of me? Or was this somehow relevant? "Did they, uh, say anything to you?"

"Not a thing," said Marguerite. "I thought they seemed preoccupied."

And with that utterly unhelpful thought, she gave me a little bow of the head and continued on her way.

15

Twists and Tendrils

When Officer Thorn found me a little while later to compare notes, I was admittedly distracted. And since she had had little luck herself, she was in no mood to put up with my halfheartedness. It didn't help when we stopped by the tavern to find that Lavender couldn't shed any light on our questions about the housekeeping staff at the tower.

"My own staff are too busy to go out that far," she said. "I leave the properties on the mountain entirely up to Daisy. If she needs help, she knows to turn it over to me, but she handles all the routine maintenance."

This was even *more* distracting. The housekeeper Luca and I had met certainly wasn't Daisy. But I was hard-pressed to say who else it may have been . . . or may *not* have been. In their cap and mask and overalls, really the only noticeable thing I could recall about them was their height—just shorter than Luca and me. It really wasn't much to go on. And then there was the fact that Luca had seemed so friendly with them—of course, he was friendly with everyone—apparently

111

too friendly, these days, some might say—

"Cinnabar," Thorn snapped as we leaned on the bar. Lavender had wandered off, and so had my thoughts.

"When did I give you permission to use my full name?" I grumped, sticking my tongue out at her.

"When you stopped responding to 'Red,'" she retorted. In an investigation several years ago, she'd learned my first name—Cinnabar—but most people knew me only as Red, my childhood nickname. For years I'd preferred it that way. Since visiting my hometown and making peace with the more magical aspects of my family, I didn't mind as much, but it was still a little jarring to be addressed in an unusual manner.

This whole morning had turned out to be jarring, in fact.

"I was *saying*," Thorn continued, "that I still have to wait a little bit for Doug to finish his shift at the market. Want to have lunch?"

I made a face, my stomach churning again as doubts plagued me. "I don't know."

My friend studied my expression for a moment before settling on a nearby stool. "You don't have to feel bad about the housekeeper lead," she said. "It's interesting, sure, but it's not like we have an established time of death or even victim identification yet. We can sweep it under the rug for now."

"Har har," I said, but my heart wasn't in it. I sighed. "It's not that, exactly. It's—"

For one moment, I did think about confiding in her, telling her all my worries about Luca and his secretive behavior of late. But in the next moment, I remembered where we were and what we were doing. Officer Thorn had an actual murder and potential cold case kidnapping on her hands. She didn't need to hear me moan about my errant partner.

"Maybe you should go see Sakura," Thorn suggested.

I startled. I hadn't told her what the mayor had said. Had she somehow heard the same rumor? Were there *more* rumors?

"I'm not saying I wouldn't like to help, of course," she said hastily, spurred by my dramatic reaction. "I would. But Maggie's always telling me I have to know when to quit. And I have to admit . . . Sakura *can* be helpful. She's better at the mushy stuff than I am."

"What mushy stuff?" I asked, still ruffled.

"Oh, nothing," said Thorn, though she did smirk at me. I glared back.

And yet—it wasn't a bad idea.

"I *would* like a proper cup of tea," I said. Lavender's was famous for its awful tea, just as much as it was known for its wonderful cider. It was the reason Saki had set up a café in town in the first place. "You're okay on your own from here?"

"I know where to hunt everyone down if I need them," Thorn assured me, this time with a genuine smile. "Go on. You're due a break."

* * *

The clouds hung low over Market Square, the chill driving me forward as I stepped into the Pomegranate.

As usual, the café was bustling. Scents of tea, cheese, and pastry filled the air, reminding me that I'd come at the start of the lunch rush. Nevertheless, Saki beamed over the counter at me once I'd made my way through the line to her register.

"Pumpkin spice chai?" she asked, one hand hovering over the register keys. "You've certainly had a steady stream of customers today."

113

"I haven't been in," I said guiltily, glancing at the blackboard behind her for the sandwich specials. Fancy grilled cheese, veggie paninis, egg salad with dill—it was overwhelming. My stomach rumbled. "I've been helping Thorn."

"No wonder you look so glum." Humor sparkled in Saki's blue eyes, alongside compassion. "If you're worn out, why not let me take over? I'll choose something for you to eat and bring it to you. Go and sit upstairs—there's a table right above us now that should have just cleared out. Go on, you can pay me later."

Gratefully, I went.

I found the table just where Saki had described, nestled near the railing on the second floor balcony. No sooner had I collapsed into a chair when Sakura appeared, her orange skirt and bright pink apron flouncing as she dodged tables and customers with ease. When she reached me, she set a steaming mug and a plated panini on my side of the table before sitting down with her own wide cup of cocoa and an enormous cheese sandwich piled high with peppers and mushrooms.

"We can switch if you want to, but I don't want to," she said cheerfully before digging in.

I took a bite of my own panini before answering, savoring the mozzarella and basil. "I guess at this point I've come in often enough for you to know what I'd like."

"And honestly, no one ever wants my sandwich," she told me, grinning rather triumphantly. "It started as a joke between me and Glacial. I told her just to use whatever ingredients she had left over, and not to toast it—I hate sharp bread. Now I think she does her best to find weird combinations."

"That one doesn't seem so bad," I said, doubtfully, as a slim bit of mushroom tumbled onto her plate.

"Oh, it's not. Especially since I waited a little too long to take my lunch and now I'm starving," Saki said lightly. "Same case for you?"

"A little," I admitted. "Though what I was really craving was your chai. Thorn and I were talking to people in the market all morning."

"I'm sure that was interesting." Saki spoke with a trace of irony, but she waited for me to say more.

I sighed. "It was something. The problem is that so far this case is entirely circumstantial. *Everything* seems to be."

If she noticed the frustration in my voice at that, she didn't mention it directly. Instead, after another big bite of sandwich, she observed, "Is it really so emotional? I thought so far it was all about long-lost sons and recluses no one knows."

"You're not wrong, not exactly." I paused and sipped my drink, uncertain how much to say about the case—or how much Saki knew. Surely people had seen Officer Thorn carry a body to the station last night, and the rumors had spread? I tried to remember if anyone had mentioned it at the market, but I could only remember Marguerite's comment. "But there's still a lot of reason to tread carefully."

Lavender, Daisy, even Rhys, by extension. And Luca. So far they were all tied up in this somehow . . .

"Maybe you're treading *too* carefully," Sakura said bluntly.

I glanced at her, then down at my panini, which was already half gone. As a shadow witch, Saki made a habit of saying what other people might skirt around. She was essentially a rogue witch, someone whose power came from facing her own darkest corners, and the result was that she didn't have much patience for those who preferred to keep things easy and unspoken.

It was one of the reasons I liked her, even though I knew I myself was not always great at speaking on emotional topics. But I had been getting better lately. I cleared my throat. "Did you go to the market with Luca the other day?"

"Did I?" Saki's blue eyes were wide and innocent.

I pursed my lips at her. "Did you want me to ask, or didn't you?"

That made her laugh. "I figured it might be best if you did. But that doesn't mean I have to answer."

"What were you doing?" I pressed. "What is *he* doing?"

"How would I know that better than he would?" Sakura smirked over the last of her thickly sliced bread. "If that was what was bothering you, why didn't you go to the bookstore?"

"The bookstore doesn't have tea," I said, irritably.

"It has answers," she pointed out.

I frowned at her as I put two and two together. "You've been waiting to tease me about this since I ran into Luca and Daisy here a few days ago, haven't you?"

"I teased you then, but you were busy," Saki said blithely. "And why didn't you straighten things out already? Like you said, it's been several days."

"I know, I tried, but—it's complicated," I protested, pushing away my empty plate and reaching for the comfort of my mug. This one was decorated with a smooth yellow glaze and an etching of a bee. All of the Pomegranate's dishware was eclectic and colorful. I sometimes wondered if Sakura picked out certain items for particular customers on purpose.

"It's really not," she observed. "Luca's acting oddly and you want to know why."

"And he doesn't want to tell me why," I amended. "That's

what actually worries me. And it doesn't help that you're *also* avoiding telling me anything, by the way."

Sakura tucked her white hair behind her ear. "It's not my secret to tell."

"Isn't that helpful." I rolled my eyes before burying my face in my mug again, inhaling the cinnamon and nutmeg.

"It's not, I know." Saki hesitated, then reached across the table and laid her pale hand over mine. "Is there some reason you aren't sure you can trust him?"

"I *can* trust him, I know I can," I said, sighing. "It's just . . . odd, like you said. And far *more* odd that everyone's so secretive about it. Even William was giving me a hard time. It's like I'm missing something, somehow."

"You'll figure it out in the end. You always do," Saki said, her eyes sparkling once more.

"So you're telling me to leave you alone and just be patient?" I glanced up wryly.

She tossed her head, grinning. "Something like that. Though do, of course, come back any time you want more chai. Or to let me in on what exactly Officer Thorn is doing. I hear Olivia and Jack might be an item?"

"This entire town is nothing but a gossip machine," I said, shaking my own head. "I have no idea what's going on with Olivia, or Thorn at the moment. You'll probably find out before I do."

"Particularly if I get back to my post," she agreed. Before she rose to go, though, she added, "Are you feeling a *little* better, at least?"

"A little," I allowed, smiling. "But I'm taking this mug and the rest of my chai with me."

It was a common thing to do, of course—the Pomegranate

did have to-go cups, which customers were expected to return for cleaning and re-use. Some people in town thought Sakura cast a spell on all her traveling cups, but I had no idea if that was true. I always returned mine promptly. I certainly stopped by the café often enough.

The walk to my shop was short but dismaying, like walking straight through a cloud. I almost wished the rain would come back and get things over with already. Rhys was helping a group of school-age children look through the little reference book section (perhaps mostly so that he could ensure that the books were reshelved properly) so William began filling me in on the morning's events. It *had* been a busy day. We were out of warming powders again, and Lumi wanted twice her usual essential oil order . . . I listened absently to William's report as I made my way into my lab to check on the ongoing experiment for Officer Thorn.

The distiller was still bubbling away, which was no surprise. Breaking a substance down into its component parts might take hours or even days, depending on the substance and any latent magic that might be involved. But my eye caught on something off to the side.

It was the grow light over the terrarium—something I'd forgotten that I'd set up in the first place. But it didn't look remotely like it had this morning. When I'd left it, it had been a little glass box with a yellow-greenish smudge at the bottom. Now, it might as well have been a living cube of moss. The glass was entirely covered.

And the moss was *glowing*.

"William," I said, interrupting his ongoing monologue. "I'm going up to the tower tomorrow. And I'm going to need you to come with me."

16

Return to the Tower

The next day dawned windy and dark, and I was raring to go.

While William slept until the very last moment, I paced my tiny kitchen collecting provisions and making traveling cups of tea. One for myself, and one for Luca, who had insisted on coming along the instant he'd heard our plans the previous evening. He'd even gone to Lavender to get the spare key again *and* conferred with Thorn on our behalf. It was clear he was determined to be helpful. Both our shops were scheduled to be closed, anyway—it was a Rest Day in Market Square—and I could hardly turn down an extra pair of eyes and hands. Not that I wanted to.

I jogged downstairs to my lab, glancing over the experiments and tucking one of Paracelsus's new journals—along with his letter, for good measure—into my knapsack. The fact that my old mentor was looking for a glowing flower and we'd just found a victim associated with glowing moss had not escaped me. Paracelsus had always had *interesting* timing like that. It was one of those qualities that either made for a terrific alchemist or a terrifically unlucky alchemist, and I could never tell if he was doing it on purpose or if he was just "in tune with the universe" or something.

When I ran back up the stairs to wake William, I met Luca coming out of the bathroom. Sugar the pixie had flown over too, and was doing her best to stand on his head.

"I'm ready, I promise," he mumbled. A tremendous yawn dislodged his passenger.

Despite my misgivings, I grinned. Of my friends, I was the only genuine morning person. Except perhaps for Sugar, who didn't seem to sleep as much as disappear until someone did something to catch her attention.

"Want to draw straws for who has to wake William?" I asked my partner.

A low growl came from the window seat. "I'm up. Though I don't see why. It's basically the middle of the night."

"It's not even early morning anymore," I retorted. "You just can't tell because the cloud cover is so thick."

"Remind me why we're going out when we *know* it's going to storm." William had yet to move.

As I picked up our breakfast off the kitchen island, I obliged. "Because I need answers, and so does Officer Thorn. And who knows how long this storm will last once it starts. If we're quick, maybe we can get up there and back before the rain comes."

Infamous last words, I thought—and then immediately pushed the thought away.

William grumbled, but under his breath. With just a little more shooing, I managed to get my companions out the door. Even in our sturdy water-proof boots and thick woolen cloaks, both Luca and I shivered a little as the wind whipped through the yard behind the shop.

"It won't be so bad once we're moving," I said, hopefully, leading the way to the street.

"There was a time when you wouldn't have left your house at all in these temperatures," William observed, trotting alongside us. He never seemed to mind the heat or cold very much.

"Well, we all have to grow up some time." I smiled ruefully down at him.

"Wait, I—never mind," Luca said, pausing before recovering and jumping up to join us again. "I thought I left the key, but I have it. The pockets in this cloak are really deep. Hate to go all the way up there for nothing, right?"

I chuckled, but I had the distinct impression that William was not amused.

"Although, Lavender said something funny to me," Luca went on. "When I went to see her yesterday about the key, I mean. When I showed up it was just after dinner, and things were a little quiet, mostly folks from out of town getting ready for Samhain. So we were chatting for a moment, she was really curious about what we might be looking for. I told her I didn't know, really, because I wasn't sure how much of Paracelsus's 'homework' was supposed to be a secret."

"Oh!" My breath huffed in the air, another little cloud. "I don't know if it *was* supposed to be, but thank you."

"Is this coming back around to something funny?" William demanded.

"Oops." Luca's stories tended to be a little long and wandering, and it was only worse in the morning before his brain was fully in gear. We all knew this, though, and he grinned sheepishly as he went on, "Um, not funny-haha, but funny-odd. So after we talked about how you wanted to go back there, Red, Lavender went and got me the key, and as she gave it to me she said something like, 'at this rate, maybe you'll find the back entrance,' or maybe it was more like, 'maybe you *should* just use the back entrance.'"

"Is there one?" I asked, startled. My mind immediately went to Officer Thorn and the suspected murder.

"That's what I said," Luca informed us. "I said, I hadn't realized that there *was* one, and then she said well maybe it was all just an old rumor."

William, who had been sniffing the air as we entered the forest, tuned back in at that comment. "Shouldn't she be the one to know if her own property has a back entrance?"

"You would think so," Luca said, thoughtfully, "but I didn't, at the time. Someone called her away for a drink or something, and I didn't think to ask any more about it."

I thought this over, too, watching the branches sway above our heads in the breeze. "You went and saw Officer Thorn afterward, right? Did you mention it to her?"

"I didn't. I was so focused on explaining your experiment, and she was distracted because she and Olivia were switching shifts soon, I think. I'm sorry," Luca added.

"Don't worry. It might be nothing," I assured him. "Everyone's a little rattled these days, it seems like."

As if to prove my point, after that we lapsed into silence. Only occasionally would someone speak up, usually to point out a particularly spooky-looking tree or to notice that the wind seemed even brisker than it had before. By the end of the hike, of course, we were all breathless anyway, even William.

The three of us stood at the edge of the clearing at last. Luca and I paused to sip tea, and I passed around a bit of pumpkin bread I'd been saving. While we lingered under the tree cover, I told them, "I want to check the area outside the tower first. Especially given what Lavender said to Luca, now."

"All I see is plain mud," William said skeptically, plopping himself down on a nearby log.

"That's why we're taking a closer look," I reminded him. "Especially since it isn't raining yet. How about we each take a section of the clearing and look for anything unusual? You've all had a good look at my sample, right?" I held up a glass vial with some of the moss I'd grown yesterday. It was as thriving and glowy-green as ever.

Luca looked closely, his own green eyes shining with a not-totally-dissimilar glow. "Any idea *where* it might be, Red? Like on rocks, or trees, or just out in the mud, like William said?"

"No, not really," I admitted. "That's why I want to cover the whole clearing, just in case. Officer Thorn found her original sample on the victim's boots, and presumably she had to walk through this area to get to the tower. But bear in mind that Paracelsus is looking for something with a similar glow. So we might not just be talking about moss."

"Walk back and forth through the wet grass looking for anything glowy," William summarized. "Got it. I call the middle section with the tower."

"I'll take the upper section, then," Luca said, smiling at me. "All set?"

"All set," I agreed, closing up my bag. "Let's get to work."

* * *

Despite what William might say, it wasn't the *worst* work I've ever had to do. Trudging back and forth through the long grass, while monotonous, became rather meditative. The smell of wet leaves and nearby pine trees rode on the wind, and with my cloak and boots—not to mention our recent exercise—I was nice and toasty. I had my goggles on and was just inspecting an unfamiliar wildflower near the cliff edge when I heard a shout.

I looked up, alarmed, to see Luca waving. His black cloak stood out against the fading grasses, marking him plainly in the middle of the clearing. But he wasn't waving at me or William. He was looking up at the sky.

I looked, too, just in time to see a massive shape soaring by. *Daisy?* I knew her at once, but I was still confused. *Why is she flying around here, especially so close to the Outlook? I thought Officer Thorn's searches were done for now.*

There was no time to wonder any further, though, because William came bounding up around the side of the tower. "Red, what about the road?"

"What road?" I asked, still thinking about dragons and flying.

"Exactly," he replied. "Shouldn't there be a road to reach the tower? Or at least a path?"

"Not if it's usually abandoned. But if whoever lived here *was* routinely going down to the market, with a cart, you'd think there would be," I realized slowly. "Why do you ask? Did you find wheel marks?"

"No," said William promptly. "The ground around the tower is totally boring. But *should* it be?"

At that moment, lightning struck farther down the mountain, beyond the trees. I stood up, straining to see if I had seen right—or if somehow Daisy had been involved? But a few moments later, there was a deafening roll of thunder.

"Let's continue this conversation inside," I told William.

"I'll get Luca," he agreed, taking off like a shot through the long grass.

I could be just as swift as he was, when I wanted to be. And with the gray sheet of rain advancing over the treetops toward us, I definitely wanted to be. I got to the tower's front door a moment before Luca and William did. The first raindrops came down riding the wind, flinging themselves into our faces. I held my arm up to ward them off as I watched Luca fumble in his pocket for the key. There was a glimmer—or perhaps another lightning strike?

In the next moment, we were tumbling into the tower's dark hall.

17

Heights and Depths

"There and back before the storm hits, huh?" William asked, shaking his black fur so that rainwater went flying everywhere.

"Hey, stop that! I said *maybe*," I reminded him, cowering with Luca against the stairwell from the wet dog terror. Outside, the storm raged with full force against the tower's stone walls. "Is everyone okay? Made it inside in one piece?"

"More than one," Luca said.

"More—?" I turned to look, puzzled. He was holding one hand out in front of him, his gaze fixed on his palm. After a moment of confusion, I realized that Sugar was curled up with her arms around her knees, sulking, in his hand.

"Sugar!" I said, half in surprise, half a reprimand. "Why didn't you just tell us if you wanted to come along?"

"She was hiding in my pocket," Luca said. "I almost squished her when I went to grab the key in such a hurry."

"Probably not, unfortunately," said William, ambling over. "Pixies are tougher than they look. But why'd you want to come out in the first place?"

This last question was directed at her, and Sugar finally lifted her head and looked at all of us. Then she stood up, shook herself—much like William had done—and rose into the air.

"Glowy flower," she said, in her thin, high voice. "I want to see the glowy flower too!"

My stomach dropped. Pixies, glowing flowers, and dragon fly-bys usually only meant one thing in Belville, and it was something I'd been half suspecting ever since Paracelsus made his request.

"I have a thought," I announced to my friends. "But first, let's go up to the second floor and get comfortable. This might take a while."

* * *

Since Officer Thorn had already had her expert assistant (me) sketch the place, and Lavender had been so accommodating, I didn't feel bad as we took over the second floor parlor with its cozy blue rug. Luca and I hung up our cloaks and shed our boots, and William soon had a fire going—a real one, since the tower was stocked with a neat pile of logs beside the hearth. The rain against the window panes was fierce. I half expected a storm to materialize over the mountains painted onto the walls. We pulled the armchairs into a little circle and collapsed gratefully. Sugar perched on a nearby end table, her spirits restored already.

"Okay, hear me out," I began. "Obviously, my first thought on reading Paracelsus's letter was Daisy's tree. The Tree of Life," I corrected, when Sugar shimmered next to me.

We'd had a run-in with rumors of this mystical tree a few

winters back. And though I, as a social being, tended to think of "Daisy's pixies" or "Daisy's tree," Sugar was right. Daisy and the pixies lived where they did *because* they had long ago found shelter in a great big cavern that housed a Tree of Life.

I'd never been to see it myself, but I knew plenty about such magical trees from my training. They were a particular fascination in alchemy. Though they were sometimes called "world trees," most people these days agreed that there was more than one hiding in the untouched areas of Beyond. That explained why there were so many rumors and fairy tales about them.

"Rhys said he didn't recognize the flower, though," said William. He was curled up in a heavy plush chair with his chin on one armrest.

"Right," I agreed. "But remember how we found out about the Tree because people thought the miners had hollowed out a cave close to where it might be? There are all kinds of tunnels and caves in Belville Mountain, and most of them are perfectly natural."

"You think the glowing flower, and possibly also the glowing moss, come from some other hidden and previously-unknown connection to the Tree," Luca concluded, his forehead creased as he mulled this over. Then he turned to Sugar. "Is that what you think too?"

It warmed my heart to see him taking her opinion so seriously, and I have to admit, I felt a little guilty for not asking her thoughts on the matter before. I'd become too used to Sugar being my little kitchen buddy; more often than not, I neglected to think about her past with Daisy's pixies.

Sugar glimmered, then rose up and flew over to sit on my shoulder. I could guess what she wanted. I fished in my belt for the vial of moss, and held it up for her to examine. She perched on my hand, bringing her tiny face close to the glass.

"I just like it," she told me. "I didn't think why."

I relayed this answer to William and Luca, who might not have been able to hear her above the crackling hearth and the thunder outside. "Is it like what you saw before, with the Tree?" I asked her.

She nodded, but then shook her head.

"Similar, but not exactly the same?" I guessed

To this, she agreed. I set the vial on another nearby table so that she could keep looking at it if she wanted to, and addressed Luca and William again. "There's something else. This is even less scientific, but bear with me. Thorn and I had a conversation about Jack's name the other day."

William perked up one ear. "That *is* unscientific."

I grimaced, but it couldn't be helped. My time with my mothers—and truly, even these past few years with my friends—had taught me that intuition had its place as well as reason. "I know, but we were already talking about Lavender's story at the time—about how it mirrors the Rapunzel tale. And in that story, names are significant. It does make you wonder, why rename a child?"

"Aside from pure conceit?" William asked. "Or just convenience and *deceit*?"

Luca pondered more slowly. "Of every name out there to choose, Jack is potentially a good one for someone who wants to keep a low profile. It's common, and mixed up in plenty of fairy tales."

"Yes, but," I repeated, "think about it. They lived—we're pretty sure they lived—in this tower. Very high up. Selling *plants* at the local market."

William yawned. "Be better if it was beans."

"But you see my point!" I said triumphantly, ignoring his sass. "It makes me think of Jack and the Beanstalk."

"Are you saying that you think there's some kind of greenhouse at the top of the tower?" Luca asked, leaning over his knees.

"I hope not," I said, then grinned at him. "Anyway I don't think it's likely that we missed anything, Officer Thorn and I. But *somewhere here* there must be. Maybe the old tale isn't exactly on the nose. Daisy and the pixies and their Tree, they all live in a cavern somewhere—essentially under the mountain. So what if, somewhere, there is a passage that leads *down* from here?"

At this, William showed interest. "It might explain why no one but us seems to use the front door."

"According to everything I've read, Vesper did come to the area looking for something to extend her life—and an offshoot from the Tree of Life would probably do it," Luca agreed. "Okay, Red, we're on board. How do you want to start looking?"

I looked over at William and grinned. "*I'm* not going to do it. This is someone else's turn to shine."

* * *

Once we were all agreed and Sugar had tucked herself safely into my knapsack, we trooped back down the stairs. William had grumbled a little, but only for show. His fluffy tail was high in the air, and I knew he was excited for the hunt.

I'd realized long ago that if anything else was hidden at this tower, it would take someone with better magical vision than me to find it. People like me, and Luca and Officer Thorn, had been all over this place and the only thing we'd been able to find was that trapdoor—arguably the lowest hanging fruit, since who would ever be up on the observation deck looking at the ceiling, anyway? I strongly suspected that when it came to hiding a magical cavern—a place that was probably more important to Vesper than anything else—more protections had been put in place.

Of course, there was no guaranteeing that the source of the moss and the tower were directly connected. But the storm was pouring down buckets of water outside, and we had to start somewhere, so we all agreed to start somewhere dry.

We stood in the entry hall of the tower once more. Luca held lightsticks aloft while I tugged my goggles into place. But the true test was William. He was already glowing, blue magic crackling over his dark fur as he began investigating the edges of the room.

Luca tapped at the windows and the door, while I examined the mirror, just in case. It was hard to tell exactly how canny a sorcerer might be. This one seemed to have a rather twisted sense of humor, based on everything I'd heard about her so far. She hadn't been the one to build the tower—it had existed before her time—but perhaps she had been the one to discover its secret, and then to add layers of her own secrecy to it . . .

"I do see something," said William after several minutes, sitting at one edge of the room. "But I'm not sure it makes sense."

"What is it?" Luca went over, and I joined them, peering over William's shoulder. Even with my goggles on, it just looked to me like William was staring at the mural on the wall.

"Technically, it's the second thing I've seen," William went on. "There used to be a teleportation circle there, in the middle of the floor." He gestured behind us with his nose, at the rug. "The magic is faint, and I definitely wouldn't trust it any more."

"Faded because its caster died?" Luca suggested.

"Most likely," William agreed. "Big spells like that do fade over time. There are things sorcerers can do to sustain them, but she might not have figured it was worth her while. After all, it was probably only in place to be convenient for her while she was alive."

"Can you tell where it went?" I asked.

"No. That's not how this works, and anyway I told you, I could barely see it at all," William said. "I didn't even notice it under the rug when we first came in. The more important thing is right here."

"On the . . . wall?" Luca asked, faltering. I, too, failed to see anything out of place about the painted trees and ferns.

"I'm not sure," William admitted, with uncharacteristic hesitance. "If it's there, someone's tried really hard to hide it."

"That could be a good sign," I supplied.

"But it's too small to be a door," William added. "Much too small."

"How big is it?" Luca prompted. I was nearly on my toes by this point, trying to see.

"See that fern, there?" William again pointed at part of the mural with his nose, and then sneezed. "It's weird. There's this very faint magical outline right there. But it's not a door and it doesn't follow the lines in the mural, either. It looks like a . . ."

"Like a what?" I asked, nearly bursting.

"You're going to laugh," he said. "But it looks like a cabbage."

I nearly fell over. "A what?"

But Luca, meanwhile, had gone rigid. "Take it," he said.

"*What?*" William and I repeated together.

"Take it," he insisted, excited now. "That's how the story starts in Rapunzel, right? You have to steal the lettuce."

"Wow, I know I figured Vesper had a sense of humor about the name 'Jack,' but that is going in a weird direction," I couldn't help but say.

"Sorcerers do that," William said impatiently. "That weird, annoying, self-aware thing. More to the point, it's a bad idea. I can't tell what kind of spell it is. It's too faded into the mural."

"Meaning?" I asked once more.

"Meaning I don't know what it will *do*," William said. "So nobody take anything."

"But we found it!" Luca protested.

"*I* found it, and it could be a trap!" William argued back. "Or just some magical graffiti!"

"Both of you, hush," I interrupted. I pulled a long set of forceps from my toolkit. "I came prepared. William, if you tell me where to aim these things, and keep us protected as best you can—and Luca, if you'll hide and be our ambusher just in case some*thing* comes out—then we should be good, right?"

William looked from my tool, to me, to Luca, who was already going ghostly. He sighed heavily. "If by 'good' you mean 'absolutely foolish,' then yes."

18

Rising and Falling

It was like a strange team building exercise. Trying to latch on to something in the wall that I couldn't see while William gave directions like a harbinger of doom and Luca literally hovered over my shoulder was *not* as easy as it had sounded when I'd come up with my plan. But just when I was ready to say *maybe there actually isn't anything in the wall to 'take,'* my forceps caught on an edge, and a piece of wood the size of my palm tumbled out of the wall.

The three of us waited as one, holding our breath.

After a minute had passed with nothing but the sound of the rain outside, I gave a long, cautious sigh. "So far, so good."

"It's too small a hole for anything *really* scary to come out anyway," William grumped.

"That *is* odd, isn't it?" Luca remained ghostly, just a shadow against the mural, as he moved toward the wall. "Given Red's description of a cavern under the mountain, I had expected William to find some kind of door in the floor. Instead, we have just a little hidey hole here, several feet up . . ."

His voice trailed off, but I could see from his faint outline that he was peering into the place where the "cabbage" had been.

"What is it?" I asked him.

"Brace yourselves," was all he said.

And then the floor beneath me disappeared.

"Luuucaaaaa!" I cried out, but it was no use. I was falling, and so was William. The world was a dark blur, but I could see his blue sparkles next to me. A pang of dread echoed through my chest as I wondered what in Beyond we were going to do *now.* But before I could think of anything, I landed butt-first on something that spat me back up. Confused and dazed, I crash-landed on a stone floor.

"Sorry about that," said Luca's voice. In the dark it was impossible to see him, but it sounded like he was gently floating down toward us. Stupid ghost powers. His voice wasn't at all as strained as mine had been.

William, somewhere nearby, sounded more angry than scared. "Did you *do* that or did you see it coming?"

"I—I did it," Luca admitted guiltily. "There was a knob in the wall behind that wooden plate. I just wanted to help and I knew we'd argue about it but if we were going to find this cavern then someone had to—"

"You're not the one who fell, are you?" William shouted.

"I didn't know! I thought it would just take me, since I was touching the knob." At this point, Luca reached me, and helped me as I was struggling to stand up. "I'm really sorry," he said. "I just wanted to help."

"Let's all 'help' as a team from now on," I told him, still a little dizzy. "Does anyone know where we are?"

"Give me a second." Luca shifted, becoming more corporeal again. I almost cautioned him not to before I realized what he was doing. When he was in shadow form, all of his clothes and anything in his pockets transformed with him—and ghostly lightsticks wouldn't be of any use. He had to transform back, even if it could be dangerous. Though, so far, we seemed to be entirely alone . . .

Light bloomed as Luca held several lightsticks aloft. I could finally see him, and William nearby, but beyond that—faintly, at the edges of our illuminated bubble, there was a wall, damp but entirely straight. The stone floor beneath our feet was cut into close-fitting tiles. We weren't in a natural cavern. I looked up. Though the surprise fall had seemed like it might have taken forever, William and I had only really fallen two stories down. Through a circle in the ceiling, the dim entry hall was barely visible.

"Some joke," William muttered.

I turned to see what he was looking at. Behind us, there was—of all things—a trampoline. It seemed to be the only furniture in the room, and it was definitely newer than everything else by centuries.

"That's what we landed on," I realized, self-consciously rubbing my backside. "Are you really saying Vesper *used* that? It seems so . . . undignified."

"Oh, it is," William assured me. "I doubt she ever did use it, on purpose anyway. But she may have put it there just in case. Since her whole reason for coming here was that her life and magic were fading, she might not have trusted her teleportation spells completely."

"Or—what about Jack?" Luca asked. "Could it have been a fail-safe for him?"

"Who knows," said William. "We don't even know yet why either of them would bother coming down here. We're in a basement. All I see is the tower foundations."

"No magic at all?" I straightened my goggles and took another look around, even growing brave enough to start walking the room. It was exactly the size of the rooms above—definitely, as William had said, a basement. And there wasn't a trace of anything there with us, not even cobwebs . . . the only thing in the room aside from the trampoline was a thick layer of dust.

"Here's your escape route, anyway," William said from the far corner. Luca and I both went over to see what he was talking about: a rope ladder that looked like it might snap at any moment. The years had not been kind to it, and it had seen *far* too many years. But it extended all the way up to the entry hall floor above us. When Luca lifted the light, I could see that the ladder ended in a hatch. But there was something wrong with it.

"Wait—hasn't that hatch been boarded over? From the inside?" I asked, as I strained to make sense of what I was seeing.

"I think so," Luca agreed. "And if I remember right, I think it would come out right under that bureau in the hall. So someone really didn't want it to be used, I guess."

"Why would she go to the trouble of blocking and hiding the actual entrance to the basement, only to make her own with a secret knob and possible transportation spell?" I ran my hands through my hair, frustrated. "There must be something down here."

"Probably a flood," William suggested dryly, "if we stay here long enough for the storm to make its way in."

Something in his words made me think. I was reminded suddenly of my first visit to the tower, when Luca and I had looked into the nearby ravine and seen that, despite the rain, there was no water flowing in the old riverbed.

"It already has," I said, slowly, as I thought aloud. "I thought I saw dampness at first, when Luca shone the lights. But everything since then has been dusty and dry. Which way were we looking?" I turned, and abruptly began to retrace my steps. Luca and William followed close on my heels. As we went, I explained, "I thought the wall itself seemed damp . . . Here." We reached the spot on the opposite wall, and I bent down to examine it.

"Looks to me like the floor's damp, not the wall," William observed, still clearly unimpressed.

"Well, I may have still been dizzy and mixing things up a little," I admitted. He did have a point: it was the row of tiles right where the wall met the floor that was wet and shiny. "But the point is the dampness."

"Why? Isn't that what water does? With all the rain lately, the water level in the dirt rises or whatever?" William said.

"Yes, normally, but not here. Remember, Luca? We talked about how mysterious it was," I said, getting excited now. "And even here, this is *weird*. It's only damp in one spot—not even as long as the wall itself is. That's not really how the water table should work. If I just—"

William barked. "Cinnabar Sunset! Do *not* touch that wall! I still haven't forgiven Luca for exactly that kind of—"

But it was too late.

The camouflaged door swung open, revealing a magical world beyond.

It was an alchemist's delight. When we stepped over the threshold of the heavy stone door, we left behind a desiccated, dead basement for a cavern filled with life. On every surface—

uneven walls, arching ceilings over our heads, far corners—there were things growing, and *glowing*. It was like stepping into some kind of deep sea reef.

The air was cool and clean, and full of the smell of fresh moss. The cavern stretched and meandered away from us, a little footpath amongst the plants marking out a trail. It should have been even darker than the tower, and yet the vibrant plant life filled every nook with a gentle, green-blue glow. Though the rock underfoot was slick and uneven, it didn't feel like a treacherous place. In the distance, somewhere ahead of us, I could hear the sound of running water, and it urged me forward.

The path rose up briefly and then dipped down, winding further under the mountain. I followed it breathlessly, my companions close behind. No one said anything. There was nothing that needed to be said, until—

Until the path spilled us into an even wider, even grander cavern, leaving us wide-eyed and panting at the edges of an underground river.

"By the stars," William whispered.

"This is incredible. Amazing," Luca said, his voice echoing against walls and a ceiling several stories overhead. "There's nothing like this in any of the old town maps or records. But it must have been here all along!"

"All along," I agreed, my eyes roaming over the stalactites, stalagmites, boulders worn smooth by age and covered in moss and wildflowers. The river itself was strong and clear as it rushed under and around the dark rock formations. In normal times it might have been safely below our feet, but now the water lapped at our boots, as though encouraged by the rain water that slipped down the rock walls from the ground above. "Luca. This is the Lost River. It has to be."

"Whatever it is, it's brimming with magic," William said.

"Even more magic than the Tree?" I asked, curious. It was truly such a wondrous sight, I would have believed anything.

"Not exactly." William sparkled blue once more, though I noticed the effect was growing faint. He was tiring himself out. "It does have that same, natural magic look, like that vial Officer Thorn had. But it's been added to somehow. As if she—"

William broke off, looking around. Then he spotted something and bounded off to the left. "Over here!"

We followed him as fast as we could, slipping over the wide, wet rocks. The cavern just continued to grow around us, forming a natural ballroom or grand hall of sorts around the river. It was an echo of the clearing above. And in the center of that space, William led us up to a spire of rock as tall as my chest. Set into the spire was the largest chunk of amethyst I had ever seen. It was easily as big as my head, and it, too, was glowing.

"An augmentation spell," William said, with satisfaction. "Sorcerers use amethyst when they want to work a spell that has to do with longevity. Even they realize that peace probably helps when you want to have a long life."

I was familiar with amethyst's association with peace and serenity, so that made sense. But I was too star-struck by such a fine crystal to say anything.

Instead, Luca beat me to it. "That had to be a massive spell," he said, looking at the stone and then at the cavern around us. "It must have used up whatever power she had left."

"In order to extend her life, she basically had to forfeit it," William agreed. "That's generally how the magic seems to work. Honestly, I'm surprised it worked at all. Most magic theory says that working such a spell for your own benefit will backfire. But maybe there was something already so vital about this place that it counteracted that."

"Effects from the Tree of Life," Luca suggested, gazing out over the rushing water nearby. "Perhaps the river itself comes from a spring in Daisy's cavern."

William rumbled. "If that's true, then she and the pixies would probably consider this place to be under their protection too."

"That's if they know about it," Luca added. "I really haven't seen anything to suggest that *anyone*—aside from Vesper, and maybe Jack—did. And I can't imagine keeping a secret like this."

"Well, she didn't," William said. "Not entirely. Paracelsus knew about flowers from this place. Give Red a shake, won't you? She's drooling all over the stone."

"I am not," I protested, snapping back into the present moment. "I'm totally fine. I want that gem, I want this whole cavern, actually, but other than that I'm totally fine."

Luca chuckled. "Maybe just settle for getting some samples, for now."

"Get plenty," William advised. "Otherwise no one will believe us about this place."

19

Into Place

"I believe you," said Officer Thorn, some hours later. But she did not sound convinced.

We sat clustered around the front desk in the police station, drenched and muddy. Though weather-proofing spells in our cloaks and boots had made valiant efforts to hold back the storm, it had been a dramatic walk back to town. Even now, the wind and rain still battered the little building around us. Luca and I huddled over our steaming mugs of green tea and honey, the best Thorn was able to offer us. William had wanted to go straight to the café, or better yet, home, but I had insisted we tell Thorn everything right away.

The officer drummed her fingers on the old wooden desk. "Maybe just take it from the top, one last time. Or would that be from the bottom?"

"Funny," William grunted.

"The Lost River is real," said Luca, more obligingly.

"Clearly the sorcerer living in the tower, most likely Vesper, knew about it and had gone to great lengths to hide it," I added.

"And it's chock full of magic," William chimed in begrudgingly.

"Magic plants, which I suspect will match with what Doug was saying The Hermit sold," I concluded. I was also ninety-nine percent sure the flowers would match what Paracelsus wanted; I had taken copious notes and samples, and could hardly wait to go over them in my lab. But that didn't have to do with murder, so I was keeping quiet about that part.

"And with the slime on the victim's boots," Thorn said slowly.

"Yes, that too," I agreed.

"I bet the water is magic, also," Luca said. "Red, did you—?"

"Oh, I definitely did." I grinned. Three bottles of the river water were stowed in my knapsack beside a peacefully sleeping Sugar.

"This is all sounding a lot like motive," Officer Thorn reflected, "and it pieces together some holes in the story. But one thing I don't understand. If you fell down two stories to find the place, how did you make it out?"

Luca, William, and I exchanged varying degrees of a guilty look.

"Well . . ." I began.

"We didn't exactly rush at first," Luca admitted. In fact, after I'd taken all my samples, we'd had a bit of a picnic lunch with the sandwiches and tea I'd packed. Just because Officer Thorn rarely stopped for meals didn't mean we, as impartial explorers, followed suit!

"And there was some concern," William added. Actually, there had been a full-on outburst, as discussing if we could get out the way we'd come in reminded William that he was still angry at Luca for getting us launched down a trap door in the first place.

"But we had help," I said brightly. "Maybe you remember Sugar, the pixie who took up residence in my kitchen a few years ago? Well, she'd come along—long story—and she came out to explore while we were eating. She was the one who found the side cavern. More of a tunnel, really. It was a steep climb, and pretty narrow in some places, but it actually came out near the upper edge of the clearing."

"Where there was also a hidden path and a covered-up cart," William concluded smugly.

"Yes," I conceded. "That too. From there, we just followed the path until it joined up with a road. It's actually quicker than the trail we were all taking before."

I'd expected Thorn to be very interested in the cart discovery, but she remained focused. "Let me get this straight. The three of you, some of Belville's brightest, went tumbling into a trap you couldn't get yourselves out of, and then you were rescued by a pint-sized bit of sparkle?"

Luca glanced at me. "Um—sort of?"

I swallowed. "I'm sure we would have found the way out eventually."

"Go on," said William. "Tell them they were foolhardy. I've been trying to for *hours*."

"You were *all* foolhardy," Officer Thorn decreed, thumping her hand on the table between us.

And that was even without us admitting that Luca had had to stop me from trying to sample a gem that was woven into an old and intricate spell that was possibly keeping the entire cavern alive.

Sometimes, curiosity makes us do very silly things.

"Still, though," Thorn mused, sitting back in her chair, "you stumbled across some useful evidence."

"Stumbled!" I sat up, my tea sloshing, indignant. "I specifically arranged to go up and *investigate* because—"

Officer Thorn gave me a pointed look, and I gave in.

"At least you had Luca warn me beforehand," she went on. "I'd have come looking for you if you'd *really* been trapped. Eventually."

"Thanks," said William, sarcastically. "More to the point—"

"Maybe I should award Sugar a civilian's medal," Thorn mused, stroking her chin.

"Anyway," William broke in once more, loudly, "what have *you* been doing? Did you find out who your victim is?"

Officer Thorn collected herself, her teasing grin fading into something more professional. "As a matter of fact, I did not. Doug came by yesterday afternoon. The trouble turned out to be the aging spell on the body. The victim I have now looks centuries old. The Hermit looked like Red."

"It could have been an *anti*-aging spell, which faded after death," I said, glancing at William. I ignored the comment about my appearance.

"It might not have even been a spell at this point," he said, panting. "Just her eating and drinking everything in that cavern to keep herself looking and feeling young."

"Either way it's no good for victim identification," Thorn told us. "I have her under all the Guild-approved spells downstairs, so it's not like she's going anywhere. But neither is this case if I can't get identification because everyone knew her to look drastically different."

For a brief moment, exhaustion peeked through the veneer of determination in her voice. I was sympathetic as I thought this over. We'd dealt with cases where the murderer altered their appearance, but never one where the *victim* was the one using magic to obscure their identity. But surely it couldn't be so unusual? Glamour spells were strictly overseen in Beyond, for the most part, but still, people did manage to create new identities, often for purely benign purposes such as reinventing themselves. "There must be some Guild guideline for identifying a body that's not based on sight," I said.

"There are a bunch," Officer Thorn told me, rather sourly. "I've been through them all this morning. There's checking magical signatures, and fingerprints, and even some divination stuff that people do. The problem is you have to have something to *compare* all that to. And since this victim most likely hasn't been living in town since two hundred years ago, and even then she was probably using some kind of pseudonym, I don't have anything to check my information against."

"And even your suspects might not recognize her, since they too dealt with her when she was 'young,'" I mused.

"The magic could tell you," William said, stirring in his chair. "There's traces of magic all over the cavern and in the entry hall, and probably in the apartment too. Everything I've seen looks like it came from one person."

"Even if she and her house match, it still doesn't tell me her name," Thorn argued. "It's not like there's a deed out there for 'secret hidden floors at the top of the old tower on the mountain.' I checked. And Lavender insists she had no idea, and no preexisting arrangement was mentioned when she bought the tower off the elves who built it."

"And Daisy never saw anyone either?" I wondered aloud, thinking again of seeing her fly past earlier.

"Haven't got a hold of her yet," Officer Thorn said grimly, "But Lavender said she never reported such a person. And

Jack, *if* he lived there too, is still not talking."

"But if you go back far enough, the magic might," Luca said, leaning forward. "William is right. You have to go to school to be a sorcerer, and schools keep records—of students, of their exams, of where their alumni go and what they do. Of magical signatures, too, which have to do with the geometry of how an individual casts their spells and wields their magic. If you go back far enough—if the records are detailed enough—"

"That'd be pretty far back," I interrupted, skeptical.

"But not *so* far, really," he said, eyes alight. "And what else is scholarly research for, really?"

The rest of us were silent, so he added, "Well, lots of things, actually. But looking into the past is one of them. And in this case if I could help put the pieces together—"

"Are you offering to look into it?" Officer Thorn asked.

Luca nodded emphatically. "I think I know exactly who to ask. Or, I know the person who would know where to start, at least. They live in Brass, where the sorcerers' university is—we met at the conference last year."

Officer Thorn sighed, her shoulders visibly lowering. "I say try it. Anything helps at this point."

"Hear, hear," I agreed, smiling. "And here's to networking."

This made Luca laugh, a welcome break from all the planning and theorizing. Despite the damp and storm, the room seemed brighter, a little more relaxing. As I grinned along, it suddenly hit me that we had had a long day so far. I was definitely ready to be home—and possibly to have a snack. And proper tea . . .

But William, apparently, had one more thing on his mind. "Speaking of networking," he said, as the amusement died down, "you should get the Witch to look at your plant samples."

"Who, me? Trent?" I struggled to follow this idea at first, then understood what he meant. Witches had a different kind of magic than sorcerers, but they still would have valuable insight. "That's a great idea. He isn't still busy looking after Jack, is he?" I asked Thorn.

She shrugged. "At this point, he's eating and sleeping okay, so it's just a matter of keeping an eye on him." I assumed she meant Jack, not Trent, and noted that nonetheless Trent had refused to let Thorn take over custody of his patient. Either Trent was becoming more bold, or Thorn was more run down, or both. "You should also," she added pointedly, "have Rhys take a look. And make him bring Daisy back into town."

"I can't make either of them do anything," I protested.

"But you can network, can't you? Give me a bit to write up everything you told me," she went on, "and then I can go switch out with Trent, send him over to you so he can take a look. It shouldn't take too long, right? Might give Olivia a break, too. I can't imagine they've had much excitement over there."

The statement struck me as *infamous last words,* much like my promise that morning to be back before the storm broke had. But I chose to keep my opinion to myself in this case.

After all, I didn't need to give William yet *another* opportunity to tease me!

20

Patterns on the Wall

Unfortunately, despite my excitement to return to my lab, I found that actually being there became overwhelming. Often, my lab was my sanctuary. It was where I felt quiet, calm, and relatively in control. However, that evening, I had bitten off a little more than I could chew.

Luca had gone to change, check in with Frank, and pick up dinner for us all. William had gone on a café run the moment we left the station, which was both good and bad. Good: I now had a half-empty mug of pumpkin cocoa on my lab windowsill. Bad: William had apparently had no luck in his *actual* goal—gossiping with his friends.

"No one even asked where we'd been," he complained from his spot behind the register, for the third time. The shop was closed, of course, but he knew better than to hang out in my lab.

My lab, indeed, was in chaos. I had three comparative experiments going on at the same time, and notebooks both old and new strewn across the counter. Perhaps I'd been a little *too* excited to learn about these new plants!

"Well," I said, adjusting the burner on one experiment and stirring the other, desperately wishing for another sip of cocoa and wondering how long Luca would be gone, "Saki and I did have a pretty serious chat yesterday. Maybe she didn't want to get into it again."

"And there wasn't even anyone there," William continued, as though I hadn't spoken. "Everyone's hiding from the storm or whatever. So no one knew a thing!"

"Where's Dusty?" I asked, now balancing several glass beakers of samples in one hand and trying not to let a terrarium full of moss overflow onto the other.

"Don't even get me started," William grumped.

That seemed promising. If he started ranting, then at least I wouldn't have to respond for a while—I might actually get my experiments settled. "Oh?"

"He's got a *new* friend," William began, and I could tell by the ire in his voice that this rant would go on for a while. "He's too busy playing tour guide to ever stop to chat. I've barely even spoken to him in the last two days. You'd think he'd at least come around to see how the new gutters are holding up in the storm, since he put them there himself, but not so much as a gnomish shadow has darkened our door! And I would know if he'd come by while we were out. But has there been any sign of him? Not a one! He meets some stranger and then all of a sudden all his old friends are chopped liver! I might as well have stayed up in that cavern for all he'd notice."

"Is his new friend Keith?" I asked, my head down at workbench level as I tried to balance out my scales, which were brimming with plant material and little brass weights. "I think I met him the other day."

"And that's the other thing," cried William. "Why didn't he

bring him to meet *me?* Why didn't he ask *me* to be a tour guide too?"

I poked my head up through the window, leaving my experiments alone for a moment. "Is that what this is really about?"

"It's about *everything,*" William retorted.

At that moment, the front door opened and Luca came in, wafting scents of rosemary and curry throughout the shop.

Not a moment too soon, I thought, smiling gratefully at him.

"Did I take too long?" he asked, making his way back to the sales counter. "You two both look like you could use a real meal."

"I could use a better friend," William grumbled.

"And I could use a hand, actually," I said through the window. "If you don't mind coming in for a minute? I was too ambitious with all the experiments I wanted to do."

"Sure," Luca said, placing two large paper bags on the counter. "William, do you want to unpack everything? How's your magic holding up? What's this about your friends?"

"I'm fine. Red just doesn't want me in her lab because she's a worrywort," was the reply.

While William began lifting containers out of the bags—with, truth be told, *very* weak magic—Luca made his way into my lab. I glanced at him with a raised eyebrow, indicating William. He made a curious, concerned face back.

I cleared my throat. "*I'm* not the friend who's in the doghouse, apparently."

"Aren't you funny," said William, sounding as though he'd never laughed in his life. "Just like Thorn."

I handed Luca a glass stirring stick. "Can you keep an eye on this burner while I finish recording these weights? Apparently,

William feels that the town of Belville was not concerned enough about our absence."

"That's not what I said," William retorted. "I said Dusty's too busy to even check on our gutters."

"Ohhhh." Luca began stirring, looking to me for approval. When I nodded and got back to my work, he settled in next to me and continued talking to William. "Is there something wrong with them?"

"No," said William. "Don't you think I would make a good tour guide?"

"Tour guide?" Luca repeated, sounding bewildered.

I just focused on checking off one task at a time.

"Of Belville," said William. "For a new person. If someone showed up in town, don't you think I could help show them around?"

"This is about Dusty?" Luca glanced at me for confirmation. "Did you tell him you'd like to help him out?"

"How can I," William mumbled. "He's too busy."

"Well, it seems like we're *all* a bit too busy at the moment," Luca said, reasonably. "Looks like even Red got a little carried away, right?"

"She sure did," William said, before I could protest. He sounded brightened by the thought.

The bells on the front door tinkled again, this time announcing Trent, town Witch and budding physician extraordinaire. He looked very much like he, too, had been too busy lately. His dark hair hung at odd angles around his head, and there were deep circles under his eyes. He was wearing no coat, only a ratty knit sweater and jeans. A very large umbrella and oversized yellow rubber boots had provided storm protection. These he left to drip beside the door.

"Smells like dinner in here," he said, his voice gravelly. "I'm starving."

"Paws off," said William, who sat like a king in front of an array of curry dishes and naan from a restaurant across the Square.

"Actually," said Luca, still standing beside me and stirring away, "I got plenty. I figured we'd all be really hungry tonight, and it makes good leftovers anyway."

"Perfect." Trent came to rest in front of the counter, just slightly offset from William so that he could look into the lab. "I heard you guys have been all over the mountain. Hard work today, huh? You could probably use the break."

"You see what kind of break Red is taking," said William pointedly.

"I'm almost done," I called, hunching over my notebook one last time. "I just want to get these things recorded before I forget them. Luca, your burner should be okay to turn off now. Thank you for helping. I'll admit, I didn't need to test *all* the plant samples at once . . . But I was too excited. Trent, did Officer Thorn fill you in on everything we found?"

As Trent gave us a wry account of his dealings with Thorn, Luca and I cleaned up and left the lab. Rain still pounded at the shop windows—the storm had more energy than all of us combined, that was certain. No one felt like moving everything upstairs. Instead, we pulled a motley collection of chairs around the counter and began to dig in.

"So, anyway," said Trent, perched on the far end of the counter, "she said you wanted me to take a look at some stuff and I figured, after everything else, I better let her win this one."

"You're learning," said William, through a mouthful of

rosemary naan.

"Very diplomatic," I agreed, amused. "We can take a look when we're done eating. How's your patient? Thorn said he's basically recovered, aside from needing rest?"

"At least she recognizes he *does* need rest," Trent said, rolling his eyes. "I swear, it's like pulling teeth to get her to acknowledge that trauma is an injury, too."

Luca, sitting beside me in one of the old armchairs, looked up at this—interested and clearly sympathetic. "Was it very intense, whatever he went through?"

"It's hard to say exactly." Trent wolfed down an entire cheese dumpling, reminding me just a little of the officer he'd been so at odds with lately. "I mean, there's obviously some sort of long-term thing going on there, if you ask me."

"We *are* asking you," William reminded him. "You're as close to a doctor as we've got."

"Scary, right?" Trent grinned lopsidedly. "I've always been good with herbs and things though. But in this case, nothing's going to magically fix what's bugging him. He isn't not talking to us just because he's had a bad shock. I think he probably never would have trusted us to begin with."

Luca looked grim. "That's what you mean by long-term. Someone manipulated his view of the outside world?"

Trent nodded, mouth full, and I laid my hand on Luca's knee. He covered it with his own and held on tight. After a moment, I recalled what I'd said to Thorn several days before. "Whatever happened just recently must have been something pretty drastic, to make him think of coming here at all."

"Yeah, that's kind of the stance that Olivia has taken," Trent agreed. "I think she's pretty concerned about him, honestly."

"So Thorn thinks Olivia's there to protect *you,* and Olivia thinks she's there to protect Jack," William observed from his stool.

"That's about it," Trent said. "And don't even ask me which one of them is right. I'm only here to help with the healing."

From there, William began telling Trent about our adventure, glad to have an audience at last. Luca and I chipped in occasionally but mostly focused on eating—true to Luca's prediction, I found I had been ravenous. By the time we were all done, there were barely a few scrapings of sauce left.

"So much for leftovers," Trent said, looking at Luca with an apologetic grin.

"I'm just glad there was enough," said Luca, smiling back. "I know where to get more tomorrow if we want some!"

"But in the meantime, come on," I told Trent as I rose. "Let's see what you have to say about these flowers."

While Luca and William began sorting dishes and cleaning up, I led Trent back into the lab. I showed him the samples I'd set aside, both of plant material and water. Some of my experiments would run overnight, so I hovered over those while he glimmered with purple light, checking things over.

"Anything?" I asked, turning around when my own checks were complete.

Generally, Trent had a certain boyish charm, accompanied by a completely unruffle-able attitude. It was one of the things that made him such a good counterpoint to Officer Thorn's working style. But now, as I looked at him, I saw troubled lines etched across his face.

"It's—" he turned, distracted, as Luca and William stuck their heads through the window. Then he shook his head. "Well, like William could tell you, my magic is more practical and natural than a lot of sorcery and arcane stuff. So I couldn't tell you stuff like specific magical signatures, not without doing a lot of spellwork, anyway. But . . ."

"All I could get off of it was that it *is* natural," William interjected.

"Yeah," Trent agreed. "I get that too. But there's more. When I look at this kind of thing, I can see a sort of aura around it. And usually a magic user will have an aura, too, and their color matches with their work, if that makes sense?"

I nodded patiently, though something about the way he was speaking was creating a pit in my stomach.

"Well," Trent admitted at last, "there's a couple colors I see here. A couple different people, maybe. One of the colors matches how Daisy looks, especially in her dragon state. And the other one . . .

"Honestly, it's exactly the same shade as Jack."

21

Spooky Thoughts

The next morning found me in a rain slicker and boots, out in Market Square. Officer Thorn had decided that, murder or no, storm or no, it was time to decorate.

She had most of the town out helping. Many shop owners had delayed their opening times, and the bakery two doors down from the Pomegranate was giving out apple cider donuts. The rain had even slowed to a misty drizzle. For most people, the morning was a festive one, as one team cleaned up fallen leaves and branches while the other team rolled out pumpkins and hung up ghostly garlands around the Square.

William was back in the apartment sleeping, and for once, I wished I could join him.

When the knot I was trying to tie slipped for the third time, one of the other decorators took pity on me. Gloria, owner of the salon next to my shop and a longstanding friend, held up the banner that I was supposed to be anchoring in place.

"Thanks," I told her. Gloria was not one for small talk, I knew, so I could have left it at that. But she lingered after the knot was tied, so I added, "I've been overdoing things a bit lately."

"'Tis the season for it," she said, dryly. Gloria was phoenixkin, a fact made obvious by the red crest of feathers that rose above her head in place of hair. As usual, she was dramatically dressed, today in an all-black raincoat and sleek knee-high boots. She put one hand on her ample hip. "You want help with the rest of those?"

I glanced down at the basket of posters and banners at my feet and sighed. "Yes, please. Officer Thorn has way too much trust in my ability, it seems."

"She has other things on her mind," Gloria said, cracking a small smile. In the background, Thorn could be heard enthusiastically shouting directions to a string of volunteers tangled up in garland.

"Yeah, well, me too." I smiled back. "Come on, I'm supposed to put one on every tree. Have you been following all the stranger-in-town, unsolvable-murder-at-tower business?"

"Only because Maggie comes into work and vents," Gloria said as we began to walk toward our next target. Though she sounded a little gruff, I knew that she adored Maggie—though not, of course, in quite the way that Thorn did. Gloria had always been clear about her aromanticism.

I smiled ruefully. "Well, I wouldn't want you to feel besieged on two fronts."

"By all means, rant away," Gloria said, waving one perfectly manicured hand tipped in black fingernails. "It's fitting for the setting, don't you think?"

"You mean the Samhain festival, or the dreary rain?" I joked back. As we reached our next tree, though, I sighed once more. "That's part of my problem this morning. We're all supposed to be coming together for Samhain, joining in the celebration and facing darkness as a united front and whatnot, and I . . . I'm not feeling very neighborly."

"I hardly ever feel neighborly," Gloria remarked, holding up another banner for me to tie into place. "And all that about facing darkness sounds deep."

"I know, I know," I chuckled. "I'm feeling philosophical. My problem is that so far, to me, it looks like the main suspects in this latest case are either victims themselves . . . or dear friends."

I tried to imagine telling Rhys that Daisy had both motive and opportunity to kill a sorcerer on the mountain who was, in a way, stealing from her Tree . . . and immediately shivered, and stopped imagining. He might be happy keeping a shop and looking after pixies these days, but he did still carry a sword.

"I didn't realize there were actual suspects yet," Gloria said. "I thought Maggie said Thorn's hands are tied since she can't investigate the body until she contacts next of kin, and she can't figure out who the person is."

"Luca's helping with that," I said absently. "Anyway, we're pretty sure who she is. It's just a matter of proof. As is usual in solving a case," I added wryly.

"Usually it's going the other way, though, right?" Gloria smiled at me as I picked up my basket and we headed to the next tree.

"Don't even get me started," I told her. "But . . . this thing about the suspects is really bothering me. Since going back home, I've been trying to lean on my intuition a little more, but—this time, what my intuition is telling me is not pleasant."

Like when I thought Luca was hiding something from me, I

realized. And had that truly been resolved?

"Doesn't matter if it's pleasant or not," Gloria said. "Right? You have to investigate all the options, either way."

"I suppose," I admitted. "But—Daisy has a hard enough time coming down into town as it is, without us also suspecting her of crime. And Rhys—"

"—is a snob," said Gloria, sourly.

I laughed. "You're still mad about the soaps."

"So what if I am?" We reached the next tree, and she grinned briefly as she unrolled the next banner.

"We smoothed that all over, remember?" I told her.

"Yeah. *You* did." Gloria could be antisocial in her off hours, but she was unfailingly supportive if she saw something to support. "Remember that when you talk to him."

"Remember what?" I asked, a little dismayed that she agreed with my gut—that I needed to talk it out with Rhys. "That he has very particular ideas about soaps?"

"That he has caused trouble around town, and you helped fix it," Gloria said. "He's not perfect and, if anything, he probably owes you. So he'll most likely be willing to hear you out."

"How very reassuring," I said, unenthused.

Gloria leaned around the tree and smirked at me. "You'd better hurry up with those knots, or you'll miss a chance to talk to him at all."

* * *

Tempting as it was to slow down our decorating efforts and remain safely in the Square—the wet, cold, noisy Square—all day, I did eventually decide it was time to go to the shop and face Rhys. But on my way down the street, I ran into another familiar face.

"Dusty!" I said, instantly reminded of William's complaints the night before. The gnome was in his customary overalls and cap, a basketful of gourds slung over one shoulder. "You've been called in to help decorate too, huh?"

"Wasn't given any choice," he said, rather grouchily. Though he was cheerful as a rule, Officer Thorn was not Dusty's favorite person. "Thought I'd stop by your place on my way to take these to the station. How're your gutters holdin' up?"

"Just fine so far." I dropped down onto a nearby bench so that I didn't feel so much like I was yelling at him from a great height. Dusty hopped up, too, clearly glad to have a break. I added, "I do think William would like to talk to you, though. He was disappointed when he couldn't find you yesterday."

"Why? What happened yesterday?"

My intuition told me not to get too involved, and in this case, I listened to it. "Oh, you'll have to get the full details from him. We made some interesting discoveries."

Dusty scratched at his forehead before tugging his cap back into place. "That explains it. I went looking for you all yesterday morning, and had no luck. Then business picked up."

"Has Lavender had you showing more people around town?" I asked.

"She had a sort of a welcome dinner for Keith last night at the tavern," Dusty informed me. "Bit of a last minute thing. Between you and me, I figure they both need somethin' to be happy about."

"'Both' being Lavender and Keith?" I clarified.

Dusty nodded. "It's hard on 'em, with the kid being back in town but not remembering anyone or talking just yet. Keith keeps tellin' me how he wished he'd have come back earlier, though as I say, he had no way of knowing. Besides, he had to cut his last job at New Dale short to get here as it is. The boy has good family waiting for him, at least."

"Yes . . . Well, he isn't exactly a 'kid' anymore," I said, thinking of what Trent had told us about Jack.

"They know it," Dusty assured me. Despite his usual penchant for gossip, his voice was subdued. "Keith told me himself. 'We've waited centuries for this, we can wait a little longer now,' he said. Centuries. Breaks your heart, doesn't it?"

"It *is* an awfully long time," I agreed. And though I didn't admit as much aloud, it did beg the question: *do patient people kill?*

"And then that Thorn goes and treats them like suspects," Dusty continued, almost as though he had heard my thoughts. "If you ask me, that sorcerer prob'ly just got ahead of herself and fell over all on her own. Evil catches up with you, you know."

I startled. "You think it was an accident?"

"Why not?" Dusty shrugged. "Don't see why anyone else would bother to do her in now, do you?"

"The timing does feel . . . off," I agreed. I couldn't quite say *random*; since Jack's appearance in town, everything else had felt like it must be a part of that same cold missing-persons case.

But that's all conjecture, I reminded myself. *And it's possible that Jack wasn't the motive at all, but came here because he was escaping a different crime . . .*

A crime of greed or anger, perhaps, related to the Lost River and Daisy's Tree. Even though it was nothing I hadn't thought before, realizing it afresh made my stomach turn.

"Anyway, I better be going," Dusty said reluctantly.

"Well, stop in later and see William," I suggested. "He's been stuck behind the counter lately."

"Smartest place to be," said Dusty. "Tell him I say good work!"

I let Dusty get a head start down the road, lapsing back into my own thoughts. Unless Luca discovered some twist in our victim's past, then the obvious motives for murder remained: revenge—freedom—a mercantile dispute—or protection of an ancient secret.

And what if it *had* been just an accident, as Dusty thought?

It was an appealing idea, but I shook my head. Officer Thorn had seemed determined that it was murder, and she had her training—not to mention her experience—to back her up.

No, there was no way around it. Everyone else was doing their part: Luca looking into the past, Thorn and Olivia sending out requests and keeping everyone calm. As nice as it would be to just focus on my plant experiments and holiday decorations, there *was* something else that only I could do. Something Officer Thorn had specifically asked me to do.

There wasn't any way to reach Daisy unless she wanted to be found: the location of her home on the mountain remained a secret. Only one person came and went. One person, who often held himself apart from town affairs and interviews . . .

It was time to get Rhys to talk.

22

Lonely Words

I entered the shop through the back door, coming into my lab first. I was eager to check on my experiments: not only did they bring me a sense of peace, they'd give me purpose, too. So far, about half of my tests were complete. The slime Officer Thorn had collected from the victim's boots most likely matched a sample I had taken from the tunnel on our way out. I was ninety percent sure in that case, and just waiting for a final distilling check to finish before I reported it to the station. The water from the Lost River *did* have magic in it, and I was running a complicated filtering experiment to figure out if its magic was, as William had suggested, entirely natural. If so, then chances were good it came from the Tree of Life—though of course I'd have to ask Rhys for a sample in order to check that theory. If not, then we'd have more evidence that the sorcerer was using magic to enhance the cavern and its plant life.

Both of those were essentially background tests. I was fairly confident of the results, but open to whatever happened. What I was truly curious about had nothing to do with the murder .

Were these plants the ones Paracelsus had been looking for?

The question led to yet *more* questions. For now, though, I was focusing on the plants themselves. I'd set up a temporary container garden at one end of my lab bench. There, I'd transplanted some of my samples in different growing conditions—in soil, under lights, in darkness, and so on. I was curious to see how the plants would do outside of the cavern. I'd even left some samples out simply to dry, to see if they matched Doug's accounts of The Hermit's merchandise. I'd also planted a few seeds I'd collected. Paracelsus had described a very particular flower: by observing the life cycle of some of these plants, I could be confident in matching the description with the physical thing.

So far, every single plant was thriving and healthy—even the ones that had been tied into a bunch and hung from the ceiling to dry.

As I finished making notes on the ongoing experiments, Rhys poked his head through the interior window. "Good afternoon. When I arrived to open the shop, William told me how you've been spending your morning. We both agreed a late brunch was in order. Would you like a piece of frittata, a muffin, or hot tea?"

"All of the above," I said, though the fact that he was being so thoughtful was *not* helping my nerves. "But do you mind if we head upstairs for a moment? I have something to talk to you about, and—and," I said, in a sudden flash of inspiration, "you might want to talk to Sugar, too."

If Rhys found this odd, he didn't show it. Instead, he bowed, and disappeared from the window. We'd been able to convince him to stop addressing everyone by title, but some habits, it seemed, would never go out of date.

I hung up my rain gear and locked up the lab once more, emerging into the shop, where a tight spiral staircase led to the landing above. Rhys was already waiting, a plate full of food and a mug of tea in hand. I sighed, a silent wish: *Please let me figure out how to say things tactfully, at the very least.*

I led the way upstairs and into the apartment, turning on the magical kitchen light with a wave of one hand. Sugar didn't greet us at first, but I knew she was probably on top of the cabinets near the kitchen sink window—her favorite spot. She'd come down when she was ready. For the moment, I paused beside the kitchen island.

"Did—ah," I cleared my throat, "did William fill you in on our adventures yesterday?"

Rhys set the plate and mug on the island, then looked thoughtful. Under his white shop apron, he was wearing a sweater that was knit with such tiny knots—and in such a vibrant teal color—that I could only conclude that the pixies had made it for him. It made me just a little annoyed. It was like he was *trying* to make me feel bad for suspecting his girlfriend and their charges.

"His words exactly, I believe, were 'You had better hear all about it from Red,'" Rhys said finally.

"Great," I replied, glum. So William had pulled the same trick on me that I'd tried with him and Dusty. *Thanks, friend.*

Rhys coughed politely. "If it has anything to do with the new plant material in your laboratory, I can't imagine why it should leave you feeling so hesitant. I should think you'd be excited."

"Well—yes—you're not wrong," I admitted. And it *was* probably for the best, I reminded myself, that William hadn't stirred the pot. I shook some of the tension out of my shoulders and decided to start over. With a faint smile, I asked Rhys, "You saw everything when you came in, then?"

"I did," he conceded. "And I couldn't help but notice that, in the time between my arrival and yours, not an hour later, many of the specimens in your pots have already doubled in size."

"I started out tracking it regularly, but honestly, some of them grow so fast it's unbelievable," I agreed, glad to share this bit of professional wonder. "I figured I'd let this set run its course, and maybe be more strict and regimented with the next group. Because—well—that's the thing. There are other people involved—"

"You have found the source of the flowers your mentor was looking for?" Rhys suggested, when I ran out of words.

"Yes, I think so—and more," I said. "Listen, I think it's best if I tell you the whole thing. Just don't go repeating it around town, alright?"

It was a silly precaution. I knew Rhys kept his cards close to his chest, and anyway, once he heard the whole story, it was doubtful that he'd *want* anyone else in town to know . . .

Nevertheless he gravely agreed, and listened to the entire tale: the missing child, and the tower, the discovery of the body—and then the rumors at the market, and my determination to go *back* to the tower to look around. He raised his eyebrow at us getting tricked by a trap door, but said nothing as I described the cavern. By that time, Sugar had drifted down and perched on my shoulder.

"She saw it too," I said, gesturing to the little pixie carefully. "She had decided to come with us. She said it was . . . the same, but different."

"The same, but different," Rhys repeated, solemn, considering Sugar.

Sugar shimmered—an action I couldn't see, but could faintly hear, just beneath my ear, like the ringing of a very distant bell. She had left the other pixies before Rhys had come to live with them, and she did not seem like she was about to knit him any sweaters now.

"Well," I said, running my hand through my hair, "you saw the plants in the lab."

"Yes," agreed Rhys. "My immediate thought was not that they are the same as the plants that surround the Tree of Life. The plants there do not grow with such wild abandon."

"That makes sense, otherwise how would anyone live there," I said, nerves making me talk too much. "Especially over centuries upon centuries. There'd hardly be room left. But— that's also something I've been thinking about. There are people *living* there, with the Tree. Isn't it possible Daisy and the pixies are tending to the plants, keeping—"

There was an immediate steeliness in Rhys's eyes that made continuing that thought aloud feel *very* impractical. Without moving, he said, very low, "You think her responsible?"

"No! Ah, that is, not for these plants, the ones we found and I sampled," I rambled. "But it was clear that—well, see, we found this amethyst set into the cavern, the biggest and clearest amethyst I've ever seen, and William said it was probably the focus of a spell. So I think it's possible that the sorcerer was using her magic to augment the magic in the cavern—most likely coming from the water, though I haven't determined its source just yet—*ow!*"

Sugar was in my hair, pulling at the roots. I was getting wound up, and it had made her wound up too. As soon as I realized this, I made myself slow down and take deep breaths.

Rhys waited silently. And while that could be considered scary murderous knight behavior . . .

I took another breath and remembered what Gloria had said. For all his faults and odd habits, Rhys was my friend. We had been through several misadventures together, and we worked together often. Besides, we both had a tendency to look after the people around us. He knew how I felt about Luca, and I knew how he felt about Daisy. *More than likely, he's just trying to make sure he understands,* I reminded myself.

"I've been nervous about telling you," I admitted finally, settling Sugar atop my head.

Rhys inclined his head, but he didn't soften much. "Why?"

"Because, no matter what else is going on there—why the plants grow so fast, or how exactly the Lost River came to be—right now, I *do* think they're connected to the Tree. Sugar does, and honestly, I don't think that more than one source of super-magical plants on this one mountain is very likely. You could take a look and see what you think . . . But also," I said, with another big sigh, "you should know that I think that this is what the sorcerer was selling, too. As 'The Hermit,' down here in the market, in town. Plants like these could go for a high price—either for spell work, or as 'miracle cures,' who knows. So I have to tell you . . . right now, I don't think it looks good for Daisy."

"Because someone potentially found, and profited from, a part of the Tree she's bound to protect?" Rhys's expression flickered, but I couldn't catch it.

"Um, no, not exactly. Sugar didn't seem to think anyone— any of the pixies, or Daisy—knew about the Lost River. So I'm not trying to say she hasn't been a good guard. I'm saying that, if she *did* learn about this . . . If maybe she found out a few days ago, while out with Luca or while searching the mountain . . . she *is* a dragon, and . . ."

The steel was back in Rhys's eyes. In fact, I may as well have been looking at a metal statue or a suit of armor. "Enough," he said abruptly. "I see the insinuation you are making. And I regret to inform you that I will now be taking the rest of the afternoon off."

"But, Rhys, I—"

"I am leaving now," he said firmly. "I am using my accrued time, as is my right."

"Absolutely, you can do that, I just . . . . And, he's already down the stairs," I sighed to Sugar. There was nothing—not even the sound of doors slamming. The silence made me feel worse. "Oh dear. I *knew* that wasn't going to go well."

Sugar flittered down to the kitchen island and sat beside my abandoned plate. After a moment, she stole a chunk from my muffin and took a large bite.

"So much for hoping for any comforting words of wisdom from *you*, hmm?" I teased. She made me smile despite the gnawing in my gut. Not only had I made Rhys upset, I'd also probably told him—and therefore Daisy—much more about the investigation than Thorn had been hoping for . . .

And now he was off doing gods knew what.

Why had I thought this was a good idea, again?

I took a small piece from the muffin, too, and considered it. "If Zady were here, she'd tell me that maybe this is what was supposed to happen. What had to happen," I mused aloud. I popped the muffin in my mouth and realized immediately that I'd been starving. I smiled again at Sugar. "Maybe your advice was more helpful, after all."

23

Write it and Regret it

I gave William the afternoon off—he certainly deserved it, after covering for me for several days. And in the wake of my conversation with Rhys, I was feeling guilty. Aside from wishing I could protect everyone, I'd never before thought about the way that me helping with investigations was difficult for my friends. Even if I *wasn't* accusing their significant others of murder, I was relying on them to watch the shop or come on hikes or get lost in strange locales.

My trip home over the summer had taught me a lot about myself, and in some ways, I was still trying to take it all in. I thought about this absently as I cleaned up my pumpkin spice novelty display. It made a nice change from pondering murder and mysterious plants, at least.

Naturally, this was when the police found me.

In this case, though, it wasn't Officer Thorn with more "volunteer" tasks or clues. Instead, Olivia came into the shop, a long blue cloak around her shoulders and a basket over one arm.

"Hello, Olivia," I called from my corner.

"Hello," she chirped back. "Trent sent me. He needs more antiseptic potions and he wants to know if you have dried lavender?"

"You're doing errands for the Witch now, too?" I asked, amused, as I stepped away from my display to help her with her order.

"The duty of the police is to help," she replied very seriously. "They tell you that every day at the Guild."

I glanced over my shoulder at her as she followed me to the medicinal shelves near the counter. She'd mentioned before that she didn't really hear people's tone, so she often missed out on jokes. But what I found more interesting was that she didn't seem to mind the fact that she'd spent the last several days cooped up in a Hut with an unruly Witch and an even more unruly patient.

"How's it been going over there?" I asked, curious.

"Jack is doing really well for someone who's been through so much," Olivia told me. "It's amazing. It's hard to believe he was living in a tower hidden away for so long."

"Oh," I said, a little surprised—this was not quite Officer Thorn's view of the situation. But, she'd never been one to dictate her opinions to her trainees. (Just orders.)

"We know now that he was," Olivia went on. "Officer Thorn said it was your idea? Giving him paints?"

"Oh," I repeated. I'd entirely forgotten that. "Yes, I did suggest it. It's not that I wanted to trick him, but I just thought, it might take some of the pressure off of getting him to talk."

"It was wonderful," Olivia said.

I began piling sparkling potion bottles into her basket, half waiting for her to say *stop*, half puzzled at her enthusiasm. "Was it?"

"He loves it," she confirmed. "He told me so. Not with words, but the flower he drew—it was happy. Not all of his paintings are happy, of course, most are very sad. But I think that's good for him. Each time he shows me one, I can feel his relief, just for a moment. I'm going to the art supplies store next to get him more things."

"Then you might still want room left, right? Is that enough potions?" I asked finally. She looked down like she hadn't even noticed them there. She counted them up and handed one back to me, and as she did so, I couldn't help but add, "Is he sad to be stuck there? In the Hut?"

"No, I don't think that's it," Olivia said. "Officer Thorn says we shouldn't jump to conclusions. She says *you're* the one who really taught her that, by the way. So I know that perhaps according to the Guild, I shouldn't say, but I really don't think that's why he's sad. It feels more like confusion—like great big swirls of dark colors, and things withering away.

"Even in the Guild handbook, it does say that not everyone speaks with words," she added. "It's not so unusual. There's a merfolk clan that swore off them, and some plants might speak using body language. Plus, a lot of speaking animals actually do better when they can make testimony based on other senses or act things out. Courts have to be very open-minded."

I smiled, thinking of Frank and his reticence. "That's a beautiful point."

Though she probably had a decade on me, Olivia blushed, a bit like a schoolchild. "I read that chapter very closely."

"That's probably part of why you'll make such a great officer," I said. Recalling Trent's request for lavender, I began sorting through the baskets that held my dried herbs, filling a muslin bag for Olivia to take.

"Ye-es." For the first time, Olivia seemed hesitant. When I glanced up, her catlike eyes were far away. "I just wonder . . . How does Officer Thorn spend so much time getting to know one case, and then move on to another?"

"Officer Thorn?" I hesitated, a bit lost. "She does set things aside sometimes, like this morning, to focus on the fair. But she's still thinking everything over and has a plan, I'm sure."

"Not just her," Olivia said, with a slight gesture of impatience. "In general. Once you solve a case, it's gone."

"Hm, I think I see what you mean now." And with my face down in my herbs again, I smiled a little. *Maybe Sakura was right about a little romance.* "I suppose what you say is true. But the people involved with the case will still be around. Especially if they're your neighbors, or friends, or—more."

Olivia seemed to be thinking this over. I looked up again to ask, "How much lavender did Trent want?"

"Four bunches," she said. "I asked him what a bunch is and he just said you would know."

"I would, would I?" I pursed my lips at the lavender I'd bundled up so far. What *size* of bundle or, better yet, how many stalks would have been helpful, but Trent had never been too interested in details. I tucked what I could into the bag and decided that if he needed more, he could just come over himself. "Alright, I think that's enough for now, at least. Did he want you to handle payment, too?"

"He said to write him a bill." Olivia followed me to the register. "You might see him out later today, but it was my turn to get out of the house, he said."

"At least you aren't all holed up in there constantly," I said sympathetically. "What's Officer Thorn been up to, do you know?"

"She's getting the Guild to send in a special sorcery consultant," Olivia replied. "I saw them give a lecture while I was in training, and they are very good with forensic magic. I thought it might be helpful."

"I'm sure it would," I agreed, as I finished writing everything out. "Good luck, to all of you."

Olivia bade me a polite goodbye, but I hardly heard a word of it. In handing her the handwritten note, I'd become distracted.

Studying the magic of this crime was one thing, and certainly something I couldn't help much with. But studying the *paper*—I'd forgotten that altogether!

* * *

Half an hour later, I had a fresh cup of earl grey and my microscope set up on the sales counter. It was nearing closing time anyway, and my lab was practically over-run with magical plants. They weren't *everywhere*, exactly, but they were still enthusiastically growing and distilling, and I didn't need any extra magic pollen or sorcified moss interfering with simple science.

Because that's all a study of Thorn's two notes would be: pure examination—and comparison. The comparison part would come later. I already knew, from examination with a special microscope lens—a gift from Officer Thorn last Yule— that neither note bore any fingerprints. So that left me with basic material evidence. For now, I was determined to be methodical about laying the groundwork.

I pulled the anonymous notes from my lab coat pocket and set them on the counter in front of me. In all the excitement with the tower, I'd put them away, thinking they wouldn't be of any more use. But sometimes the tiny, everyday things were more helpful than the big, flashy clues. I laid out a fresh notebook and began to bring my thoughts into order.

Naturally, I focused on the earliest note first. *A child has been kidnapped and is being kept on Belville Mountain,* it read. I copied down the message, both as a way to identify which note I was observing, and in case anything happened to the original. So far, I was only looking—not burning it up and doing flame or ash comparisons—not that I ever would destroy evidence, of course! But in this case it wouldn't hurt to be *too* careful.

Next I made some notes about the handwriting. It was in all caps, but still clearly an old-fashioned cursive, steady—no dashes or wobbles or half-closed letters indicating haste. The ink, I'd already examined; I wrote down a few notes about that, as much as I could remember. It was standard black ink, nothing too noteworthy: the kind Olivia would see bottles and bottles of at the art shop, no doubt.

But the *paper.* Though ink is essentially a potion, and fun to mess with, I've always found that paper is more distinctive. There are so many ways to make it, and so many uses for it, that a careful alchemist can be very specific. This paper was bright white, the kind preferred for writing, as opposed to wrapping or printing. It was thin, and cut into a rectangle no bigger than my hand—most likely it had come from a pad of note paper, then, as opposed to being sold for artistic purposes. But while the bottom and the sides were cut cleanly, the top had been torn away. Like the handwriting, the tear was clean and even, not hasty but purposeful.

With those observations down, I turned to the second note. This one was even more interesting. *Check the Lost River*

Outlook for important information on the case, it read. That was even more direct than the first.

From there, the differences continued. It was in old-fashioned cursive, too, but this time the writing seemed far shakier. Perhaps someone had been trying to copy the first note, or writing in a way that was unfamiliar to them? That suggested they were trying to disguise their own handwriting, which was interesting. I made my notes and moved on.

The ink, as far as I could tell with only my eyes and my lenses, was the same basic black writing ink used for the first note. What was more strange was that the paper, too, seemed similar. In fact when I measured the notes against each other, they matched—as if they'd been torn from the same block. But the second note had been torn farther down on the paper, and much more unevenly, as though the writer was tearing a piece off fast and not totally paying attention.

Why be purposeful with one note and hasty, almost distracted, with the other? I sat back as I looked over my work so far. I couldn't decide, yet, whether there had been one note writer or two. But it *was* clear that there had been one source of paper. An unlined notepad like this could be found at the art shop, most likely, or even at some of the businesses around town that wrote out bills and receipts, just like I had. They were common in homes, too. If I wanted to look for the source of the paper, I had a lot of potential comparisons to work against.

I glanced out the windows. Evening had fallen, and the shadows were thick. I smiled to myself.

There was a lot to do, and if I moved fast enough, the cold and dark couldn't catch me.

24

Picking up Pieces

I had closed up the shop and thrown on my warmest cloak in a flash. It was still just a little before normal closing time for most of the shops on the Square, and I was determined to visit as many as possible for paper samples.

My first stop was the Pomegranate—it was closest, and yes, I'll admit: in this weather, another hot drink was always welcome. Besides, I'd need the energy. But my investigation didn't quite get off to the speedy start I'd envisioned.

It wasn't because of Saki: she was cheerful and efficient, and the notepad she kept at the café register was, naturally, tinted pink. The trouble came after I'd collected my drink and turned to go. I nearly tripped over William and Dusty bringing their used snack plates up to the counter.

I recovered quickly enough, and beamed at them, happy to see them together. But, conscious of my time, I said, "Sorry to run into you! I'm off on an errand. Don't let me—"

But William pounced. "What are you doing out of the shop?"

"I closed up early. Nothing important," I lied, as Dusty looked curious.

178

"Liar," William declared. "I'm going with you. See you later, Dusty."

"I have to get back to the tavern anyway," the gnome agreed.

I breathed a sigh of relief. William and a friend meant gossip and questions. Just William still meant questions, but it also meant he might help.

"What's all this about?" he demanded, setting the tone as we left the café, trailing after Dusty.

"I need paper samples," I confided to him. "Everything else is just going along smoothly, but I never did follow up on the whole note business."

"So Thorn is keeping you busy?" William asked.

"No, I gave myself this task. I just—I don't know," I admitted, once we were out in the darkened street. "There's so many unanswered questions still, and I don't like it. Plus, I made Rhys pretty mad earlier. It'd be nice to do something to help the investigation that isn't . . . talking."

William looked up at me with his head on one side. "I *knew* you didn't give me the afternoon off just to be nice."

"Well, you're welcome anyway," I retorted. I kept an eye on the shops as we walked past. The curiosities shop and the bakery were closed already, but they hadn't been high on my list to begin with. "You and Dusty seemed friendly again."

"He told me all about it," William said, with satisfaction.

Normally I might have been curious, but in this case I was itching to get more paper. I paused to explain things to William. "I can meet you later if you want, for dinner, and we can go over everything. But right now I really want to get to the shops before they all close."

"What about Luca?" William demanded.

I blinked. "What about him?"

"He runs a *bookstore*."

"Oh. Yes. He's on the list," I said, metaphorically speaking, because he in fact had *not* been on the list I'd brainstormed earlier. "So is the art shop, and any restaurants that write down orders, and the tavern."

"And the grocer should be too," said William. "I'll go there first, and you go to the art store, and we'll meet at the other corner of the Square."

"Yes, that could work, but—"

Before I could rattle off my newfound worries about overworking him or dragging my friends in general into drama, William was off like a shot. I could barely make out his black form running across the Square toward the market. Apparently, he'd decided we were racing.

Honestly, I thought to myself, *not a bad idea.*

I started running, too. At first the cobblestones were hard under my boots, but soon the feeling of the wind took over, the joy of speed and *getting things done.* I burst into the art supply store like a tornado.

The shop bells jingled ferociously, and everyone in the store looked up. Olivia had gone, probably long before, but there were still some kids browsing and a rather tired-looking employee behind the counter. Another employee, this one decked out in a dress depicting cats in Halloween hats and a spiderweb headband, asked me what I needed.

"Paper, any kind you have, about this size on a tear-away pad," I declared, holding up my hands for scale.

I don't know if it was my entrance, or the breathless quality of my voice—or perhaps a prudent desire not to keep me around their wares for too long—but between the two of them, the art shop employees had me in and out of their store in under five minutes.

Back out on the street, I considered running again. But this time, a heavy cloth bag of notepads weighed me down. I could only imagine the scene it'd cause if I accidentally knocked someone over with it. It was damp and shadowy out, and most people were inside, but there were still enough spectators around that I could get myself into trouble.

I eyed the far corner and, seeing no sign of William, decided to check in at the diner. But as I reached for the front door, it opened, revealing Marguerite.

"Red, what a nice surprise," she said.

"Um, yes, nice to see you," I agreed, trying to pretend to the mayor that I *hadn't* just been thinking of traffic accidents and trouble. "Here, let me hold the door for you."

"Been shopping, have you?" Rather than continuing out of the restaurant and on her way, Marguerite paused on the doorstep, looking over my bag. "Got everything you need for Samhain?"

"Oh, yes, I—it's just paper," I said, waving the bag as though it had been put on trial. I couldn't help it: talking to the mayor often gave me the creeping sensation that I'd tracked mud where it shouldn't be or offended some important town personnel.

Marguerite's gaze sharpened on me. "Still helping the police?"

"Um, yes?" I said, wondering if the town had recently passed a law against it.

The mayor smiled. "Here. Take a sheet from my notepad, too."

I watched, amazed, as she pulled a large canvas-covered notebook from the back pocket in her jacket and meticulously tore out a clean page. As she handed it over, I swallowed. "Thanks. I'll add it to the collection."

"Very good." Marguerite watched with approval as I tucked the blank page into my bag, and then bid me a perfunctory good night and walked away.

I ducked into the diner, but only for a moment. When I emerged again, I still felt dazed. The diner used lined paper pads.

The mayor, apparently, did not.

When I got to the far corner of the Square, William was already there. He was sitting up on a park bench, panting, and seemed rather pleased with himself.

"What's eating *you?*" he asked as I came up.

Since we were alone on this part of the street, I filled him in on my encounter with the mayor. "Plus I have a dozen or so examples from the art shop, and a page from the diner," I added, more practically. Glancing back along the block, I realized aloud, "I should have checked to see if Leo was still in at the paper."

"Don't bother," William advised me. "She only uses those tiny black notebooks, and the newspaper itself is way thinner than Thorn's notes. If you really want, get Maggie to bring some samples to Thorn later."

"Not a bad idea," I admitted. "How was the grocer's? Were they even still open?"

"Got there just in time," he informed me. "And guess why? Olivia was there, arguing with one of the sons. She wasn't letting them close."

"Why would she care about that?" I asked, confused.

"She didn't—not about closing time. She was arguing with them about vegetables. Something about some kind of lettuce that grows on the mountain.

I had set my bag down and was drawing my cloak around me, but this made me pause. "Not *more* lettuce?"

"That's basically what they were telling her," William said, chuckling to himself. "All out of winter greens, come back tomorrow, that sort of thing. She wasn't having it."

"It seems like a strange thing to fight over," I mused. "Are you sure there wasn't more to it? How did things end?"

"Well, she couldn't just *make* them conjure up a lettuce," William observed. "She saw me there and we started talking about something else. And they weren't really 'fighting.' That is, the grocer's sons definitely were, but Olivia wasn't, not really."

"That makes more sense," I agreed, aligning the story now with what I knew about all parties involved.

"And I got paper from her *and* from them," William said, triumphant.

"From her too?" I hesitated. "Why? Did she guess what we were up to? Don't tell me you stole it."

"I told her I needed to write a note to you," William said, as though he'd won a prize for spywork and I was just a bumbling initiate. "And then when she was gone I stole some from the grocer."

"William!"

"What? They'll never notice. Anyway, *look*." With sparkling blue trails of magic, he held up two sheets of paper. One was lined, thin, and grimy along the edges. The other was pristine and white, and had been carefully separated from a glued binding—the kind of binding that allowed you to tear off a piece of paper without actually *tearing* it along the top.

"Don't tell me," I said, with a sinking feeling.

"Interesting, isn't it?" William agreed. "She made a point of telling me about getting a special notepad so that she could easily separate out certain pieces of paper."

"Still, though, Olivia's sheet is too small to have been one of our notes," I said, taking both and tucking them into my bag. "Okay, where to next? Do you want to keep going? You can always head home, and—"

"I'll go to the pizza shop and the bookstore," said William, before I could finish my thought. "You never even put Luca on the list, did you?"

"No, I didn't," I admitted. At first I wanted to add, *and I won't apologize for not suspecting my boyfriend,* but my conversation with Rhys was still eating at me, and it seemed too hypocritical. Besides, someone could have easily come into the bookstore to use or buy a notepad. William was right: it was worth checking out.

"So I'll get Luca and then we'll meet at the tavern," William concluded, his tail waving. "Dusty says Lavender's food's been really good lately. And we've been missing out on the gossip."

"Hasn't it only been like two days since we were there?" I rolled my eyes, but made no further protest. Given how wholeheartedly he was helping, William was absolutely within his right to request dinner out. "Alright, sounds good. I may walk by the print shop just in case while you do that."

"Don't forget to actually collect paper at the tavern, too," William reminded me. "And save us a good spot."

I shook my head, amused, as he ran off once more. It was like he didn't trust me to do my own investigating!

Of course, I did fall into a trap just yesterday . . .

Ruefully, I grinned to myself. Maybe William's worries were *somewhat* valid.

I retraced my steps up the block. The print shop, headquarters for Belville's local newspaper, was on the second floor above the art store. I had a feeling that if Leo, the reporter-editor-printer extraordinaire, had any leads like "a child has been kidnapped" or "a murder has occurred," she would go investigate them herself instead of writing the police a note. For that matter, she'd publish them in her own paper before giving out the information anonymously. Still, it seemed like too big of an oversight *not* to collect paper from one of the main sources in Belville.

As I walked up below the windows, though, I knew I was out of luck: every light was out. For a moment I thought I saw a shadow in amongst the printing machines, but the windows were high up and my vision in the dark wasn't great.

I was just turning to leave when I noticed the paper stand on the corner next to the building. I hadn't caught up with the latest issue of *Belville & Beyond*; there had been too much on my mind. But as I paused now and looked at the issues behind the pane of glass, my stomach dropped.

Tragic Cold Case or Modern Murder? The headline asked. *Local scholar investigates!*

25

Shattered

I tried to explain to one of the servers at Lavender's Tavern that I was collecting paper for an experiment, but honestly, I was barely listening to myself.

What in Beyond could Leo mean by putting that in the paper?

The server was actually very helpful, fetching a hotel pad of paper for me to look at.

Did Luca know she was reporting all that??

It was a nice memo pad, featuring the same "clean tear away" technology as Olivia's notepad, along with a tavern logo in the bottom right corner.

What if Luca becomes a target now???

I dutifully tucked a few sheets in my bag, but I was distracted to say the least.

The tavern, meanwhile, was rather jovial. Most seats were filled with families visiting and townsfolk still proud of their efforts decorating the Square. Talk of Samhain was everywhere. I hardly heard a peep about cold cases, kidnapping, or murder.

I sat at a booth along the front wall of the tavern, cozy

and warm inside but with a view of the Square through the window. The bag of paper to test was tucked next to my feet. In light of what Leo had written, it felt a bit like a fool's errand. And yet at the same time, more crucial than ever.

Despite the impact the headline had made on me, I hadn't bought a copy to read the article. Leo and I had clashes from time to time, and this felt like one of them. In the moment, I had been too aghast to consider paying her money for printing such stuff. I didn't want to encourage it. I felt righteous.

But now, sitting alone with nothing to do but wonder, I wished that perhaps I *had* bought a copy. At least then I might know exactly what to worry about . . .

A mug of hot cider and basket of complimentary rye bread arrived, and in its wake, Luca and William showed up.

"Hey, Red," said Luca, leaning over to kiss my cheek as he slid into the booth beside me. William immediately sprawled across the booth opposite and began quizzing the server about the night's specials.

"Luca," I said, low so as not to interrupt William's conversation, "did you know Leo wrote an article about you?"

"Ah." He glanced around, then focused on me, leaning in. "I was going to tell you. I knew she interviewed me, of course, that was a day or two ago. Mostly I had wanted to tell her about my new display."

"*You* reached out to *her?*" I summarized, entirely unreassured.

"Yes, but," Luca hastened to say, "not about the case, or anything recent at all, really. Only by then, of course, she'd heard. And I'd just been doing some research on Jack's case in particular, so then she noticed that and we were talking about it . . ."

Luca's voice trailed off as I sighed heavily. It was all *very* like Luca.

"You don't think I did something wrong, about the case, I mean?" he asked. Worry was clearly visible in his green eyes.

"I don't know," I said. "I didn't actually read it—I just saw the headline. So I don't know what she said. I'm sure Thorn will fill us in if it's something important. I wasn't worried about the case, Luca, I was worried about—you."

"Me?" Luca frowned, but in a moment, understanding settled across his face. He took my hand. "Red, I never thought of it that way. Of course you would worry if I'd done something to endanger myself. I'm sorry."

I found myself at a loss for words. In fact, I felt a little choked up.

"Are you two done yet?" William called across the table. "Because if you aren't I'm going to order for all three of us."

"As long as you don't *eat* for all three of us." Luca looked up, smiling. "Sorry, William. Red saw the article in the paper, and it made her worry."

"About time," William said. "Dusty and I talked all about it over tea. It's old news now."

"You did?" I gathered myself and sat up to join the conversation, though I still held on to Luca's hand. "What did it say?"

William huffed. "Dusty says it didn't really say anything. Just vague stuff about Jack and everything that happened here at the tavern two hundred years ago. He thinks Leo's losing her touch."

"Or becoming more conscientious," Luca offered, now smiling at me.

"Or distracted by something bigger," I said, still plagued by that sense of foreboding. But I did my best to sigh it out. "Oh, well, we'll find out soon enough. What are we getting to eat, William?"

As though conjured by a magic trick, the server reappeared, and William oversaw our orders. He barely needed our input at all, and I thought about teasing him for it, especially since he'd interrupted us. But, I decided, it was probably a good thing to have been brought back into the present moment.

* * *

In a blur of relief and laughter and squash risotto, the evening passed. It wasn't until we were walking home that Luca pulled me aside again.

William trotted on ahead of us, tail in the air. There were some breaks in the cloud cover, and I knew he'd be happily basking in the starlight for a while. Meanwhile, Luca and I walked much more slowly through the Square, avoiding low-hanging decorations and piles of fallen leaves.

"There *is* an investigation I'd like to talk with you about, though, Red," he said quietly. "I didn't want to bring it up before. You know how I offered to look into Vesper for Officer Thorn?"

"I know," I said, amused despite myself. "I was there."

"Of course you were." He smiled fondly at me for a minute before going on, "Well, I've had some luck."

"Already?"

"Already," he confirmed. "We were just wiring about it this afternoon. My friend in Brass said she's always wondered about this connection a bit—she wrote a paper on it once, but she couldn't find anything more at the time."

"More than what? What connection?" I asked, dodging a particularly large pumpkin.

Luca put his arm around my shoulders. "Okay, so, I asked her to look into any of the sorcerers' records, two hundred years ago and older, dealing with efforts to extend life, student records of plant-based magic, or even any record of that huge amethyst. It was a lot, and I really didn't expect to hear from her for a while. But she wrote back almost at once.

"She said she remembered there *was* a sorcerer who got really into immortality magics, because there was a big scandal about it at the time. The council of sorcerers in Brass all got together and voted to kick her out, and it was the first unanimous vote they'd ever had, in their entire history. What made them so mad apparently wasn't that she *wanted* to live forever, but that she was willing to give up her magic and all of the secrets of sorcery to do so. She'd been caught trying to make a deal with a minor deity from the northern mountains."

"How would kicking her out of the sorcery club out stop her?" I asked.

Through the shadow, Luca looked grim. "It's a little more than a club. They use magic and blood oaths on their members a lot. The implication is that they erased her memory of the particular rites she was willing to betray."

"Yikes." I shivered, drawing my cloak closer. "I mean, I know magic *can* be used to do things like that, sometimes, but to actually hear about it . . ."

"Yes," Luca agreed vaguely. His arm around me tightened, even though we stumbled across the uneven ground. "Well, it took the combined power of the entire council to carry it out. That's usually how it goes with big punishments like that, in the sorcery world, I think. You have to break rules and make a lot of people mad first, but when you do, they come down hard."

"Sounds familiar." The year before, we'd dealt with a sorcerer being punished similarly. "When did you say this was?"

"Two hundred and thirteen years ago," he said precisely. "My friend wrote a big paper for the two hundred year anniversary. It's a big deal—things like that don't happen very often in the sorcery community. But there's more.

"The sorcerer that was cast out, they make a point of not recording her name," he went on. "But that's just the sorcerers. The newspapers at the time were constantly writing about it, and they give all the details that they could find. Her name was Vivian."

"Vesper." I shivered again.

Luca paused us beneath a tree near the shop, turning slightly to face me. "There's been some studies that suggest people often choose a new name that honors their old initials, and honestly, it makes a certain amount of practical sense," he said, lapsing for a moment into his usual inquiring self. But then with more gravity, he added, "Vivian was recorded as having attended the sorcery school three hundred years ago, and getting top marks. Her specialty wasn't plants, it was arcane mastery—controlling the elements, especially water. There were instances of her getting into trouble, too, often for manipulating other students. And most of all . . .

"One of the few times she made the news after leaving school, and *before* the trial with the sorcerers, was because she reportedly discovered the largest natural amethyst in the world at the time. In fact, she still holds the record."

"So she's not afraid of dirt," I mused. "And the control thing—

it could factor in to what we saw at the tower. And of course, wanting to preserve her own life—"

"Even going so far as to sacrifice her power to do so," Luca agreed solemnly. "Frank took my report to Officer Thorn earlier. There's records of Vivian's magical signature that can be used, I hope, to identify the magic at the tower and maybe on the body."

"You did it, Luca," I said, amazed. "And in the course of one afternoon!"

"A little more than that," he said modestly. "And, um, there's something else, Red. Two somethings."

I waited, excited by this success, but he paused to take a deep breath. "First is that she *did* have a terrible disease—an incurable affliction in her blood. That's the last record the sorcerers kept that has her actual name. She disappears from Brass and from all records after their trial, and not even the papers knew where she went."

"Was that the second thing? That she disappeared?" I asked, when he'd been quiet for a moment.

"Oh! No, that was extra," he said, refocusing. "No, the second thing is—there was one other story about her that got into the papers at the time. Just a rumor about a relationship. It's probably made up, but it was in the papers a *lot* for a few years, and even a comment made in the trial kind of hints at it. We can at least say that they did know each other, even if it isn't true."

"Who did?" I asked. "Who's 'they'?"

"Vivian," said Luca, slowly, "and your mentor . . . Paracelsus."

26

Vertigo

Needless to say, I didn't sleep too well that night.

As a rule, alchemists don't tend to go in for hero worship. Having the scientific method drilled into your head when you're an apprentice leaves you with a permanent, cautious skepticism—at least, it did for me, and many others I knew. Besides, a lot of alchemists become famous not for being *good*, but for being . . . shall we say, quirky? Swallow a rock from a goat's stomach, harvest blood for an elixir of life type quirky. Some harmless, some downright appalling. Alchemists who simply do quality work and maybe make a discovery or two throughout their life don't often make the history books. The ones that do are dubious at best.

And yet, I'd always thought of Paracelsus as an exception to that rule. He had been a kind mentor, inscrutable and odd at times to the young apprentices, but always well-meaning and wise. Nurturing a kind of friendship with him over the past year, on somewhat equal footing as professionals, had honestly been something that made me proud.

Now he was suddenly at the top of a very short list of "people who knew Vesper well enough to bother killing her." Granted, one possible affair two centuries ago didn't necessarily make a motive—but then again, did living on the same mountain and possibly dealing in the same magic as her make a good motive, either? I could still picture Rhys's face the moment I brought up Daisy. I tossed and turned between guilt and self-doubt and stubborn belief in the investigative process.

I finally gave up and got out of bed just as William was finally getting home. It wasn't odd for him to have a late night out, though, and it was just as usual for him to head straight for bed rather than stay up and chat. I let him pass me on the landing, deciding to keep my worries to myself for the time being. Instead, I went down to my lab to fiddle with my new plants.

A fuzzy robe was hardly a lab coat, but then, I didn't plan on doing anything too dangerous. The light in my lab was cool and silvery, just a bit of starlight and early dawn coming in through the high windows, mixed in with the shine from the lantern I set on the workbench. I checked on all the experiments that had been running. By now, they were mostly complete. Everything checked out: the victim's slime was the plant matter from the tunnel, was the plant Paracelsus wanted. My samples hanging to dry had finally stopped growing, and now shed moss all over the floor beneath them— just as Doug had complained. Not quite conclusive there as of yet, but I could take the plants to the market later and get his confirmation.

The only thing I didn't know, and couldn't expect to find out soon, was whether these plants matched the ones that grew around the Tree of Life.

Well, and one other thing—*how had Paracelsus known about these plants? If it was because he'd heard from Vesper over the years, why not just say so? And why ask me to find them* now?

Idly, I pulled my notebook over and began writing down these questions. After forgetting entirely about the paper lead, I didn't want to overlook something again. No matter how awkward it might be. After all, how much *more* awkward could things get?

Reminded of the paper samples, I went out into the shop to grab my bag. I'd dumped everything on the counter last night and left it. Comparing paper samples under a microscope while fuming over what your mentor may or may not have told you and therefore what he did or did not set you up for was hardly advisable.

Now, though, I felt a little more calm. I arranged everything into an orderly row, writing directly on each piece of paper its source. The art shop, the mayor, the diner, the grocer, the police assistant, the tavern, the pizza shop, the bookstore. All told, it was a pretty good survey of town. First I would conduct an exam of each one, like I had the previous day with the original notes. Once I'd identified the few that might match, I could move on to performing actual experiments.

I decided to work backwards, leaving the pristine notepads from the art supply shop for last. For each piece of paper, I dutifully made notes on my observations. Some were obviously not right, though. Luca's note paper, for example, was a coarse, brown material, because he often tried to make it himself from recycled scraps around the shop. I'd actually helped him with that a number of times, and enjoyed it. The pizza shop paper was at least white, but it was much thinner than the original notes had been—and besides, there were greasy marks along the edge.

Both Olivia's note and the branded note from the tavern were a better match, but not quite the right size. The grocer's and the diner's were no help at all. Then there was the mayor's . . . it was too large. Of course, it might have been trimmed down . . .

Of the dozen or so notepads from the supply store, some were again the wrong size. I dismissed the ones that were too little, leaving only four left. There was one among them that was perfect. And yet, I distinctly remembered the employees telling me that that size was usually only used for custom orders. And they had insisted there were no custom orders lately.

That wasn't saying someone hadn't found someone else's custom order and used it . . . But I'd now looked at most of the custom notepads in town. Who was left?

The sun had come up as I'd been making my notes and growing increasingly frustrated. A little voice in my head warned me, *you're too close to your work. Emotion doesn't make for true results.* But that little voice sounded a lot like Paracelsus—in fact it was nearly a direct quote from my apprentice days—and that just made me more annoyed. It was definitely time for a break.

I went upstairs and got ready for the day, William's snores a constant backdrop as I went through my routine. But even that was not quite settling enough. So, when I got back down into the shop, I decided to make a delivery instead of hanging around. Leaving my paper piles out on the counter for now, I gathered up a basket waiting by the back door and stepped out into the morning.

It was a nice day, really—not a clear one, but a little lighter than it had been recently. There was a heavy dew on my back patio plants, but no rain. Counting that as *one* blessing, at least, I made my way down the little alley beside my shop and knocked at the salon's front door.

"You," said Johann, as he unlocked the door and let me in, "are far too early. What are you doing up at this hour?"

"*This* hour isn't too unusual. It's the hours before this one that were tough," I said, grinning.

Johann, an old friend of Gloria's and now her assistant at the salon, shook his head. He had deep brown eyes and lovely dark brown hair, of course, and exactly the kind of refined bearing one might expect at an up-scale salon in a city. He maintained that he wasn't interested in hair—just in helping out a friend—but, nonetheless, he'd been working with Gloria for nearly two years now. He made no secret of being part vampire, and had once told me that heritage was what made him feel that there was no hurry to "find a real job."

"Gloria isn't in yet, but she should be soon," he told me. "I was just going over the inventory. I'm guessing you're about to make my job more complicated?"

I laughed. "Not more complicated. More satisfying, maybe?" I handed the basket laden with soaps to him. After getting off to a rocky start with my neighbor, I now made several of the products she used in her salon.

Johann sniffed at the basket. "Hmm, since you did autumn scents, I'll take it. Is that apple pie?"

"The golden ones are, yes," I told him, relaxing against their sales counter instead of my own for a change. Hair and Beauty by Gloria felt very different from my shop: the counter near the door, the sleek black and silver designs, sparse potted plants and long mirrors visible in the main part of the store where Gloria and Maggie did their work. It was very spa-like. "The brown ones are cinnamon spice, the orange ones are pumpkin of course, and the black ones are a more cool, floral scent in case some people don't buy into all this warmth and sugaryness—"

"Hold on," Johann interrupted. "Tell me you wrote this down somewhere?"

Meanwhile a door opened at the back of the shop, and Gloria's voice rang out. "What am I missing?"

"Soap delivery," I called, unnecessarily as she rounded the corner into the reception area a second later. To Johann, I added, "Yes, it's all written down. There should be a paper in the basket."

"Ugh," I added, turning back to Gloria. "If I never see another piece of paper, it'll be alright with me."

"More investigation woes?" she asked, raising perfect eyebrows.

"Yes, and I've given up trying to make sense of them at the moment," I said. "I came over here for a distraction."

Gloria smirked. "How's this for one: Maggie volunteered to be a ghost at the Samhain festival."

"Wow, she's really come a long way since settling into town. And is she making you two join her?" I asked, glancing from Gloria to Johann.

Johann shuddered. "I *hate* Halloween."

I glanced at Gloria, incredulous. She shrugged. "We're working on it."

"Not by putting me up in a tree in a sheet, you're not!" her assistant retorted.

I chuckled. "You could do spooky face paint in—"

Before I could finish another thought, a knock sounded

at the door. Johann frowned, diving for his schedule book. Gloria frowned, too, as she looked through the window at the would-be intruder.

I followed her gaze and gulped. Rhys.

"You'd better," Gloria told me, answering my unspoken question.

I sighed, and crossed the tile floor to let him in.

"Miss Red," he said. Cordial. So far, so good? He also bowed to Gloria and Johann in turn. "I called at the potions shop, but no one was there."

"You don't have to call me 'miss,'" I said, rather miserably. Now that the initial shock had worn off, I clocked his attire: tall black boots and a long green cape, and a fabric bag that was alarmingly lumpy. "Um—are you running errands or something? I didn't think you were scheduled to come in today."

"I am not," he informed me. "However I am, as you say, on an important errand."

Next to me, Gloria crossed her arms. "Judging more soaps?"

Rhys cast a surprised but polite glance at the basket on the counter. "As I work at the store which prepared those soaps, I do not feel I could be an impartial judge. However," he said, with emphasis, "I have come to make amends."

"With Gloria?" I asked, startled.

"With you," he corrected. "I spoke the matter over with Daisy, and she informed me that the proper thing to do would be to reach out."

"I thought she was worse than Maggie," Johann whispered loudly to Gloria.

"Maybe she has better taste in soaps," Gloria grumbled back.

I glared at them over my shoulder. Not only were they not

helping, they weren't even *trying.*

Gloria stared back, and Johann grinned.

"Well," I said, "since we seem to be the only adults in this room, perhaps we'd better remove ourselves."

"Excellent," said Rhys. "In that case, you might find it edifying to accompany me on my next errand?"

"Where to?" I asked, ignoring Gloria's ire and Johann's silent laughter.

Rhys shuffled his bag, looking as cool as ever. "The police station."

27

The First Step

The idea of reaching out and making amends stuck with me as we left a chuckling Johann and Gloria behind.

"Did Daisy really tell you that?" I asked, once Rhys and I were walking down the road.

"She did," he said primly. "And she reminded me that, given that I have chosen a role as liaison between herself and the pixies, and the town, it wouldn't do for me to abruptly 'storm out' whenever someone tells me something unpleasant."

It was hard to look at Rhys. But I also found myself wanting to smile. "She really said *that*, too?"

"She did," he agreed, more seriously. "And—I owe you an apology, Red. I was emotional yesterday, at the turn of the investigation. And while Daisy assures me there is nothing wrong with that, in itself, I should not have left you so abruptly without any explanation. Who knows what you must have been thinking."

"Who knows, indeed," I said, thinking of all the many things I'd been thinking in the last twenty-four hours. "Rhys, I think

201

that's very well put, thank you. And to be honest, I owe you an apology too, for not treating you with more compassion. Even Gloria was trying to tell me to see things more reasonably. I've let this case get me all twisted up, somehow."

"Sometimes it is difficult to see these things in the moment," said Rhys, as we turned the corner and began heading toward the police station. "For example, I do not wish you to think there was anything unreasonable in what you said yesterday. It is only natural that you should wish to investigate a potential connection between the Tree and this Lost River. I merely reacted poorly because I saw danger to Daisy."

"I saw it too, even though I didn't *want* to," I assured him. "That's part of what made me so upset about it. Especially because, Rhys—I *saw* her flying near the tower, the second time we went up there."

"You took Sugar with you that day," Rhys said—not so much a question as a statement of fact, but I nodded anyway. He went on, "The pixies at the Tree noticed her presence on the mountain and asked Daisy to go looking, just in case. They originally went into hiding because of a dispute with other pixies."

"I didn't realize they would be so sensitive," I said, surprised. "Sugar didn't say anything."

"Pixies have a tendency to be both sensitive and forgetful," Rhys said dryly. "Daisy is infinitely patient with them, but I confess this is not the first time they have unwittingly caused trouble with their anxieties."

I had to chuckle, thinking of a swarm of upset Sugars and one very large, very long-suffering dragon. "I think I can understand all that. I hope I didn't cause too much trouble, too—at least, it was never truly my intention."

"I don't doubt your intentions in the slightest," said Rhys.

I smiled, genuinely this time. "Friends again, then?"

"We were never not friends," Rhys replied, glancing down at me as we followed the road. "And friends work to maintain their connection."

"Sounds very reasonable to me," I said, my spirits lifting despite our destination.

"Of course it does," said Rhys, contentedly. "Daisy said it."

I laughed, and was still chuckling as we walked up to the station. Rhys held open the door, leaving me to walk in first and confront Officer Thorn behind the desk.

"You look jovial," she said, clearly resenting the fact. "Haven't been up half the night sending wires back and forth with *your* Guild, have you?"

"Actually, I was up pretty early going over some experiments," I admitted cheerfully. "And I have another 'wire' for you to send. One to Paracelsus. Ask him about Vivian."

Officer Thorn started. "Him too! I read Luca's report last night. Or this morning? What does it matter? And what are *you* doing here? Did you know this supposed Vivian too?" she asked Rhys.

Rhys had closed the door, and made a point of looking around for a coat rack. There wasn't one—I could have told him that. When we'd come down from the mountain, we'd had to dry our cloaks on extra chairs. "I don't recall any person named Vivian," he said at last, clasping his hands over the handles of his strange bag. "I have come at Daisy's behest."

"Daisy! Another one I've been trying to get a hold of for too long." Officer Thorn sat up, running her hands through her hair. "Hold on a moment, both of you. Let me get a bite to eat, and maybe I'll be able to do more than repeat whatever blasted name you bring up. No one tell me any more names! I know Maggie was in here earlier," she continued, almost to herself at this point, as she got up and stalked around the waiting room. "She must've brought something . . . aha!" Thorn dove through the door to her actual office, and came back in a moment with a little tray covered in a tea towel. She plopped herself back down at the visitors' desk and removed the towel to reveal yet more muffins.

My stomach rumbled. I'd forgotten breakfast . . .

"Help yourself," said Officer Thorn, her voice much more cheery now that her mouth was full. "Maggie was right. I've been at this too hard. I *hate* cold cases," she decided, as I took a pumpkin crumble muffin and Rhys took a toffee one. The officer went on, "What was it you two were saying?"

"I was saying you need to get in touch with Paracelsus—he might know something," I said, much more evenly than I'd felt before. "And Rhys is on a mysterious errand."

"Daisy sent me," he put in, eating his muffin one little piece at a time, like Sugar would.

Officer Thorn, on the other hand, was already through her first baked good. She eyed him sharply as she selected another. "What's in the bag?"

"This." At last, Rhys reached down into the fabric carry-all and pulled out a clump of dirt.

From the clump—which held together quite well; an indication of a good strong soil, I couldn't help but think—a small, and rather sad, seedling was struggling to grow.

"What's that?" Thorn asked, through a mouthful of chocolate chip.

"Is the Tree dying?" I asked, with considerably more alarm.

"The Tree is fine," Rhys insisted. "And Daisy has suggested

a plan."

* * *

Eventually, once we'd eaten our muffins and arranged ourselves more professionally around the little plant on Officer Thorn's desk, things started to make more sense.

"Let me get this straight," said Officer Thorn. "Daisy says the plants in the cavern *aren't* growing because of her Tree?"

"That's right," said Rhys.

Officer Thorn then turned to me. "And you think they *are* growing because of the Tree."

"Well," I said, "that's my best guess at the moment. There definitely is something special about them. But I'm not the expert in—"

Officer Thorn was clearly not listening any more. She'd turned back to Rhys. "What do *you* think?"

"I am in the middle," he said, serenely. "I believe them both to be right, in part."

The look on Thorn's face was sour. "They either are or they aren't."

"I believe that the plants did originate from water affected by the Tree of Life," Rhys said, patient. "However, while that may be why they originally grew, it is not why they grow now."

Officer Thorn sighed, her elbow on the desk and her fingers tugging at her ear as she thought this through. "You know that bringing down *this* plant from your Tree of Life could essentially confirm Daisy's motive, right?"

Rhys was steadfast. "She believes it will exonerate her."

"But wait," I interrupted. "What does she actually want us to do with it, Rhys?"

"She wants us," he said, pointedly, "to take the plant to Jack."

* * *

"This would have been easier if you just ran some tests," Officer Thorn mumbled to me. We trudged along the muddy path to the Witch's Hut, led by Rhys and his lumpy fabric bag.

"I don't think an exact comparison is what Daisy is getting at," I whispered back. "I think she must want to prove something else."

"Well, it'd be a whole lot easier if she came down to the station and told me herself," Thorn complained.

I grinned. The sun was fully up now, and even with the mist on the hillside, it was plain to see my friend's irritation. I couldn't resist teasing her a little. "Because you're so easy to talk to?"

"Everyone at the Guild seems to think so," she retorted. "Kept me up all night with their 'confirm this's and 'try that's and 'positive identification required's. I've about had it with this case, Red."

"I know," I said sympathetically. "Me too. Remind me to tell you about my efforts with your anonymous notes later."

We were coming up to the garden gate now, and it was clear from the lit windows that Trent and his guests were already up. Rhys paused, waiting for Officer Thorn to go first and announce her intentions.

The atmosphere as we entered the Hut was celebratory, an almost startling change from the rest of my morning. Trent and Olivia were standing around the kitchen table, beaming. Dirty dishes from breakfast were scattered around, and the place still smelled like toast and jam.

"Officer Thorn!" Olivia said, as the three of us entered. "Look what Jack made!"

She held out a small canvas in her hands. On it, quite clearly, had been painted the Hut with the sun breaking through the clouds above it, casting one bright ray down onto its rounded walls.

"Nice," said Thorn, with the air of one who is uncomfortable passing opinions on art. "Is that what has you two so excited?"

"We think it's a good sign," Olivia said.

To the side, slightly behind her, Trent caught my eye and made meaningful glances at the top of her head, like, *see? Told you.* But he seemed just as pleased by the picture as she was.

Rhys cleared his throat.

"Oh," said Olivia, who may as well have been elected speaker for the gathering. "I know you. You work at the potions shop."

"Sending goons to collect payment now, Red?" Trent asked me with a lopsided grin.

"Not quite." Since neither of my friends seemed willing, I explained a little further. "Actually, Rhys brought something in today that we'd like Jack to take a look at."

Trent settled his hands on his hips. "And what is it exactly?"

Wordlessly, Rhys produced the ailing plant.

Both Trent and Olivia looked very confused. "But why?" she asked. In a much quieter voice, she added, "Is it from the tower?"

"It's from the mountain," said Thorn, with the tones of finality. "And it's not going to poison him, so don't worry, Witch. We just need him to—"

She glanced at Rhys, suddenly uncertain.

"Hold it," Rhys intoned.

Trent scratched his neck. "Should be fine, I guess. Here, let me take it."

Olivia's face betrayed her misgivings. But when Trent took hold of the ball of soil and didn't immediately die, they both seemed to relax once more. Like a motley, indoor parade, Olivia, Thorn, Rhys, and I fell into step behind Trent as he crossed over to Jack's door.

He knocked, and then entered, the rest of us streaming behind him. Jack was sitting cross-legged on his bed, dressed in an old sweater and jeans that had probably once belonged to Trent. If he was surprised to see us all, he didn't show it. Actually, his gaze was fixed on the little plant, from the moment it entered the room.

"Rhys, the one over by the door, tells me that he brought this down from the mountain this morning," Trent said by way of introduction. He held out the plant to Jack as we all stood round. "Would you take a look at it for us?"

Jack reached for the plant without hesitation.

The moment he touched the soil, the air in the room around us changed. There weren't any sparkles or spell words or other signs of magic, but there was a rush of wind around Jack and the plant—and all at once, the sapling was straight and tall, a vibrant green. This was what William sometimes called "quiet" magic, an affinity, a natural power—a power with plants specifically, which members of the Drus did often have . . .

. . . But it was also much, much more. We'd run into elves who could make vines move before, but even I could tell that Jack's ability was even stronger than that. The little plant in his hands wasn't just green, it was growing. Growing with only air and a little bit of dirt . . .

Exactly like the plant samples in my lab.

28

A Quiet Life

Olivia and Trent may not have had any idea what we were up to, but every single one of us was surprised. Jaws might as well have been on the floor. Jack looked around at each of us in turn, his eyes lingering on Rhys. Rhys was the only one without his mouth hanging open; in fact he looked centered and yet slightly censorious, like a teacher whose student has just given a wrong answer on purpose.

Jack held his gaze, and I watched them watching each other for a moment.

Then Jack opened his mouth.

It took a few tries. At first, nothing came out. Finally he drew the plant down into his lap, and looking at it instead of at us, he whispered hoarsely, "I should have known."

"Jack!" Olivia fell to the floor, her hand resting on the blankets beside his knee. He looked down at her, but didn't say anything more just yet.

I glanced at Thorn. She'd pulled out her notebook and was scribbling furiously. When I met her eyes, she gestured with her head for me to *go on.* I could see the reason in that: I wasn't in a police uniform, and might be able to be a neutral third party.

"Jack," I said, echoing Olivia more gently as I stepped forward, "I know this is rather sudden, but it's not any kind of trap. You're not being accused of anything. We met before—my name's Red, and I'm the local alchemist." He was watching me calmly, but had no more to say just yet. I went on, "I've actually been to the cavern—I don't know if they told you. It's *incredible.*"

Officer Thorn kicked the back of my boot, like she disapproved of how much I'd said. But the understanding in Jack's face was worth it.

"You . . . know," he said slowly, focusing on me.

"I don't know much at all," I told him plainly. "Just that those plants are special. And—have you been helping them grow? It was you?"

Jack looked down at the sapling, which now might rival any respectable potted plant for size, health, and sheer number of leaves. "I . . . don't know . . . how not to."

At the end of the room, Trent tapped thoughtfully at his chin. "Any magic that strong would be a pain without proper control," he commented. "Is that why you were in that tower?"

That idea—that somehow Jack had wanted to hide away, or that it had been for his own good—had never once occurred to me. I looked up in surprise, and Jack followed my glance. But then he shook his head.

"I like it," he said, his voice still low and hoarse. "It doesn't pain me. But I knew . . . I could never get far."

"The chains in your pictures," Olivia said quietly.

"You know," Jack agreed, looking down at her. "You could see it. I like it better—talking that way. It seems safe."

"You can keep on communicating that way," I said. "There's nothing wrong with that. Only, we're trying to put some big pieces together here, and fast. So just for now, if there's anything you want to say. . ."

Jack looked down at his plant again, and at Olivia.

Trent cleared his throat. "Did you get that magic from your parents?"

"Don't remember them," Jack said, his gaze now far away. "I used to think . . . that I didn't have any. That I grew from a seed. Like these." He looked down at his plant again, then up at me. "But I do know . . . about alchemy. We had books on it—so many books. Two things together, turning into one."

"Right," I agreed. That was a fairly standard principle of alchemical processes: you could distill things into their many parts, and then bring the parts back together, into solution. The fact that *this* was what he'd thought of made me venture a suggestion I'd been mulling over in the back of my mind. "There was a really big amethyst in the cavern, and my friend, William, who can see magic, said that it was the source of a powerful spell. So was it two magics coming together—yours, and Vivian's?"

Jack shook his head. "Vesper."

Officer Thorn moved up, and I felt her glance. This was yet more confirmation. I tried not to sound inordinately pleased as I clarified, "It was your magic, and Vesper's, then?"

"They have magic in them already," he said softly, looking down at his plant again. "This one has even more . . . than the others. Vesper said . . . she was making sure the cavern's magic stayed strong. But she couldn't make anything as strong as this."

"We think we know the reason for that," I told him. "That

plant comes from a different place on the mountain. So she was enhancing the magic in the water, in the cavern . . . but it was you actually keeping the plants themselves alive?"

Jack nodded. "The water. Yes. You could taste it . . . the magic in it. But I only tasted it once. It wasn't for me. That's what she said."

I knelt down to look at him. Given everything he'd said about Vesper so far, I didn't have a great feeling about where this was going. For just a moment, I wished that this fairy tale had turned out differently—that maybe Jack *had* wanted to stay there, that he hadn't been lied to and kept secret. But if being with Luca had taught me anything, it was that brightness would follow facing the dark. "Jack," I said very carefully, "what did Vesper say about us? About the world outside your home?"

Jack returned my gaze intently. "Is she dead?"

I glanced up at Officer Thorn, who nodded. "She's gone," she said.

Jack sat back. One hand trailed away from his plant and found Olivia's, on the bed. It was Olivia who spoke up. "I know how he feels about her," she said. "He showed me the painting. I knew it was some*one*, not something. You can see it." She glanced up at Jack, and when he nodded, she fished a canvas out from a stack of finished paintings under the bed. They spilled onto the rug at our feet. We all leaned in to look. In the one Olivia had chosen, a mass of chaotic dark clouds completely overwhelming a small, trailing vine.

I couldn't see the meaning as clearly as Olivia had, but a look at Jack's face completed the picture. His normally nut-brown skin had gone gray. "She said . . . it was war," he whispered. "That everyone had turned against us . . . against her. She said

. . . we had to survive, to prove them wrong. She said nothing else mattered."

"But you wondered," Olivia said, tracing the swirling clouds in another of the paintings.

"I wondered," Jack agreed, "why the plants would grow. If the world . . . was only hate . . . why would there be magic? Why would the plants be here?"

Despite the gravity of such a wonder, I smiled faintly. "That's an interesting point."

Beside me, Officer Thorn spoke up. "Did anyone else know about the cavern?"

Jack didn't look at her, but he did seem thoughtful. "No one could know. Even I—felt bad for knowing. We would travel there using magic. She said no other way was safe. But . . . she took the plants away. Cuttings. For people who were trying to survive, but who were far away, she said. She would go often . . . And the last few times she came back . . . She was mad."

"Can you say any more about that?" Officer Thorn leaned in.

Jack glanced down at his paintings again. Following his glance, I saw one where rocks had crushed a little flower. "She was terrible when she was mad," he whispered.

"Terrible how?" I asked softly.

"She would do anything. She would have got rid of me," he said, and though his voice was small, it was firm. "I knew that . . . I always knew. She was mad at the people outside. Sometimes they were good . . . But sometimes they asked too many questions. Or tried to make her pay."

I glanced at Thorn beside me. Market fees hardly seemed like a usual motive for murder. But if Vivian was truly so volatile, perhaps she wouldn't see things that way. And perhaps a confrontational grocer had sent his son after her one day . . .

. . . But truthfully, equally likely was that, one day, she'd started a fight with Jack, and it hadn't ended well.

Perhaps Olivia saw it in my eyes as I was looking at Thorn. Perhaps she realized the danger in his testimony herself. Immediately, she reached across the pile of paintings and pulled out another, a symphony of cool, pale blues and greens flowing across the canvas—a river.

"He wouldn't have acted," she said, holding this up. "He was trying to let things go, to live in the moment."

As one, Officer Thorn and I glanced at Jack. He looked faintly puzzled over this turn in the conversation, but he did nod at Olivia. "It did me no good. To linger on things."

"But you do remember," said Officer Thorn, purposefully, "what happened to make you run away?"

"Nothing happened," said Jack, turning his head. "I don't remember."

"Would it have been a market day?" Officer Thorn pressed.

"I'm not sure," Jack said, with effort.

"But you remember everything leading up to that day?"

"I don't remember anything," Jack insisted. "My head—my head was hurt."

He glanced at Trent as he spoke. The Witch cleared his throat. "That much is true, as I had told you repeatedly, Thorn."

"I know, I know." Officer Thorn leaned back, making a few more notes. "But you said he *might* remember."

"Sometimes the memories do come back," Trent agreed, placidly. "But that's not a guarantee, and there's no forcing it."

By the door, Rhys shifted. I'd entirely forgotten he was there. As I stood up and looked at him, curious, he said mildly, "Self-defense is a mitigating circumstance."

"I know it is," said Officer Thorn, cross. "But it still has to be proven."

"The cavern was the main thing," Jack said, as though he'd barely heard us. "She always wanted . . . just to protect the cavern."

And she needed you to make sure the plants grew, I thought, my heart going out to him. Aloud, I said, "Thank you, Jack, for talking to us. You could tell Olivia if you think of anything more."

It was a whim, but it made Olivia smile as she looked up at him. "Or you could paint another picture," she said.

Jack looked down at her silently and smiled back.

* * *

Officer Thorn, Rhys, and I clustered around the garden gate after saying our goodbyes.

"I have to hand it to you," she told Rhys, taking a deep breath and a look around, "that plant idea really took root."

"It was Daisy's idea," Rhys said, placid as ever. He shifted his weight, usually a good sign he was about to take his leave.

Before he could go, though, I piped up with a question. "Rhys, why did Daisy want you to take the plant to *Jack* specifically?"

He smiled at me. "My lady's reasoning was thus: the plants you found grew at an incredible rate, unlike the plants where she and the pixies call home. Therefore, though they might be similar, someone else must be using their own magic to tend

215

to the plants. Her belief was that such a connection would be very strong, but would not last beyond death. As the sorcerer was dead and the plants continued to thrive, she doubted the sorcerer could have been the 'gardener,' so to speak. So she asked me if anyone else had been shown to live at the tower," he concluded, with a little bow.

"And you reminded her about Jack," I mused, seeing how the pieces fit. "Nicely done."

"Yes, nice. But tell her I still want to talk to her in person!" Officer Thorn yelled. By that point in the conversation, she was yelling at Rhys's back. He merely waved over his shoulder.

Officer Thorn turned to me. "We probably won't hear back from your Paracelsus for a while yet."

"It may take time," I agreed, glancing at the sky. The sun was high, but the cloud cover was thicker, and a breeze had picked up. And I couldn't recall if I had warned William I was going out or not . . .

"—whole thing sideways," Thorn was saying.

"Hm?" I asked, trying to pay attention.

"I said, Daisy gave us that plant and turned this whole thing sideways," Officer Thorn repeated emphatically. "Everything I thought I was going to do with my day, upended. Now I'm thinking I'd better go over to the market again."

"Or to the tavern," I said vaguely. That phrase, *sideways,* was bothering me. But in another moment, I'd realized why. "The tavern!" I said again, taking Thorn's arm. "That's exactly where we need to go next!"

29

Stacks and Sheaves

Of course, we didn't go *exactly* to the tavern next. I dragged Officer Thorn with me to the potions shop, where we found the faithful William behind the counter and the store open. (There was a distinct possibility that it hadn't opened on time, of course, but wasn't that also my fault for getting distracted?) All my paper bits and observations had been moved to the counter in the tea nook. (Again, my fault for being distracted and taking over shop space with lab work!)

I rifled through the papers, leaving Officer Thorn to catch William up on the events of our morning. He was interested, and very gratified to hear of Rhys and Daisy's role. I could distinctly feel the smugness of his expression on my back before I turned, having gathered what I needed.

"I'd like to see the day when you suspect them of something and they *have* done it," he commented, a doggy grin plastered on his face.

Thorn eyed me and my handful of papers. "You suspected Rhys?"

"I suspected Daisy, and I wasn't happy about it," I said. "With any luck, that'll be the last time. Here, look at this."

I put the two original notes down on the counter between them first. Then I pulled out my two most relevant samples—Olivia's notepad, and the tavern memo sheet.

Officer Thorn frowned. "Does that one say 'Olivia'? You suspect her now?"

"It says Olivia because it's from her notebook. We were gathering all kinds of things yesterday to compare," I informed the officer. "This is not accusations—just science. See how both your original notes are roughly square, with evenly cut sides and bottoms, torn along the top?"

"Depends which way you're looking at it," panted William, who was seated across the counter and therefore had a different view than Thorn and me.

"Exactly," I agreed. "I assumed the top was torn because that's the way the notes were written. But you might flip the paper around before you write, especially if you're moving quickly, and it's unlined, so it wouldn't matter anyway. It was your comment about 'sideways,' Thorn, that made me think of it. I just couldn't get my mind to function properly this morning, but I *knew* there was something going on."

I turned Olivia's notepaper on its side. The plain white rectangle was now exactly as long as the two notes were, but it wasn't quite as tall.

"It only barely fits," Officer Thorn was quick to point out. "And why would she tear the side of her paper, not the top?"

"Olivia's notebook uses tearaway glue, so the tops of her paper come out nice and clean—just like the sides of these notes," I said. "But, as for why she'd pull the sheet out so nicely and then tear along the edge like that, I have to admit I have no idea."

"To make you wonder," William suggested dryly.

"Let's see the other one," Officer Thorn said, giving William a dirty look.

"This is from the tavern memo pad," I said, setting it beside the others. "Like Olivia's, the weight and color of the paper matches the notes. But the shape didn't make sense. Their paper tears out cleanly, too, so you wouldn't get that torn top. However, they have the tavern logo there at the bottom."

I turned my sample sheet over so the logo was upside down at the top, and then carefully ripped it off to make the paper unidentifiable.

Officer Thorn whistled. "I'd say that looks like a perfect match."

"Why tear it two different ways, though?" asked William. "The first note is nice and even."

"While the second one is on a sloppy diagonal," I concluded in agreement. "It is something else to wonder about, as you said."

"It's something else to ask Lavender about," said Officer Thorn. "I think you had the right idea, Red. Time to go to the tavern."

"Wait one moment," William said, just as I'd gathered up my evidence. "Red, someone came in looking for you earlier. The faun from the market?"

"Oh, Doug." I exchanged a quick glance with Officer Thorn. "Did he say what he wanted?"

"He remembered something else he wanted to tell you, but he wouldn't tell *me*," said William, sounding rather miffed. "And he was very interested in your plants."

"Well, as an herbalist, he would be." I did wonder for just

a split second, and then I pushed the thought aside. "We can stop at the market after the tavern, maybe."

Officer Thorn gave me a friendly push toward the door. "Only if you get moving!"

* * *

We got to the tavern shortly before the lunch rush. Officer Thorn charged straight in and toward the back, and honestly, none of the servers looked surprised. At the end of the bar, Lavender was talking to someone in the kitchen—probably about the day's specials, I figured.

I trailed after Thorn with my papers in hand, as though I might be called upon to make a presentation. Actually, I felt a little nervous. Luca, William, and I loved coming to the tavern. Just like suspecting Daisy, implicating Lavender in evidence of crime felt unsettlingly personal and wrong. The facts were there, but when it came time to confront her with them, I felt somehow like an impostor—like she'd see through my charade at once.

Fortunately, Officer Thorn took the lead. "Lavender? We've got a new development in the case to talk to you about."

Lavender turned abruptly from her conversation. "Should we go back to my office?" She asked, her amethyst eyes worried as she looked at both of us across the bar.

"This may only take a minute," said Thorn. "I need you to confirm something. You have a memo pad handy?"

"I'm sure I do, somewhere." Lavender smoothed her hands over her apron pockets and, finding nothing, began to look down the bar at the rows of bottles and glasses. "There—by the sink. Let me just grab it and be right back."

It took her no more than a moment, but my heart was in my throat as she came back to us and set it on the bar top. "What's this about?" she asked.

Officer Thorn nodded to me, and I placed my three sheets of paper on the bar: the first two notes, and my own sample. My hand shook just a little. I thought I caught a glimpse of something in the dark mirror behind Lavender's head, but the impression was fleeting.

"You heard about the notes I got," Officer Thorn said to Lavender, her voice low and confidential. "Looks like they match the tavern stationery. Wouldn't you agree?"

Lavender's face, pale and rosy at the best of times, blanched. She toyed with the edges of one of the notes. "I have to say, I might. Especially if the sheets were turned upside down."

"That's what we thought too," I said, relieved that she saw it. "I didn't realize it at first, but it came to me this morning."

Lavender gave me a wan smile. "Funny how these things catch up with you."

"You know what I have to ask next," said Thorn, settling her elbow on the bar as she leaned in.

Lavender looked over her shoulders, at the kitchen, the slowly filling up restaurant. She, too, leaned in. "You'll want to know if I know who wrote them, dear. But I'm afraid I can't tell you for sure. You see, we hand these out—do everything but stick them in customer's bags for them. I've always thought of it as a sort of marketing."

"Not such good marketing to be caught up in murder," Thorn said, watching her closely.

"In this case, it can't be helped." Lavender shrugged her shoulders heavily, and as she tilted her head, the low light caught the deep circles under her eyes. "There's no way the tavern *couldn't* be implicated in this particular story."

"Do you think someone knew that?" I asked, on impulse. "Maybe they wanted to tie the tavern in to everything going on?"

"We've got a full house right now. It's our busiest time," Lavender said slowly. "I've hardly kept track of guests the way I usually do. Any of them might know, especially after it was in the paper."

"The notes came before the article was published," Officer Thorn said. "And why would someone use the tavern paper but tear *off* the tavern logo?"

"Maybe they thought they were doing us a kindness." Lavender's voice, usually so full of life, sounded flat.

I still felt uneasy and very bad for her, but Officer Thorn remained focused on business. She pulled out her notebook. "So you didn't send the notes?"

"No," said Lavender.

Thorn made a note. "Does Daisy have one of these pads?"

Lavender started, and so did I. "Yes, I think I did give her one," she said.

Before I could decide whether or not to protest, Officer Thorn went on. "How about Jack? I noticed tavern takeout at the Hut."

Lavender looked even more rattled than ever. "I *have* been sending over care packages, Officer—Trent said it was alright. In the first one I think I did include a pad with a note on it to Jack, but—but surely *he* couldn't have—why, he's been watched, since the moment he came into town!"

"Just running through possibilities," said Thorn. "Anyone at the market have one?"

"There's no reason they couldn't." Lavender's distress was

evident.

"That covers that, then." Officer Thorn snapped her notebook shut. "And you haven't noticed anything odd lately about the memo pads—them going missing, or turning up unexpectedly?"

Grim-faced, Lavender shook her head.

At that moment there was a commotion over by the front door. Glad for a distraction, I turned to look. Someone had collided with people coming in for lunch—someone who was still stuck, lingering by the door frame. I had a clear line of vision through the crowd, straight to them. It was Doug.

"William said he was looking for me," I reminded Thorn. "I'm going to go catch him while you finish up here."

"We're done for now." Officer Thorn nodded to Lavender, not unkindly. Lavender smiled faintly back at me before staring at the memo pad on the bar.

I slipped through the crowd, leaving Thorn to fend for herself. Lunchers were everywhere now, it seemed, but I managed to catch up with Doug on the tavern's porch.

"Doug!" I called, and he turned as though rooted to the spot. "I heard you were looking for me. I was going to go to the market—it didn't occur to me to look anywhere else!"

I meant it as a joke at my own expense, because of course Doug didn't *live* at his little stall. But his gaze slipped over my shoulder, unamused and frankly, a little frightened. I glanced back to see Thorn catching up with us. *But they got along just fine at the market the other day . . .*

Concerned now, I turned back to him. "Is everything alright?"

"Couldn't be better," he said, but his voice was thin and a little too loud.

"William seemed to think you'd thought of something," Officer Thorn huffed over my shoulder as she joined us.

"Not—not about the case," Doug said quickly. "Just something for Red. Some plants I saw on the mountain. It's nothing, really."

"Oh," I said, a little surprised by his manner. The case seemed to have him on edge, and we weren't such good friends that I was comfortable asking him why. "I'm always glad to hear about new discoveries. William said you saw the plants in the lab, right? I was going to bring some over to you for ID, when I got around to it."

"I'm sure there's really no need," he said. "I wouldn't know them, really."

Behind me, Officer Thorn crossed her arms. "What's this all about, then?"

Doug sidled. "Nothing!"

"Doug," I said slowly, "did you run away when you saw me and Officer Thorn?"

"I remembered I didn't lock up my stall," he said, agitated. "So I'd better go check on it. See you later! Goodbye!"

He ran off, bouncing lightly on his hooved feet. Officer Thorn and I watched him go, amazed.

Glancing back toward the tavern door, Thorn waved a server over. "Doug come here often?" she asked.

"Nearly every day," said the server brightly. "We always joke we should name one of the salads after him."

"Has he ever asked for a memo pad?" the officer said.

The server tilted his head, uncertain. "I don't know. Want me to ask around?"

"No, that's enough. Thank you," said Thorn, dismissing her informant. Once we were alone on the porch again, she said to me, "So much for your paper lead narrowing the field."

30

Thrown a Line

"Red," said Officer Thorn, in a more serious tone as we crossed the park, "I need a favor."

"Other than helping you investigate, you mean?" I said, smiling. It was nice to think that the morning's tasks and confrontations were behind me now.

"You'd just meddle if I didn't give you tasks," she informed me. "I knew it from the moment you showed up in town."

I gasped. Two and a half years, and this had never come out? "Excuse you! How do you know that I'd meddle?"

"Alchemists and their inquiring minds," said my friend, looking just as smug as William. "I saw you show up and start asking questions and I said to myself, I'd better nip that in the bud."

"That'd better not be a pun about the state of my lab right now," I retorted. I didn't even want to address her larger comment. Especially because I had a feeling she wasn't wrong. "Now that you've upset me, what's this favor you wanted?"

Officer Thorn laughed, the force of it startling a papier mâché spider hanging from a nearby tree branch. "I want you to loan me William. Just for the afternoon."

"You'll have to ask him if he feels like meddling," I said. "He isn't a microscope."

"Given the trouble yours got me into this morning, that's for the best," sighed Officer Thorn. When I gave her another affronted look, she put up her hands. "Not that you haven't turned up some useful things. It just seems to be the *same* useful things over and over, twisted around, doesn't it?"

"It does," I agreed, sighing. "I feel like I can't see things quite clearly. Is that why you want William?"

"The forensic sorcerer comes in from New Dale this afternoon." It seemed like good news to me, but Officer Thorn said it grimly, and she paused beside a haystack rather than join the passersby on the street in front of my shop. I lingered next to her, waiting for an explanation. She tossed her hair over one shoulder and went on, "I had to go back and forth with the Guild to get him here at all. The road up the mountain from New Dale has been washed out for days, apparently, and they had to approve his extra travel expense."

"And you don't seem pleased about your success?" I prompted.

"At this point, I'd welcome just about *any* extra pair of eyes at that crime scene. There's nothing there, as far as I can tell. Not so much as a stray whisker. The place is clean. But . . ." Thorn tugged at her ear, a habit when she was uncertain. "The purpose is to identify Vesper, who we now know is Vivian, thanks to Luca. 'Course, I started arranging all this before he came through. I'm not saying we don't need the magical expert any more, but . . ."

"You're regretting bringing in outside help?" I suggested. It didn't seem entirely like Officer Thorn: usually she was happy to recruit whomever she needed.

"It's this particular outside help I'm wondering about," Thorn admitted finally. "He wired before dawn to ask me if I had cheese crackers on hand, Red. *Cheese crackers.* What does he think this is, a lunch date? Olivia was awfully excited about him, and I hate to disappoint her, but let's just say I'd be glad if William came along and helped keep him in line."

"It's a good idea, and something I bet William would love doing," I said, amused. "Come on, let's ask him."

I led the way across the street and into the shop. William, naturally, was very pleased at the idea of keeping a sorcerer "in line." He trotted out the door with Officer Thorn, his tail held high. Despite the stresses of my day so far, it was fun to see them go off together in such a mood.

Meanwhile, I settled in to run the shop alone for the afternoon. It was Rhys's day off, and I didn't mind having the time to myself. Between my paper comparisons and the various plant experiments, there was plenty of cleanup to do. Plus, after seeing how everyone had gone all out in decorating the Square, I was starting to feel like my window displays needed some extra love.

All the same, there was *something* still bothering me . . . Something that had me jumping at shadows, as though I'd seen someone moving out of the corner of my eye.

"Boo!" Saki's voice cut through the quiet, making me leap about two feet straight up in the air and drop all my notebooks.

I whirled. "Sakura! Need I remind you it is not yet Halloween?"

"Can't help it, it's my favorite season," she said, giggling and sparkling and, generally, not looking at all sorry. In her hands was a large lidded basket.

"And why didn't the shop bells ring?" I asked, as I bent to pick up my mess.

"It's a game William and I play. I managed to sneak all the way to the counter once. Where is he? I was bringing him a 'poor you, Red forgot all about you' care package, but I guess it's a 'poor Red' package instead?"

Sakura had deposited her basket on the counter, revealing her outfit: a flared purple skirt covered in toadstools and ferns, topped with a green jumper and a purple bow holding back one side of her bobbed hair. Looking at her was like getting hit over the head with seasonal spirit. I shook my head and chuckled. "It's his turn to be out helping Officer Thorn. Does your care package include lunch?"

"Obviously," she said, hopping up to sit on the counter before unloading sandwiches and cupcakes. "Glacial's covering my lunch break, so I have a minute to eat with you. You're never as good a gossip as William, though. Is there anything new you'd like to share?"

"Did you read Leo's article?" I asked as I joined her. "I'm afraid I still probably don't know as much about the case as she does. Or *thinks* she does."

"Leo's been rather distracted lately," Saki commented, licking hummus from where it had leaked out of her sandwich, which I noticed was made of one piece of wheat bread and one piece of sourdough. "The article was fine, but honestly *everyone* knew that much already. And how is Luca?"

I faltered, my hands hovering over my grilled cheese. I hadn't seen Luca this morning. That wasn't *so* unusual; why did it feel so unsettling? "He—he actually helped Thorn a lot, yesterday," I managed to say. "He's doing well. One of his scholar friends was able to tell him a lot about the case, so—he was pleased."

"And worried about you, I shouldn't imagine," Saki said, leveling a pointed look across two warm drinks and a plate full of extra goodies.

"Well—" I wanted to argue the point, but it was no use. "I hadn't thought about it much, but yes, I suppose so. Maybe a little."

"Hmm. Far be it from me to make things worse," said Sakura, "but I did find this tucked in your door when I came in."

She reached under her box and pulled out a piece of plain white paper. It was small—precisely the size of Officer Thorn's mysterious notes, in fact, though this one had been torn across the top and then folded in half.

I set down my sandwich and took it, a little dazed. "You did? Just now?"

"Just now," she confirmed. "I hate to unsettle you more, but something will need to be done about it, I suppose."

"Yes, it's better to know," I agreed, meeting her eyes before unfolding the paper and reading it aloud. "'A good potion-maker should know when to stop stirring the pot.'"

"That's all it says?" Saki twisted on the counter so she could look at it, too.

"They've all been fairly brief, like that," I told her.

"Have they all been threatening?" she asked. There was a distinct note of protectiveness in her voice. Had she been a cat, the fur along her spine would have been standing up.

"No," I admitted. "I think it's pretty clear we managed to make someone *else* worry."

* * *

When Luca came over after closing time, he insisted we go straight to the police station. We got there right in time: William and Officer Thorn practically met us on the road. What had been an autumn breeze during the day was now a wind that tore down the streets, whipping our cloaks around us. As we ducked into the station, the first roll of thunder cracked overhead.

"What a season," Officer Thorn grumbled, as she scooped up the afternoon's mail and made her way to the front desk. "Some weather. No one gets killed on the mountain when it's perfectly nice out, do they?"

"I'm guessing today's visit didn't go too well?" I asked William, as we lingered by the door. I couldn't help but notice there was no strange sorcerer with them.

"He's a total quack," said William, panting happily. "An entertaining one. But he didn't do anything. *I* was the one who noticed a faint tracing spell on the cloak, while *he* just went on and on about magical geometry."

"Then decided to head straight for the post office's teleportation service after William asked him what color 'the magic of the dead' is," Thorn commented as she settled into her chair. "Sit, sit! Why are you all here, anyway? I was just going to check the mail and then go check on Olivia. Oh, Red, it looks like we got a wire back from Paracelsus."

I was still musing over the fact that the sorcerer had been so happy to get away. Post offices around Beyond had started offering teleportation links, but they were considered dangerous magic, and usually only the very desperate or the very foolhardy used them. Either William had been quite rude, or the sorcerer quite egotistical, or both. Neither was too surprising.

Without mentioning my own news, I crossed the room and took the paper from Officer Thorn's hand. It was a short note—wires often were; most people still preferred letters for longer communications. Paracelsus had said:

> *Greetings Officer Thorn and Belville. Vivian and I were once acquainted, yes. I always worried what had become of her. Anything she found and devoted her life to would have been extremely valuable. But a good alchemist knows when to let the experiment end.*

I swallowed hard and showed the note to Luca.

"Doesn't answer many of my questions," Thorn commented as she finished sorting her mail. "Does he often talk like that, Red?"

"*Somebody* does." Luca was practically vibrating with indignation at my side. What had made me uncertain and unsure of myself had made him angry. He tossed Paracelsus's message on the table and threw the mysterious note from this afternoon down beside it. "Red just got this, at her shop. In broad daylight, when anyone could have been walking by!"

Thorn looked it over, her face becoming serious as she clocked the similarity in the messages. "You didn't see anyone, Red?"

"No. That is—I saw Saki—it was Saki who saw the note. She was coming over because she thought William was there." I shook my head; everything was so confused. "I was busy cleaning after you two left, and I didn't notice a thing."

William put his paws up on the table, shining faintly blue as he looked at both letters, too. "This is too close to home," he growled.

"I agree," said Luca. "And I insist we do something about it."

Officer Thorn glanced between the three of us. "Well," she said, sitting back, "the one thing our fancy Forensic Sorcerer was good for was some basic facts. We know we're dealing with Vivian-turned-Vesper, and we know she was killed five days ago. My own time of death was too recent—the anti-aging effects on the body made visual determination of time of death inaccurate. Five days ago was the last time any of her spells were used."

"I could have told you that," William rumbled.

"We also," continued Thorn, determined, "now have several experts telling us that this magical flower business is valuable. Paracelsus, our consultant, even Daisy. Seems like quite enough to kill over, according to any one of them."

"And Red is the one who found the cavern," Luca broke in. He was starting to shimmer at the edges, like he might actually go full curse-mode and try to—what? Hunt down the criminal?

"Paracelsus asked me to," I said, still bewildered by the timing of it all.

"And then he told you basically the same thing the murderer did," William pointed out. He was shimmering, too, a deep starry blue. Thunder rolled outside again, shaking the little police station.

"Let's not be hasty." Officer Thorn paused as she considered all of us. "If it starts to rain as hard as that thunder is going, then no one's going to want to go anywhere or carry out any threats."

"Are you suggesting we *wait*?" Luca seemed to grow a foot taller and darker in his frustration.

"No," said Officer Thorn, calmly. "I'm suggesting we go round back and see if Maggie made anything for supper."

234

31

A Long Climb

Poor, sweet Maggie. If she was alarmed by the three extra guests who turned up in her living room, all soaked to the bone from the sudden rain despite the fact that the door to the station was about ten yards away, it didn't last long.

"Oh my goodness, it must be awful out there, come on," she said, literally taking my arm and drawing me through to the spare room at the back, talking the whole while, "you should change, you can wear one of the sweaters from Mina's mom, she sends new ones all the time. They're very big and warm. Go on, change, and we'll have soup ready!"

Both Luca and I had been efficiently shooed into the room by someone half the size of either one of us. The door snapped shut. Maggie had once been a performing acrobat, and she had lost none of her athletic vim and vigor.

I stared at Luca, still a little lost. I hardly even knew where I was—Maggie had clearly been redecorating Thorn's little house, turning what had been a utilitarian cave of sorts into a place where painted walls, colorful curtains, and plush pillows abounded. It was a stark contrast to the rain and the talk of threats.

Luca didn't say anything, but crossed the carpet at once and pulled me into a hug.

"I'm sorry," I said, squeezing my eyes shut against his shoulder. "I didn't mean to get into trouble."

"You never do." Luca held me tighter, so tight I could feel rather than hear him chuckle as he relaxed. "Think of all the times you've gotten me out of a scrape. This is just the same. It'll be okay."

"I'm not sure how," I mumbled.

"Me neither. But we'll figure it out," he promised, leaning back to kiss my forehead. "Soup first is probably a very good plan."

Heartened, I did my best to shed my outer clothes quickly, pulling on a sweater from the closet over my tunic and tights. As advertised, the sweater nearly hung down to my knees, and it was immediately cozy. It was knit with a red yarn that was vaguely fuzzy and impossible not to touch.

Across the room, Luca grinned, attired in his own oversize sweater of forest green. A pattern of lines and trees had been knitted in.

"These are amazing," I said. "Thorn's mom should open a store!"

"My guess is she's too busy with the farm," Luca said. "Come on, let's see what the others are up to."

The others, it turned out, were clustered in the kitchen. It was nearly claustrophobic, particularly with Thorn—fresh in her own striped sweater—and a wet William taking up one corner, but Maggie was still chattering happily.

"We never have anyone over," she was saying, as we joined

William at the wraparound counter. "Of course, I hardly know anyone, except Gloria and Johann, and Glacial and Leo of course, and Rose—that's Mina's mom—but her family lives a little ways away. And Olivia, too, she's been really nice. I keep saying we should do more, but somehow it's already fall already."

"The house wasn't in any shape for guests," Thorn said when Maggie finally paused for breath. From the look on her face, it was clear she was besotted.

Maggie was bustling around a truly enormous pot on the stove. "It's good I was thinking of having leftovers," she said. "I like cooking, but somehow I can't ever get the proportions right. Mina said I could ask you, Red. If you don't mind?"

"I don't, at all," I said, clearing my throat. "In fact, if you'd like help now—"

"Oh, no, don't worry. Mina said you all have something important to talk about?"

"That's right." Officer Thorn shifted from her position by the end of the counter to look at Luca. "Someone was very insistent."

"I have every right to be," he returned at once. "Unless you want vigilante justice on your hands—"

Thorn coughed. "Enough, I was only teasing. Though at this rate, I'm not saying it wouldn't be more effective. If we just had a better idea who was behind it, I'd be more confident."

"Obviously you can stay here if you're in danger?" Maggie chipped in, looking over her shoulder.

"That's very kind of you," I said, musing. "Maybe we should try to go over everything, from the top, once more."

"Especially," grumped William, "since some of us were stuck in the shop most of the time."

With amusement at William, and encouraged by Maggie, Officer Thorn and I took turns recounting our investigation so far. Luca was silent, a little more serious than usual—even in his goofy sweater. By the time we'd gotten up to the present moment, Maggie was passing around bowls of stew. Though she had been reserved when she first settled in Belville, it was clear to me now that she enjoyed having friends to look out for.

"I have no idea how you all do it," she told us, leaning on the counter as she ate, too. "I tell Mina that all the time. My brain just doesn't work that way."

"Your brain works fine," said Thorn, fondly.

Maggie laughed. "I know, I guess I just take a different approach."

"A different approach," I agreed, slowly. "Maybe that's what we need to take here."

Luca looked up. "You have an idea?"

"Just a thought. We don't have a good idea who's behind this . . . But we have a fairly good idea why, right?" I asked, glancing at Thorn over my bowl. "If it's about the cavern, then we could use that to draw the person out."

"I get what you're saying, in principle," Thorn agreed. "But how could you make the perpetrator so worried about an entire cavern that they're willing to show themselves?"

"Not about the cavern," William piped up. "About *hiding* the cavern."

"William's right." My thoughts were finally gaining speed. "The secret at stake here is the location of the cavern and all its magic. So if we do something—if we told everyone—"

"—the whole town," Luca agreed, perking up. "Make the rumors and gossip a *good* thing, for once."

"—Right, so if we let it be known that, maybe we'll show everyone where the cavern is," I continued.

"And the amethyst," William interjected.

". . . Then the criminal might try to clean it out first," Thorn mused. "If we give them enough time."

"But how could we make everyone interested in going all the way up there?" Luca asked.

Maggie sat up, her eyes shining. "It's a big cavern, right? Maybe have a party there! A costume party, for Halloween!"

I glanced around the counter. To varying degrees, everyone was beaming.

"I'll go out and tell the mayor tonight," said Officer Thorn. "We'll tell everyone the plan is to lead the parade to a secret, special location, and that the party will happen there."

The rain was pounding hard on the wooden roof. From his spot in the corner, William sneezed. "What about us?"

"I meant it when I said you should stay," said Maggie. She looked at Thorn, who nodded. "We both mean it. Just to be safe. And while you're here . . . want to try making ghost-shaped sugar cookies?"

* * *

Halloween in Belville was a big deal. Drawing in out-of-town visitors and covering the Square in decorations was proof enough of that, of course, but also, town festivities lasted longer than a single day. So even though Samhain itself was still two days away, there was an evening market planned for the very day that our rumor made its way around town. It was meant to be the opening of the holiday events. Now, it was also the laying of a trap.

We woke that morning buried under blankets in Thorn's spare room, rain still tapping at the window. And naturally, we didn't make it out of the house without a tray full of the sugar cookies we'd helped bake and decorate the night before. We hardly made it out of the house at all, actually. Officer Thorn came back from her morning check on Olivia, Jack, and Trent looking particularly stern.

"It's already all over town," she informed us, joining us at the counter for coffee, tea, and scrambled eggs. "I swear, gossip in this town is a force of its own. How word got out so fast when everyone was stuck inside last night, I'll never know."

"Maybe you had ghostly help," Luca commented. It was largely a joke; though Samhain *was* a time of year for heightened ghost activity, most specters weren't interested in the actual news and drama of the living. They had their own concerns.

"It's exciting news," Maggie said more practically, handing Thorn a steaming mug. "And everyone needs something to think about other than the rain. Besides, isn't this what you wanted?"

"Be careful what you wish for," William muttered next to me.

Thorn glared at him before tossing her head. "What this means is, it's now officially 'go' time. Red stays here. Trent and I will go up and keep an eye on the cavern. Maggie, if you—"

"Hey, wait," I protested. "This is the last day shops are open before the festival begins, and I have orders to fulfill! I can't just sit here all day."

We had a brief staring contest over that, but Officer Thorn eventually chose to compromise. "Fine, but one of you stays with her at all times," she told William and Luca. Focusing on me again, she asked, "Are Rhys and Daisy coming down?"

"I know Rhys is, but I'm not sure about Daisy," I admitted.

"Well, keep me informed," she said. "Trent and William can pass messages. Right?"

"I'm going to start charging you for that," William warned. In the past, he and Trent had communicated with each other via magic, allowing Officer Thorn to relay orders from afar.

"Bill it to the Guild," Thorn told him, before turning to Maggie. "I have to go in just a minute—Trent is waiting. You have the link-charm to reach me if you need me. I'm sorry—"

"Don't be," Maggie said, smiling up at her. "With any luck you'll be back before you know it. I already packed a bunch of cookies for you last night."

It was hardly a balanced lunch, I couldn't help but think, but it was easy to see that Officer Thorn didn't care in the slightest. She leaned down to kiss the top of Maggie's head before picking up her bag of sugary ghosts, giving the rest of us one more *stay in line* glare, and swiftly heading for the door.

Maggie put her hands on the counter and sighed. "I guess it must start to feel normal, after a while?"

"Some times are harder than others," Luca told her, putting his arm around my shoulders.

"Only for you chumps concerned with romance," William huffed.

Romance. The word made me remember something . . . but in a flash the memory was gone.

Luca, meanwhile, was grinning past me at William. "You only pretend you don't care."

"Whatever," said William. "Let's hope the criminal, whoever

it is, gets tired of pretending today."

32

Unsavory Company

That evening, Luca, William and I found ourselves surrounded by ghosts and ghouls . . .

. . . But like Maggie's sugary confections, they were the totally innocent kind.

We lingered on the corner outside my shop. A bonfire blazed in the center of Market Square, and strings of fairy lights filled the park with light and dancing shadows despite the heavy-hanging twilight above. Market stalls had been set up in rows throughout the Square, and many of the merchants from the grocer's, as well as businesses throughout Belville, were now hawking special holiday wares to passersby. Saki had set up a stall outside the Pomegranate selling "spooky" hot chocolate, and across the Square, a stall from the tavern was selling candied apples and buttery corn on the cob. Maggie and Johann were running a station for the salon, selling magical nail art—things like little spider stickers that would crawl from one nail to another. My potions shop had a stand, too, selling glow-in-the-dark face paints and lightsticks that shone purple or orange. Rhys had insisted upon running that himself; we'd made the arrangements long ago, in fact, and even at the time I had felt bad for leaving him on his own, but he had been steadfast. *You ought to enjoy the holiday,* he had told me.

He'd repeated something similar tonight, glancing between Luca and me before going off to set up shop. I thought it seemed a little odd, given that we were still waiting for our trap to spring.

The news from Officer Thorn had been frustratingly dull, all day.

"The mayor will make her announcement from the stage by the bonfire," William told us as we watched the festivities begin. "Should only be another minute or two."

"But even so, everyone already knows, right?" I asked.

"Even Frank knew, when I checked in at the bookshop," Luca agreed.

"And it's not like much will happen *here,*" William added. "I see Dusty over by the paper stand."

"Go on, then," I said, answering his unspoken question. "Maybe he knows something. We'll meet you over by the stage."

"It's not just me, right?" I asked Luca, as we began making our way through the crowd. I glanced over at Saki, conjuring ghoulish visions from the steam rising from a customer's hot chocolate. It seemed to me that she gave me a strange look, just for a moment. But then onlookers came between us, and I refocused on my companion. "Something feels off."

"It is kind of supposed to, since it's the start of Samhain," Luca reminded me. "Remember your first Halloween in town?"

"I remember you almost getting arrested for murder," I told him, my spirits not quite rising to the occasion.

"How about the Halloween afterward?"

"The year after that?" I faltered. That had been the year that Luca and I started dating. In fact, two years ago, not far from this spot, had been our first kiss. It seemed almost surreal to think of it now.

We passed a clump of children waving fake, enchanted "torches" they'd just purchased from the candle-maker's booth. A set of ghosts lingered by a nearby tree. Luca started to say something else, but his words were drowned out as an amplification spell carried the mayor's voice across the Square.

"Welcome, everyone. Just a few opening remarks, and then I'll let you enjoy the night," Marguerite called. Noise from the merchants' stalls effectively ceased. She went on, "I'd like to thank everyone for joining in Belville's sixty-sixth annual Samhain fair. I'm sure you'll agree with me that it is bigger and spookier than ever!

"As for this year's events," she said, "you can find a printed schedule at the stand of our local newspaper, Belville & Beyond. Be sure to thank Leo for her continued support of town events! On that schedule, you will find tonight's market and opening ceremonies. Tomorrow will be the scavenger hunt culminating in a potluck dinner, sponsored by Lavender's Tavern. And on Samhain itself, the event everyone is looking forward to: a costume parade, starting promptly at sundown. This year's parade will take us to a secret location on the mountain. Be ready for a ghostly ball like none other in a hidden, cursed cave!"

A collective *oohh* went up from the crowd, and the nearby children cheered. Luca leaned in. "She sure is playing it up."

"It's honestly not a bad idea, either," I said, looking around at the excited faces. "As long as everyone stays safe."

The mayor went on, mentioning accessibility provisions, warnings, costume prizes, and the like. I stopped listening as I scanned the crowd for William. We were close to the stage now, and he ought to be nearby . . . Of course, finding a black dog on a shadowy night was never going to be easy. Just as I was about to make a comment to Luca, I noticed a familiar face behind the stall at one corner of the stage. It was Doug.

I pointed him out to Luca. "I want to go talk to him, just for a minute. He seemed upset yesterday."

"I'm coming too," Luca informed me. "I'll keep an eye out for William."

As we crossed through the crowd, applause went up: the mayor's speech had ended. People were dispersing to the stalls, more jovial than ever, just as I managed to catch Doug's attention.

"Happy Halloween," I called to him, through the noise. I came to a stop at the edge of his stand, Luca right behind me. Little ferns in ceramic pots shaped like pumpkins, cauldrons, and ghosts decorated his table. "These are your holiday wares? They're perfect!"

"Th-thank you," Doug said, stammering slightly but nonetheless looking proud of his choice. He adjusted his glasses. "I made a deal with the pottery school down by the lake."

"I love them," I told him sincerely. "In fact, I'd love to buy one. How has your night been going?" I added, as I pulled my coin purse from my belt.

"At this rate, I may sell out this evening and have to think of something else for tomorrow," Doug told me, relaxing a bit as he rattled off his prices. I knew from my own experience selling that every merchant developed those phrases and quips that they could repeat in their sleep. Doug's seemed to comfort him. He shuffled over to me, and then stood straight and tall behind his tabletop.

"That's amazing," I said while I looked over my options. "Will you be joining the rest of the fair? The parade and everything, too?"

"Red." His voice had changed from routine merchant to breathy tones of disbelief. "Did you really find the cave?"

I paused, my hand still stretched over a lacy fern spilling from a round ghost's head. Doug sounded more worshipful than worried. I watched his face carefully as I said, "It was a collaborative effort, but Officer Thorn wanted to keep it secret until now. Eventually we decided everyone should know."

"The plants there," breathed Doug. "Are they really everything The Hermit always said?"

"I have reason to think so," I said slowly.

"I tried and tried, but she never would tell me *where*," he said.

I was more conscious than ever of Luca behind me. "Did you ever think of following her?"

"Of course, I—" Doug broke off, his eyes shining oddly in the flickering firelight. "Didn't you know? Oh, I wanted to come clean yesterday. I put a tracking spell on her—it was *me!*"

I stepped backward just a tiny bit, bumping into Luca's side. *A faint tracing spell on the cloak,* William had said. Now it made sense. "Oh? You did? So you know where the cavern is already?"

"No, *no,*" Doug cried, though I couldn't tell if he was earnestly clearing his name or just earnestly frustrated. "Every time she went into the valley, she disappeared."

"Physically?" I puzzled.

"No, the traces of the *spell*—they disappeared! And then they would reappear when she got on the path again."

"So you never found anything?" I asked.

"Not a thing," Doug said. "I thought she must be toying with me! *Was* it there? Oh, tell me!"

"I think Thorn wants to keep it a secret until Halloween," I said, stalling. "Doug, where did you get a tracking spell?"

"One of her customers. He knew she was overcharging, and he came to me one day when she'd left early and he wanted to know—he asked if I was willing—it wasn't *wrong*, since anything on the mountain should be—"

"Uh huh," I said, seeing where this was going. "Well, in any case, you'll have to tell it to Officer Thorn."

Doug shuffled back with a little *eep!* "But he specifically said not to!"

"I still think you'd better," I said, firmly. "Who was the customer?"

"A man from Pine. An alchemist," said Doug.

That gave me a shiver. While I was fairly certain now that Doug was not our suspect, I didn't like thinking there was someone else out there to worry about—and someone potentially so familiar.

"He said he'd report me," Doug went on, looking at me anxiously.

"It's best if you report yourself," I told him. "Truly. You know Officer Thorn. She'll get to the bottom of things."

"Yes, yes," he said, wringing his hands. "Oh, very well. I thought I'd take tomorrow morning off, anyway."

I felt a little bad for him. Quickly, I picked out a fern in a purple cauldron and another in a glittery pumpkin and paid him for them. Technically I only had his word that he had never made it as far as Vivian's home . . . but at this point, I believed him. He certainly seemed desperate enough to learn where the cavern entrance was.

As I finished saying my goodbyes, I bumped into Luca again, this time hovering over his shoulder. "Did you hear any of that?" I whispered.

"Some," he muttered back, "but I've been watching William."

"What?" I glanced in the direction Luca indicated, over at the edge of the Square nearest the tavern. It was hard to see exactly, but there was a little cluster of people on the tavern porch, and amidst them was William—and he was glowing. While we watched, that glow flared bright blue and then receded, like a lighthouse warning.

"Has he been doing that this whole time?" I asked, scandalized.

"That's the first flash," Luca said. "It looks to me like someone is arguing, but I can't tell who."

"We have to get over there now," I decided. "That's an old signal from when we were on the road together. It always means danger!"

33

See the Light

L uca, the ferns, and I tore through the Square, dodging children and tables and even right through a disconcerted, actual ghost. The happy hum of shoppers faded as we reached the corner near the tavern. Now, we could hear shouting instead.

I got there first. "What is it? What's going on?"

"William! Are you okay?" Luca added, panting heavily as he stopped beside me.

We were looking slightly up at the tavern's wooden porch. William sat at the edge, his glow fading as he looked over his shoulder at us. Beside him, half shaded by a large jack-o-lantern, was Dusty. And just past them, in the shadow, stood Dusty's new friend, Keith.

"Hello, Red," said Keith, pleasantly. "And you must be Luca. I've heard so much about you."

That didn't sit well with me. But I couldn't pinpoint why . . .

"Keith was just leaving," said Dusty, bitterly.

"No he is *not*," said William. "It's wrong and I won't allow it."

"I can appreciate your point," said Keith, smiling down at William, "but you've got no say in the matter."

"Together, we do," said Luca. He nudged me, and I nodded, taking over.

"Why would you want to leave in the middle of the market?" I asked Keith.

His eyes were hard as he returned my steady gaze. "Would you believe I already did what I came here to do?"

"No," I said, still getting my bearings. "You came here to see to Jack, right? And he's still in custody, and only spoke to us . . ."

At that, for the first time, Keith faltered. "Purslane spoke to you?"

"Think it over, for the boy's sake," Dusty chimed in.

"No," Keith said, recovering his control. "It's too late. They'll be all over the place now, closing in. I should have known it wouldn't last forever."

"What wouldn't last?" I asked, trying to distract him from the fact that Luca, in ghostly form, was now sneaking along the porch behind him.

But Keith suddenly whirled. "It won't do," he said, addressing Luca's shadow. "You think I didn't see it, the first time I saw you? You think I don't know who you are?"

Luca blinked back into his normal form, shock written across his face. The night was so dark and chaotic—it was silly to think Keith had seen everything about Luca just a few moments ago. And that's when I realized . . .

I hopped up onto the porch between Dusty and William, desperate to draw the attention back to myself. I knew now what had bothered me about that *I've heard so much about you.*

"The first time you saw us, in broad daylight," I said. "Halfway up the tower at the Lost River Outlook. You *saw* Luca there. I didn't think anything of it when I met you in the market, but I see it now, with the shadows hiding your hair and ears. You look a lot more like you did then, with a cap pulled down over your face and a cleaning mask on. But you were hunched over then, smaller. You were *trying* to deceive us . . . You said you were a housekeeper for Lavender. But was that even true?"

Behind me Dusty, too, was rattled. "You said you only got to town a few days ago!"

"*I* said that." Another form stepped out of the shadows. It was Lavender herself. "Just tell them, Keith," she added, her voice weary. "It will all come out."

"No! You think he needs that weighing on him, too?" Keith shot back. "Better now to make a clean break."

"Dusty's not helping you get away, and neither am I," William growled. Blue magic lashed around Keith's feet. "How dare you implicate my friend?"

"Because this has been collaborative all along," I said, thinking, glancing between Lavender and Keith. Officer Thorn's comment about the sorcerer clicked into place. "Keith has needed a lot of help . . . Because he didn't plan anything out. Not even his alibi. Dusty said that Keith had been working a job in New Dale, but the road from New Dale is totally washed out. And if we assume he was in town earlier than Lavender told us, then the timeline makes sense.

"At the market," I said, sparing a look down at Dusty. "The market he already knew just fine. It could have started there. Doug said The Hermit's last day selling was the day *before* Jack showed up in town—the day Officer Thorn got her cryptic note, *on tavern paper.* So maybe Keith came through town. He did say he often traveled the area. Only this time, the fates aligned. Vesper, or 'The Hermit,' would come in for two days at a time. On her first day, he's there too. He saw a familiar face in the market. Someone he's never been able to forget . . . Someone who was never brought to justice.

"So he starts out by trying to alert the justice today, Officer Thorn. But what can he really say? He doesn't have any actual proof. He needs her to *find* it. To find Jack. So he sends his note and starts the search. But it isn't enough. It's been so long—the whole family is so distraught—" I looked at Lavender, whose sad eyes agreed. "When she shows up again the second day, carefree, it's too much. So Keith follows her—it must have been in person, since thanks to Doug we know that magic wasn't able to trace her. And in person, he could have used her teleport link to get to the top of the tower, right after she did—but then she would certainly notice him . . ."

Lavender had her head in her hands, crying. Keith looked at her, then at me. "Listen," he said, his voice choked. "You're right. This isn't me. I had no idea what I was doing. I didn't even know Lavender owned the tower, I just went where I had to. I wasn't thinking of anything except my brother's little boy. I did follow her—we're good at the woods, my kind. But not so good with the magic. I didn't think it through. I went down into the tunnel, the cave, after her. Then she disappeared in a magic ring. When I stepped after her, I showed up in that apartment and she already knew I was there. She was yelling. Purslane—poor Purslane—"

Luca spoke softly. "Why did he run?"

"Because I told him to," Keith burst. "I was frantic. I didn't even know where he might go. She was trying to hold on to him and I pushed her out of the way. He went into the ring and disappeared."

"He must have teleported and ran out through the cave," I mused. "Otherwise Luca and I would have seen him. But like William said, we never saw any indication that anyone came and went from the tower. Because Vesper always came and went via the tunnel, leading into the cave and her magic shortcut."

"But you did kill her," William reminded Keith and the group at large.

"I did," Keith agreed heavily. "It was like I could see her kidnapping him all over again, but this time I could do something. I shoved her with all my pent-up anger from all these years. She hit the wall, and then the floor."

"The wall?" I was surprised. It fit with his story, but not with the crime scene Officer Thorn and I had found.

Keith sighed. "When I came back to my senses, I knew it wouldn't do. It was too obvious. No one falls backward into a wall. But maybe if it looked like she had only hit the floor, it might pass as an accident. I've picked up my share of cleaning jobs in my time. All I had to do was throw on some old clothes of Purslane's and clean up the apartment real good, and then leave by the trap door. But by then, you two were there."

"And you were scared we would go upstairs, find the entrance, and see what had happened," I supplied.

"Should've known somebody would eventually. But I couldn't think of anything except the boy." Keith looked at Lavender again. "By the time I got down here, he'd already been picked up by the police."

Lavender cleared her throat. "He told me everything, but not until late that night. It was my idea to hide his arrival in town. But neither of us was happy about it."

"And that's why *you* sent the second note," I concluded. "That's why the writing was different, and the note torn in haste."

"I could hardly think straight," she admitted. "I knew what Keith had told me, and I believed him, but—but part of me still couldn't believe she was dead."

"So you had Thorn tie up the loose ends for you, and then you hoped to skip town," said William. He sounded much more skeptical than I was capable of being in the face of so much emotion.

"It was never about the cavern, the plants, or the amethyst at all," Luca added quietly.

At this, Lavender startled slightly.

Something that had been nagging at the back of my brain finally came forward. "Except for Vivian—Vesper," I said. "For her, it was all about the cavern. Do either of you know why she took Purslane, or Jack, in the first place?"

Lavender exchanged a weary look with Keith before sighing. "When I heard the rumors about the crystal, it was almost as bad as the rumors about Purslane. I remember it very clearly. Vesper had given it to my daughter . . . And on the same night when she stole our little baby, she stole it back, too."

"Makes sense," William said. "If she found the cavern, she would have known she needed the spell power—and someone with plant magic, too."

"But why didn't you say that earlier?" I asked Lavender.

"The crystal was never the important thing, to me," she answered. "I thought it was a bad omen when Violetta first brought it home. It was too big a gift, from too uncertain a source. But she didn't listen . . . and the first few reporters who came to town were too interested in it, not interested in poor Purslane. Oh, Red, I see now I should have told you. But after years of keeping quiet—when only Purslane himself returned—I didn't want to make things worse for him, to have him be the victim of fortune-hunting or accused of theft."

"Like I said, none of it was planned, by either of us," Keith said. "Maybe I shouldn't have stayed. Maybe if I had known going in I'd kill her, I would have thought of a getaway. But with Purslane injured—and not talking—and what if he knew—*it was his own uncle who did it—*"

Keith broke down. His feet still strangely still and captive under William's magic, his shoulders shook violently as he covered his face with both arms. I looked down at Dusty just as he looked up at me, and in that moment I completely understood why he might have been tempted to let Keith go. The man—the whole family—had they already suffered enough?

It was at that moment that Officer Thorn turned up. A breathless Trent holding a flying broom, a bright-eyed Maggie, and a rather smug Gloria clustered behind her.

"See?" said Gloria. "I *knew* that ghost was telling the truth. Leave it to them to find a criminal at a holiday market."

* * *

Officer Thorn and William took Lavender, Keith, and Dusty back to the station. Dusty assured me before he left that he hadn't ever been told anything, at least until the fight we'd interrupted on the porch, but he knew his testimony would be important.

Gloria, who had apparently noticed the ghost I'd disturbed

as Luca and I ran to the tavern and had been the one to get Maggie to reach out to Officer Thorn, soon went back to her booth. No doubt she'd continue keeping a sharp eye on the crowd. But Maggie lingered, looking up at us all with worried eyes. It was only when we decided to get some hot chocolate and rest over by the Pomegranate that she lightened, and let us go.

"I could use *something*," Trent admitted, as he fell into step with Luca and me. "I'm not saying Maggie's cookies aren't great, but it's been a long day with not a lot of food to go round."

"I'm not sure hot chocolate is going to round out your daily nutritional needs, exactly," I said, starting to scan the stalls for actual dinner food.

"No, hot chocolate is definitely what I need," said Trent, firmly. "Stick to the plan."

With that settled, I glanced up at Luca, who walked just behind me. "Okay?"

"Just drained. As you must be," he said, one hand on my shoulder.

"Yes," I admitted, with a sigh. "But it makes sense, now, at least. I knew there had to be something—when William mentioned romance this morning, it stuck with me. I know people *do* kill over discoveries and money and the like, but everything about this crime felt so much more personal than that somehow. Maybe especially because of the way it affected Jack."

"I think he pieced it all together yesterday," Trent said. "And I don't think that's a bad thing. He's a resilient kid. Between his plants and his paintings and Olivia, he'll get through it."

This made me smile, and playfully, I punched Trent's

shoulder. "A *kid* who is practically two hundred years older than you."

"Everyone is vulnerable and little in the face of my new medical powers," Trent replied with a grin.

So emboldened, he flirted shamelessly with Saki as we ordered our drinks. I exchanged a tired but amused glance with Luca, realizing *why* Trent had wanted to come to this stand at all. Samhain was turning out to be a rather romantic time of year. Despite all the danger . . .

We sat cozily ensconced on the Pomegranate's porch this time, a far cry from the confrontation at the tavern. The market was still going strong, though the noise was muted. Sakura's special hot chocolate came with different flavors, toppings, and ghostly visions in the steam. My dark chocolate with cinnamon and chili was delicious, but it was only when Luca's salted caramel vaporous cat phantom made him smile that I felt like I might relax.

Dusty and William found us there not much later, and took their own seats at the table.

"Everything came out pretty fast," Dusty said. "Just like you thought, Red."

"That last note was Keith," William added. "He swears he didn't mean anything by it, really, but he heard you talking to Lavender and was worried."

So he had been the one in the kitchen, then. I nodded, noting that William sounded like he still had not forgiven Keith in the least. And, to be fair, he *was* a criminal.

"So the note from Paracelsus was coincidence?" Luca asked over the dregs of his hot chocolate.

"Probably. But I have a few things to follow up with him about, anyway," I said, thinking of the "alchemist" from Pine.

"So we should know soon. How about the cave? Are we really going to have the party up there after all?"

At that, Trent stirred. "Oh, I forgot to tell you. A dragon crashed Thorn and my vigil today."

"You mean Daisy?" I said, half anxious, half amused.

"Yeah," he admitted, grinning. "And she's helping with the party. Plus, she said that you, Red, should swipe that huge amethyst."

34

A New Dream

"Let its new life begin," Rhys declared, as he mounted the amethyst on a little pedestal in the very center of my shop.

A day and a half had passed since Keith and Lavender confessed, and it was now officially Samhain. The store was closed, but that was for the best: we'd had to rearrange a lot of shelves to accommodate our new prize. William had felt the need to strengthen our security spells, too, something he grumbled about—but only until I pointed out that the amethyst itself was probably a helpful grounding tool for him to tie his spells into.

Especially since it no longer bore any trace of Vivian's magic. Daisy had been willing to reveal the Lost River to the town, even with its connection to the Tree of Life, but she had proposed that Vivian's spells be dismantled. That way the plants would return to a more normal level of merely somewhat-magical, and the whole place would be less of a draw for those looking to make a buck or extend their life. In this proposal, Daisy had two people's support—aside from

Rhys, who nearly always supported everything she did.

Her first supporter was me. I'd done enough experiments on the plants to know by now that the life-extending effects were limited to the specific magic user tied to the cavern—that is, Vivian. Though the plants did grow fast and glow and were otherwise impressive, they would not grant anyone else immortal life, nor cure any ills. This solved a puzzle I had been privately wondering about: 'The Hermit' and her limited sales success. She hadn't managed to attract lots of interest, because her wares hadn't really worked all that well for anyone but herself. And honestly, she probably had preferred it that way.

Daisy's other supporter turned out to be Jack. He'd decided to remain in town, and had adopted his new-old name, Purslane. But he said quite firmly, by word and by picture, that he did *not* want anything further to do with the tower or Vivian's effects. Instead, he had set up in one of Lavender's other little cabins on the western edge of town, where rumor had it he already had a promising garden growing—even at this time of year.

Lavender herself was still running the tavern and its properties, though like Keith, she would be formally tried and sentenced at the next full moon's court date. Punishments in Beyond tended to be creative and flexible, owing to the fact that they could be magically enforced. The general consensus in town was that she deserved perhaps a lifetime ban on owning strange towers on the mountainside and lying to police, but little more. Keith, too, was expected to get a sentence amounting to service and therapy, and a picture from Jack hung in the cell where he awaited trial.

Oh—and did I mention that Olivia had decided to stay in town too, once her apprenticeship was done, and hoped to be appointed as cold case investigator for Pastoria?

I grinned at Rhys. "Who knew Halloween was such a time for new beginnings?"

"With every end comes a new chance," he agreed, smiling back. "You said you heard back from your mentor?"

"I did, and he sent his blessing on our new use of the stone, too—not that it was ever his," I said, looking at the way the purple facets gleamed in the morning light. "He insists that he had no direct contact with Vivian, but admitted that he *did* try to trace her. The alchemist from Pine was one of his recent students, in fact, but once he realized which market she'd likely been spotted in, he decided to reach out to me directly. He apologized for the danger we all got in . . ." In fact, my lab was currently overflowing with new equipment and rare plants, tokens of just how sorry he was. "Apparently he hadn't ever heard about the kidnapping scandal, or Violetta and Vesper, any of that."

"Not too surprising," Rhys commented. "Belville *is* remote."

"And Paracelsus has plenty to do other than follow true crime," I agreed. "I think he really was just worried about her. The word he used was 'consumed'—he was worried she would be consumed by her quest, which in the end, she was. It's a little sad, thinking how he spent so long wondering what had become of her, and if he would ever see her again."

"It makes one think," said Rhys, rather purposefully, "of the importance of appreciating one's loved ones while they are present."

I squinted at him. Usually, when he became vague and philosophical like that, it was because he was trying to make a point. But before I could figure this one out, there was a *bang* overhead and William's voice sounded from the landing.

"What, you already put it up without me?"

I chuckled. "With how you were snoring, I figured you were going to sleep until noon!"

"And you both will have plenty to do to get ready for the costume parade, I am sure," Rhys said, with another enigmatic smile. "Daisy and I will be very glad to see you at the party."

* * *

The path through the forest had been marked and lit with magical torches. Marching up there, surrounded by everyone, it was impossible to get lost. People shared campfire stories and sang haunting songs as they walked, each scare ending in laughter. Friendly ghosts weaved through the trees. I could hardly wait to see what Officer Thorn and Daisy had done with the cavern—rumor had it that the pixies had helped decorate, just for the occasion.

But as the mouth of the tunnel came into view, Luca pulled me aside. He nodded to William and Trent, who had been walking along behind us. They both grinned, and then went on their way.

"What's going on?" I asked, confused. "You don't want to go in yet?" And yet, it had seemed like William and Trent had known he would pause . . .

"Not quite yet," said Luca. He sounded a little nervous. "Come on, let's go look at the ravine."

"We know where the Lost River is, and it's not above ground—nor will it be any time soon!" Though I protested, I followed him as he cut across the valley, past the old tower. For once, the night was clear and full of stars.

Luca climbed onto a boulder jutting out next to the chasm,

and then turned. I took the hand he offered, but I was still looking up at the tower, lost in thought.

"It's, ah, it's really too bad," he said, glancing up as well. "I really was hoping to rent it. It would have made a fun getaway . . . aside from everything."

"I do wonder what will happen to it now," I admitted. Then, as I climbed up next to him, I recalled his project. "Are you still going to do the brochure?"

"Brochure? Oh." His gaze slid out, to the forest beyond the ravine. "Well . . ."

I kept my gaze fixed on his face. "There never was one, was there?"

"No." He swallowed hard.

"What were you doing?" Saying it aloud finally broke a little hole in my reserve, and everything that had been bothering me came pouring out. "Going around with Daisy, and Saki, and— I'm not saying I've been jealous, exactly, but why didn't you ever tell me the truth? All along it's felt like there's something I don't know that everyone else does. Why wouldn't you just tell me?"

Luca ducked his head. "Actually, I was really worried you'd figure it out."

"Well, I figured out there was *something*," I said, my temper flaring. But my intuition told me to wait, to hold on one more moment—and I listened.

And at that moment, light and color bloomed around us.

It wasn't Samhain colors, black and orange—it was every color, magic sparkling everywhere. Twinkling lights of every hue lit up the valley, the ravine, even the forest beyond.

"What in Beyond—?" I gazed, awestruck, as they danced and twirled. "Pixies?"

"Yep," said Luca, watching them too. "Good thing William didn't come, right?"

They filled up the night, like so many fireflies. I could just imagine him trying to catch one, and it made me laugh out loud. "Luca, what is this?"

"Um—this is how I feel, about you, Red," he said, eyes earnest now as he turned to me, a wide smile tugging at his lips. "This is what it's been like, since you came to town, and became my friend, and then started going out with me. It's felt like—all the pieces were there, just dark and gray. And then you came and—you showed me how to truly see things this way."

"Luca," I said, alarmed to find tears at the back of my throat, "that's impossible. *You're* the one who always makes things brighter. This was your idea?"

"Not exactly," he confessed. "Actually, I wanted to take you somewhere—to go on a trip, for our anniversary, even if it was somewhere close. Maybe it's better we ended up staying in town—of course, it did end up for the better. But—"

"Our anniversary," I repeated, stuck. I felt awful in that moment. I hadn't thought of doing anything to celebrate; just thinking about the holiday, and all the other drama, had been distracting enough.

"I know." His voice was warm. "I know it's hard to believe, but doesn't it also feel like—like it will be forever?"

I lifted my eyes to meet his gaze, finally understanding. Slowly, I smiled. "Forever would be just fine."

Luca pulled his hand from my shoulder, opening it between us to show me two engagement rings in his palm.

"You'd better hide those, before the pixies decide to steal them," I said, unable to help myself.

"Or you could wear one, and I the other," he told me.

I closed my hand around his and kissed him, passionately.

Later, as we walked down the tunnel to join the others, a trail of pixies all around us, I was still grinning. "I do love Halloween, but I think this was better than anything the town could have come up with."

"Oh, they know," said Luca, contentedly.

"They—" I paused. "I was right, wasn't I? *Everyone knows.* They all knew, all along!"

"Of course, why else would everyone be so interested in helping me?" Luca beamed. "You should have seen Daisy's face when the pixies offered to help too, since we couldn't use the tower. Originally she was helping me find the perfect spot, since she knows all the buildings on the mountain, but then there turned out to be a murder at the Outlook, so that obviously wasn't going to work. Then Rhys suggested the forest instead. And I thought, maybe the location doesn't have to be perfect . . . the perfect thing is always just being there together, anyway."

All at once, all of Rhys's little comments—William's, too, and Sakura's—came back and hit me with force. I turned to Luca with wide eyes. "How long have you been planning this?"

"Oh, you know," he said, smiling back at me. "Basically forever."

And with that, we turned and continued, arm in arm, down the path to join our friends.

Epilogue

A letter from Olivia

To Red:

This is to let you know that I was chosen for the local Cold Case Consultant position with the Police Guild of Pastoria. Your recommendation letter was essential for me getting the role—so thank you, very much!

I'll be responsible for looking into old cases all around the county, not just in Belville, so I'm not sure when I'll next be around. That's why I wanted to make sure to write. But when I'm in town, for now, I'm staying at the tavern. Lavender has been very kind. She says to make sure I take time off for Yule, to "really enjoy" a town celebration.

Getting a job like this has been a dream of mine since I was a kid. I never really thought I could do it, until my first day training at the Guild. Maybe even my first day with Officer Thorn. Both she and you have been such good teachers. I'm so glad to have found Belville—and Jack. Like you said, sometimes the people you meet in cases, even cold cases, never leave you.

Thank you, again—
Olivia

Recipes

The recipes included here have been submitted by the residents of Belville, collected (and at times translated) by the author. Mistakes might have been made at any part of the process, but with any luck, these will bring a bit of fun and inspiration to you, our readers! Always feel free to experiment with the recipes included. And if you do, reach out to info@ellehartford.com to let us know how it went!

That said, without further ado . . .

Lavender's Perfect Gnocchi

Tavern keeper Lavender is famous for never writing her recipes down, but here are her tips for making Red's favorite pasta!

Types of Gnocchi to Consider:
  Shelf-stable gnocchi, made with potato flakes
  Fresh potato gnocchi, made with mashed potato
  Ricotta gnocchi

Lavender's Method of Preparation:

1. Briefly boil the gnocchi (following recipe directions, depending on which gnocchi you choose), making sure

that none of the pieces are sticking together.

2. Melt butter in a non-stick frying pan over medium-high heat.

3. Add gnocchi and cook for 2-3 minutes on each side, until golden brown.

4. Remove gnocchi with a slotted spoon and discard extra oil.

5. *Note: Lavender admits that it is also possible to bake the gnocchi, drizzled in oil, at 400 degrees F for about twenty minutes.*

Sauce Recommendations:
Tomato sauce
Pesto (Red's favorite)
Browned butter & herb (a good seasonal option)
Sauteed vegetables with olive oil and garlic
Cream or cheese sauces (especially good in the winter!)

* * *

Sakura's Spooky-Good Hot Chocolate

Delight your friends and loved ones with this gourmet hot chocolate recipe! Steam-ghosts not included.

Makes 4 Cups

Ingredients:
1/4 C sugar (or more if you like your drinks sweet)
1/4 C unsweetened cocoa powder

4 C milk (for a thicker drink, use 3 C milk and 1 C cream)
1/2 C semisweet chocolate (chips or chunks)
1/2 tsp vanilla

Instructions:

1. In a saucepan off the heat, whisk together the sugar and cocoa powder. Add milk, chocolate chips, and vanilla, then stir.
2. Place over medium heat and bring to a light boil. Stir constantly until the chocolate is fully melted and incorporated.
3. Let cool to taste, then serve and enjoy!

Suggested Toppings:
    Whipped cream
    Sprinkles
    Caramel drizzle
    Dark chocolate drizzle
    Cayenne powder
    Cinnamon
    Chocolate shavings
    Peppermint (fresh leaves or sticks)
    Halloween candy!

* * *

Trent's Simple Salve

A salve is a soft medicinal spread that can be used to soothe skin or aching muscles. The recipe is very flexible: Trent encourages you to make it your own!

Ingredients:
    1 C oil of choice: jojoba, olive, sweet almond, herb-infused
    1/4 C beeswax pellets
    1 - 2 Tbsp shea or cocoa butter (optional)
    1 tsp essential oil (optional)
    Water

Instructions:

1. Add the oil, wax, and butter (if using) to the top section of a double boiler. Fill the lower section with enough water so that the upper pan is resting on the water.
2. Heat the double boiler over medium heat until all ingredients are completely melted, stirring.
3. Remove from heat.
4. Add any essential oils.
5. While still warm, pour the mixture into glass jars. (If the mixture starts to harden, just warm it up again until it's soft!)
6. Once the salve has cooled and hardened in the jars (several hours or overnight), add lids and labels.

* * *

William's Recipe for Finding Rivers: The Milky Way

"This is a big one," says our favorite familiar, "but not everyone has seen the Milky Way. In the Northern Hemisphere, it's easiest to find between April and October—and in the Southern Hemisphere, it's even more visible. But if you live in a place with a lot of light pollution, you may never get a chance to see it. It'll look like a faded stream, or even a cloudy path, winding among the stars from east to west.

"In the past, people came up with all kinds of explanations for the Milky Way. Some told legends about it being a river, or literally spilled milk. Get out to a quiet, dark place sometime, and take a look for yourself!"

The Milky Way

the river among the stars

Acknowledgments

We have a big milestone in this book for Red and Luca! And I am at my computer writing this shortly before my own wedding. As such, I simply have to recognize the unending inspiration from my fiance that makes my writing career possible. Being an author requires a lot of self-confidence, something that I was sorely lacking in just a few years ago. Erich's love and encouragement has been indispensable!

I have also been very lucky to have a wonderful writing group go through this book, chapter by chapter. Thank you so much for the close reads and the fun conversations, as well as the questions and support! On a similar note, every reader who has reached out to me online or at book fairs—those interactions are so much more precious than you could know.

And finally, as always, I am eternally grateful to the other authors who encouraged me, to Sisters in Crime and Mystery Writers of America, the wonderful book community on Instagram, the Cozy Mystery Tribe, and my amazing ARC readers!

On top of that, I'm thankful to *you*. That means you, reading this! And if you've enjoyed the stories in these pages, I hope you'll take a moment to tell someone or write a review.

About the Author

Elle adores cozy mysteries, fairy tales, and above all, learning new things. As a historian and educator, she believes in the value of stories as a mirror for complicated realities. She currently lives in New Jersey with a grumpy tortoise and a three-legged cat.

Find more stories of Red and her friends at **ellehartford.com**. And while you're there, sign up for Elle's newsletter to get bonus material, behind-the-scenes sneak peeks, and terrible jokes!

Also by Elle Hartford

The Alchemical Tales, a cozy mystery-meets-cozy fantasy series, includes:

Beauty and the Alchemist (book one)
Cold as Snow (book two)
Mermaid for Danger (book three)
Cry Big Bad Wolf (book four)
Cinders to Dust (book five)
Death Pulls the Strings (book six)
A Thousand and One Alibis (book seven)

A spin-off series of cozy fantasy romance, Pomegranate Cafe Romance, includes:

Worthy in Love (book one)
A Tale of Rowan and Daisy (extra novella)
Strong in Love (book two)
Steady in Love (book three)

And a cozy fantasy spin-off series, Marine Magic, starting with:

How to Care for Cursed Fish